Running With

Wolves

Abigail L. Marsh

Consonus esto Lupis
si cum quibus
esse cupis.

Acknowledgements

Firstly, to my parents and my little brother for being so supportive of the journey I have been on to complete this book. I know I've been a pain in the bum!

And...

Secondly, to the two English teachers who never gave up on me- I hope if you ever read this, you don't still have your red pen.

Thank-you

Abigail L. Marsh

Chapter One: An Unsettling Evening

Standing rigid, I stared dead-pan out of the window, motionless except for my fingers which drummed against the windowsill impatiently. The rain poured down, the pitch black blinding me from the world just outside my reach. He was coming though, I was sure of that, and he was bringing my past back with him.

I'd lost count of how long it had been since I'd been kidnapped in the dead of night from a neglected children's home in upstate New York and brought to England, but I reckoned it had to be getting on for almost a decade. Before that? I don't talk about Illinois anymore, that's where my demons lurk. A place I'd rather forget.

"Stop your drumming!" A man shouted gruffly from the armchair across the dimly lit room. I knew who it was without having to turn around. It was Kurt, my kidnapper's partner in crime, quite literally. Slightly aggravated by his tone my fingers came to a rest, although I knew that I would come to no harm if they persisted, it didn't hurt to keep him happy.

Abigail L. Marsh

In the other room, the radio was playing quietly away to itself,

"And the next song coming up will be 'Down to the second,' By Zach

Berkman." With a swift back-kick I slammed the kitchen door shut.

Kurt grumbled at me, but my focus was pulled back to the darkness.

Cain was bringing back a girl a little younger than I was, who I would

have to train to become just like me. And what was I? A downright

criminal, I had been since the day I completed training. Training had

changed me, for better or for worse? I was never really sure.

You see a kid makes a better criminal when trained in the correct way,

because their appearance translates to innocence. Not a single sole on

this earth would allow a fully gown man they didn't know, into their

home or into a secure building willingly, at least not any sane person. A

upset or scared child is much more plausible, they let you right in and

promise to call Mummy or Daddy to come and save the day. It's almost

laughable how easy it is. We play on the minds of the innocent- cruel

right? My seven-year-old face had grown up, it didn't make the cut

anymore, my time was slowly but surely coming to an end. Hence the

new kid.

As I stood there, my mind churned over and over all the questions I

desperately wanted answers to. Who was she? What did she look like?

Abigail L. Marsh

Who were her parents? Would they come looking for her? Where was she from?

"Tilly! Stop tapping, or I'll rip your fingers off one by one and feed them to the bloody dog!" Kurt yelled. I glanced down at my fingers, sure enough, they were nervously tapping to the tune of 'We will rock you.'

I stepped into the hallway and closed the living room door so that I could tap in peace. The radiator was on so I sat at the bottom of the staircase staring through the glass porch to the driveway. What was taking him so long?

My mind drifted again, I was back in the kitchen the night before, when I had stumbled through the door out of breath and rosy-cheeked after a race to the next town and back. Melanie was stood at the fridge eyeing up its contents.

"Is he back yet?" I breathed heavily grabbing a bottle of orange juice from the table and pouring it straight down my throat, with little regard to the civilities of a glass.

"Give that here." Melanie said snatching it out of my hand and splashing it all down my new lycra. I scowled at her.

"Don't give me that look; we're the only two girls in this house so don't you *dare* start turning into one of those pig-headed men. We have to

Abigail L. Marsh

stick together."

Rolling my eyes, I scraped a wooden chair across the stone floor and sat down to untie my shoelaces.

"We won't be the only two for much longer." I said.

Melanie shook her head as she finally made her mind up and pulled a pack of chicken out of the fridge.

"I don't know about all this. It's very wrong."

"As opposed to bank robberies and murder?" I grinned sliding off the first shoe and lobbing it in the direction of the muddied rack.

"She is a child Tilly, your perception of what's right and wrong, it's been twisted."

"I was a child, a real child, but no-one cared one bit about that, did they?" I snapped, suddenly feeling attacked. "No-one stopped to think maybe I didn't want to be here. Arggg get off." I gave a final tug on the shoes still attached to my left foot, without warning it gave way and flew across the room colliding with Jamie as he staggered through the door, sweat dripping down his beet red face.

"Oi!" He yelled smacking it away. Mel looked momentarily shocked as we watched the giants sized man suck in a lung full of air, gripping the doorframe for support.

"Jesus grandpa, don't have a heart attack." I laughed as Melanie held her hand out to stop him stepping on her clean floor. "Where've you been? I got back hours ago."

His piercing eyes met with mine, and I shut my mouth.

"Do not step one foot on this floor, go around, go on, you're not coming through here; you're worse than Tilly." Mel interrupted his glare by shooing him out. "And don't be a sore loser. Off you go." Jamie didn't have the breath to argue the toss and disappeared back into the darkening sky.

Shutting the door and cutting off the cold air filtering through, Mel turned back to me, an expression on her face I had seen a thousand times. I knew what conversation was coming.

"I know, I know, don't wind them up." I grumbled getting up to leave. "But Mel there is nothing else to do around here, if I could have a friend or someone who…"

"I thought you were excited about the girl coming."

I shrugged.

"It won't be the same. Will it? You're right. She shouldn't be here. It's not right that they steal money and people whenever they feel like it, and Mel I do know that, I know it's wrong, but what can I do about it?" Mel lost her infuriating know-it-all expression, and I was met with something I hadn't seen in a long time, sadness. She came over and pulled me into a hug.

"I know. You are so brave Tilly, this place, it's far from right for a child to grow up in. One day you'll go home; I just know it."

I pushed away from her.

"I don't want that either." I grumbled, all endorphins released on my run had died a hard death. I stepped away from Melanie, shaking off her unexpected hug. "And I don't want chicken."

"Tilly." Mel said as I headed out of the room. I stopped, expecting her to tell me not to be so rude, but her face was still soft, almost concerned. "Don't let them push you around. You're better than that."

A spike in my heart rate pulled me sharply from my memories. There was a set of headlights approaching the gate at the end of the drive, I punched in a code in the panel hidden behind the curtain on the wall. A moment later the car was coming up on the house and parking on the courtyard patio. I unlocked the front door with shaky hands. I didn't want to do this, I didn't even know her name, yet my chest constricted at the thought of her being trapped here- for all the pain she was going to live through. This poor kid had been dragged away from her parents and would never see them again. The worst bit was I knew how it felt, but I couldn't ignore the strange pang of relief as it fluttered through my stomach- I wasn't going to be alone anymore.

Abigail L. Marsh

A few seconds later Cain opened the door dragging the girl in by the scruff of her neck. All silver lined thoughts left my brain as if they had been chased out by a rabid dog, and the fluttering butterflies of relief died on the spot. I stood there gormless; this girl couldn't have been more than thirteen. Gagged tightly and handcuffed she was denied any chance of escape. Blood trickled down the edge of her face from a deep gash above her eye and dripped from her chin as she struggled in Cains steel grip.

Cain was obviously growing tired of her already, and with one swift flick of the wrist, she was thrown to the floor with a violent growl. A groan escaped her lips as she laid face down on the hard wooden panels unable to move.

"Give over." Cain snarled. I caught the fear running wild in her eyes as she peeked up at me through her fringe, queasy didn't even begin to describe the feeling stomping around in my stomach. I gripped the banister tightly and looked over at my kidnapper. I had come to like him over the years, and I had cottoned on to the fact he liked me too. He made me panckaes, taught me how to do the things I struggled with... After training he'd changed, he'd taken care of me like you'd expect an uncle to. Maybe it was Stockholm Syndrome talking, but I wasn't in a hurry to

Abigail L. Marsh

go back to the corrupt social system, where no one gave a damn about anyone except themselves, even if some days knocked the wind out of my chest.

"Tilly." He spoke calling on my attention. I re-focused on his stoney face and nodded briefly. "This is Isabelle."
"Isabelle, this is Tilly."
I waited praying she would have the sense to respond. When she didn't, Cain took action, yanking her to her knees and giving her a shake. Once her eyes stopped spinning around her brain, she gave me a nod, the colour of her face paling by the second.
My heart ached heavily; she was already dragging up memories, things I didn't want to think about.
"Max!" Cain shouted. As my brain caught up to the words Cain had bellowed through the house, my stomach churned. I glanced nervously down the hallway, was he here?

Not two seconds later my black, bull-necked Alsatian trotted into the corridor. He may have been a dog, but in the half-light, he could be easily mistaken for a wolf. That dog would fight with jagged teeth and talon-like claws, and never back down if called to. Trust me, you did not want to be on the wrong end of his brutality when he attacked. I had seen first hand the blood he could spill.

Abigail L. Marsh

The dog stopped when he saw the scene before him and cocked his head innocently.

"Here." Cain commanded.

He moved stealthily towards us, stopping feet away.

"Max, this is Isabelle, the *trainee*." Cain said. Max's ears pricked up at his words, immediately he tensed, he'd been trained for this, his teeth bared he took a step closer asserting his dominance.

Isabelle let out a frightened cry and tried desperately to back up, but Cain stood behind her firmly, laughing at her pathetic state. Anger bubbled in my stomach as my clenched fist ached. A few more minutes and this meet and greet would be over, if that's what you could call it. My weakness finally forced itself to the surface and shined through as I saw tears enter her eyes, I instantly shoved Max away.

"Out Max." I snapped. Max was my dog, Cain had given him to me, and my commands would not go unheeded. He sloped around my legs and sat down by my side, still baring his teeth dangerously.

"You are going to have to toughen up." Cain said looking at me seriously. "To train her successfully, no mercy, no feeling, got it?"

To prove his point he then threw Isabelle forward onto the stairs, with hands tied firmly behind her back she had nothing to break her fall, and landed face first.

Abigail L. Marsh

I glared at Cain.

"Take her upstairs and give her some water, then I want you down here for a pack meeting, the guys are coming over." I nodded curtly then turned to Isabelle, who was lying face down on the stairs still. I grabbed her shoulders and hauled her up as Cain disappeared; she was shaking like a leaf in my hands. I guided her up the stairs with Max following at our heels.

Chapter Two: Do or Die

A white door covered in a multitude of locks stood isolated at the far end of a corridor. I walked towards it struggling to block out Isabelle's whimpers. Once inside I glanced around. The room was as bare as a prison cell, only a bed sat against a wall in the far corner and a small desk and chair stood next to it.

"Sit down." I said pushing her gently over to the chair. The floorboards creaked underfoot as we walked and I shivered involuntarily, noticing a definite chill in the air, and the stench of musty paint. I knew it was all designed to make the trainee uncomfortable, but I for one was pleased I would be taking a long jacuzzi-bath in my own room shortly. I was aware of my dog as he slunk into the room like a sketchy shadow you'd cross the street to avoid on a dark and rainy night, he'd keep an eye on her whilst I was gone.

Atop the desk sat a water bottle. I picked it up and unscrewed the tight lid before realising that since Isabelle's hands were tied, I would be doing the pouring. You would have thought I was holding out a dead cat to her the way she reeled backward; shaking her head violently; pleading with her eyes for me just to leave her alone.

"I promise it's just water." I said softly. "See." I took a swig and waited for her reaction. Nothing.

The doorbell chimed through the house, The Pack was here, and if I wasn't along soon Cain would be up to see what the matter was, and neither of us needed that.

"Listen to me. This is the only chance you're going to get. It's just plain old water."

Moments later she relented and leaned forward allowing me to pull her gag down, so it was hanging around her neck.

I tipped the bottle, pouring a glug of water down her throat. She started to choke on it, splattering icy water all down my top.

"For Gods…" I stopped mid anger, this wasn't her fault.

Placing the bottle back on the desk I stared at her, making sure she wasn't going to choke to death. The coughing fit quickly diminished to a

Abigail L. Marsh

couple of hiccoughs, then a frosty glare. I pulled the gag back over her mouth.

"Tilly!" I heard a familiar voice bellow up the stairs. "Cain wants your scrawny arse down here now."

It was Harley, the biggest brute you would ever lay your eyes on and one of the few men in Cain's pack that disgusted me to the very core. His morals were all out of whack; let's just say you didn't want to be alone with him, not ever!

"On guard Max." I said, not satisfying Harley with an answer.

Max sat down at her feet, hackles up a low grumbling emitting from his core. I looked back at the sorry scene. It was horrible, and just to confirm my thoughts a familiar sinking feeling clouded my stomach. Isabelle reminded me of everything I had worked so hard to forget, and when I couldn't take looking at her anymore, I turned and left.

Back downstairs I felt slightly sick, but the sound of all Cain's crime buddies tore my mind away from Isabelle, and I followed the noise into the kitchen.

All of them were present. Cain, the mastermind at the head of the wooden oak table, Kurt, with his greying brown hair and Jamie, the one with the big ears- Cains best friends sat next to him, and Rick and Wes, the getaway drivers, perched next to them, each one had a beer strapped to their hands.

Following on down the row, and opposite one another was Mel our cleaner, cook, girlfriend and all round carer, and Tate, one of the most muscular guys I have ever met. Next to him an empty chair, the only one with no arms and no cushion - funnily enough, I expected that to be mine. Opposite Tate was Harley. I despised him thoroughly. Then his buddy Chris, who was nearly equally as mean sat beside him, a large scar etched down his face, just like one you'd imagine on a pirate and he had the curly ginger hair to go with it. I teased him mercilessly for it, calling him Captain Red-Beard, (behind his back of course). Finally, there was Lucas; he was there to help Tate. They were best mates, I couldn't help staring at his bulging muscles and tanned arms, as far as crushes go when your trapped with a load of middle-aged men, with no real connection to the outside world, the way my stomach flipped from pain to butterflies the moment I saw him, I was in for a ride. No one turned to look at me as I walked in; every single man at that table was listening to Cain intently.

Cain was forty two and still in his prime, he had short jet black hair that always seemed to do what he asked, except for a little flick in his fringe that drove him insane, and required copious amounts of hair gel to

Abigail L. Marsh

tame. He had a slight stubble which made his jawline ridiculously de-fined, *not* that I was jealous. His bright blue eyes connected briefly with mine as he looked around the group, and he smiled. He flicked a piece of imaginary dust off his sleeve before looking back at the paper in front of him. Cain almost always wore a suit, whether he was going shopping, going to a meeting or going out to murder someone. All of them were tailor made to fit him by Carnaby Hanson, an old friend who owned a discreet backstreet business in London. He had the awful habit of smoking; smoked cigars by the pack full. Cain had a horrible back-story, full of things not even I could imagine- and that's saying a lot, but I'm not going to delve into that too deeply because this is about my sto-ry.

"What's going on?" I asked, purposefully interrupting. I sat down in the only seat available, in-between Tate and Lucas. As I leaned back in the chair, I realised I was sitting way out of view, lost in the muscles of the men. I sat forward as Cain threw me a glance, annoyance etched all across his face.
"The next job." He said as if it were obvious.

There were plans laid out all over the table but at a quick glance I couldn't make head nor tail of them.

"What do you want me to do?" I asked ignoring Harley's stony glare; they had been talking about his part to play before my appearance, quite clearly I had enraged him. Bonus!

"Nothing. You are staying here with Chris and Rick to train the kid." He reminded me. I frowned in disgust, how boring.

"But stay here and listen in case we need back up, or someone drops out." He added, quick to appease my bitterness.

"Do I at least get my dog?" I asked bluntly, tempted to give Harley a good kick under the table as a grin had erupted onto his face.

"Yes, Max will stay with you." Cain smiled, writing it down on his pad of paper.

Grudgingly I stayed and listened to the whole plan. They were planning a reasonably small time, low-risk robbery in Bury St Edmunds, about an hour inland from the house out on the Norfolk coast. We always, always, always carried out crimes away from the homestead. It meant we could be out of the picture faster, and let things die down.

All the details were gone through bit-by-bit, and eventually, after two and a half of the most tedious hours plagued with constant talking and bum numbness, the plan was set.

Cain let everybody go apart from Rick, Chris and I, he spoke to us directly. As I stared across at my two new partners, my lips curled into a grimace.

Abigail L. Marsh

Rick was an ex-con done for fraud, theft and numerous other crimes. He had served five years in jail before becoming friends with Cain and joining The Pack.

Chris? He hadn't been imprisoned for anything; he was just a cruel man who made things happen and got things done no matter what it took or who he hurt in the process; that made him dangerous. I didn't like him either. The problem with The Pack was, no matter who I liked or disliked they had all proven themselves to be loyal members, and Cain was a stickler for loyalty. Now I was working with them, I was going to have to watch my back.

Cain said in no uncertain terms that unless he called and told us to come down, that we must test and train Isabelle; push her to her limits by using whatever force necessary. I looked uneasily at the smile on Chris's face; sure he was happy to hear this.

I remembered training as a distinctive memory in my past. It was absolute torture, but I had become so much stronger braver and tougher. I prayed then and there to whoever was listening that this would be the case for Isabelle. I couldn't bear to think of what would happen if she didn't pull through.

In its defence, training wasn't the most gruelling time of my life, but it was up there at the top, a lot of blood, a lot of sweat and a lot of tears accompanied me through that period of my life. I had trained for fourteen to sixteen hours a day; running, swimming, cardio, biking, and combat, they even taught me to drive. If I refused? You didn't refuse, end of story. The pain inflicted the first time I refused was enough to put me off for life.

At the finish line two months later I was fit and ready, both physically and mentally. I had no real family around anymore, so Cain and Mel made do.

"How do you want me to do it?" Rick piped up with his nasal fuelled voice which always got under my skin.

"I don't." Cain said. "Tilly is going to. You are to act as guard and guards only." Cain said flatly.

"Okay boss." Rick said, I smirked at Chris.

"Tilly, I'm counting on you, Isabelle needs to be ready for the job in London. If she's not ready, and something goes wrong, she could end up dead. If that happens, you will be responsible." He said looking down on me with eyes that told me I was five years old and doing something wrong already. I didn't like the sound of that one bit.

"Hold on. I've never done this before, cut me some slack!" I snapped, angry that he had thought of that before I had even made a start.

Abigail L. Marsh

"You have four months, that's more than enough time, it's okay; you can do it, just stay focused." He smiled at me, and my features softened without my consent.

"Now get upstairs, get her correct clothes size and draw up a timetable." he said, his smile vanishing completely. I turned abruptly and left, deciding to get her trained up as soon as possible. The sooner she was ready, the sooner the torture was over.

The rest of the evening was spent pouring over a time table. I finally finished the masterpiece and took it upstairs to pin on her wall.

"Are you going to kill me?" She spoke for the first time as I pulled down her gag. I was taken aback at her small voice. It was weak, almost frail. I choked on my response,

"I'm not going to kill anyone." I said rubbing the goosebumps that were now peppering my arm.

"Will they?" She asked fearfully. I bit my lip turning this question over in my mind. I doubted it very much, but there was never any real way to tell what Cain was about to do, or going to ask you to do. I shook my head.

"No, not if you do what they say. Go where they tell you to, and respect them no matter what."

There was a pause where her eyes wandered across the depressing room, and she seemed to take in what I said, at the very least she under-

Abigail L. Marsh

stood her demise was not imminent, and then her eyes landed on the timetable I had written.

"Why are you doing all that?"

I smiled sadly.

"That's not just for me, or I would have stuck it up in my room. It's for you."

Horror shot across her face as quick as a bolt of lightning.

"Why?" She demanded shakily.

"You've got to train up." I said as a wave of sickness passed through my stomach. "To get into The Pack you have to be quick, agile, brave. You have to…"

"No, I'm not… I want to go home!" She yelled suddenly interrupting me, shocking me with the volume explosion, before launching herself off the chair. I reached out to catch her, but I wasn't fast enough, and she crashed face first into the rough wooden floor. Max grumbled warningly at the commotion, I put my hand out to shush him, and he fell silent, dropping his head back to his feet with indignant attitude.

"Well done…" I sighed crouching down by her head. "Isabelle, I know it's first instinct, but don't try and run, you can't get out of here… Believe me. It's pointless trying."

Using her handcuffs, I helped her to her feet. We faced each other off. She was much smaller than me and scrawnier, training would sort that out, but the look of pure defiance on her face concerned me.

Abigail L. Marsh

"There are seven grown men in this house, all with loaded guns, and two German Shepherds, so heed me when I say any attempts at escape will be met with your painful and gory end." I said purposefully switching tactics, attempting to put the fear of God in her. "Now I won't hurt you but the others will, so just stick with it, do everything I say and you'll survive this."

I pushed her back onto the bed and cuffed her to the frame, her eyes boring into my head as I did so.

Uncomfortable at being glared at by someone who probably very much wanted to strangle me, I spun around, finally deciding to head for that jacuzzi I had promised myself. However luck was never on my side, I had a track record for disappointments, and this was clearly not the time for anything new. Cain strode in through the open door and destroyed my beautiful plan.

"Why is this door wide open? And what on earth was that bang?" He demanded. I stepped back so he could see the cuffs, and Max sprawled out across the floor, not dignifying him with an answer. A wry smile spread across Cains' face. It was slightly off-putting.

"And how's our guest doing?" He asked striding around the room, his arms wide open, admiring his own genius. "Like the room?"

"I want to go home." Isabelle spoke sharply. Cain turned on his heel and clapped his hands together, still smiling.

Abigail L. Marsh

"Yes, yes, I'm quite sure you do, but never mind." Cain turned to me.

"Tilly I think you and I should have a nightcap before you go to sleep, don't you?"

I nodded uncertainly.

"Max, on guard." Cain said, his voice shifting from annoying to deadly serious. I watched as my dog turned from his lazy self back into the notorious killing machine and slink across to the bed, baring his teeth.

"Don't move off that bed, he will bite you and no-one will come." I said trying desperately to warn her, without Cain seeing through to the weakness I knew I had.

"Come on darling." Cain said taking my arm and leading me out of the room. Isabelle's screams that followed shot straight through me to the core. I watched as Cain fastened the locks up tight and tossed a single key through the air to me jovially. I caught it.

"Don't lose it."

Unable to listen to the screams for her Mum that I knew were futile, I left the hallway. Cain patted my back and steered me down to his office.

I had only been allowed to have sips of alcohol before, as much of a lawbreaking, hell-raising human being Cain Black was, he wouldn't let me touch his bottles, or any bottles at that. So it was more than slightly odd when he poured me a small shot of his prized Bourbon and collapsed back in his armchair.

"What's this in aid of?" I sighed looking at the foul-smelling brown liquid.

"Dutch courage… Training her isn't going to be easy, but I think you're old enough now to take on this responsibility."

"I don't know." I admitted rubbing my forehead stressfully.

"What's the motto?" He asked. I cringed, he was referring to the motto that had been drilled into my head during my training years ago. I will never forget it.

"We train because blood will spill, and it isn't going to be mine." I droned, trying to figure out how I was going to get rid of Cain's prized drink without him being offended.

"Repeat it. Come on Tilly, give it some more oomph." Cain sighed taking a sip from his gold-rimmed glass.

"We train because blood will spill, and it is not going to be mine!" I said with as much fake gusto as I could possibly muster.

Cain sat up and smiled.

"Good, now drink your drink and get to bed."

I looked down at the shot glass and sighing mentally tipped the whole lot into my mouth, swallowing hard as the fiery liquid hit the back of my throat. Cains hearty laugh echoed around the room as I coughed and spluttered.

"Goodnight honey."

I headed straight for the bathroom and washed my mouth out with copious amounts of mouthwash before finally sinking into the hottest bath I could manage and switching on the jets.

I laid in my bed, freshly scrubbed clean, hair up in a bun balanced, on the top of my head, still feeling severely dissatisfied with all that had gone on that day, then to top it all off the news came on on the TV poking out of the bottom of my bed. There was a whole story on about Isabelle, but I didn't want to watch it. I wasn't scared that someone was going to find her, because they had been looking for me for nearly a decade, and no-one had ever come close. Apart from the fact I didn't want to leave, I had given up all hope that I ever would. So I changed the channel over and put a pre-recorded episode of Eastenders on. I tried to keep up with the story, but something in my stomach just wasn't sitting right. Where did the girl come from? Who were her parents? Why did Cain choose her? I fell into a troubled sleep, with no answers.

Abigail L. Marsh

Chapter Three: The Runaway

Numerous beaches in the south of England are quite pleasant as the summer season dies down and Autumn sweeps in, but not at the cove at Western Point, a hundred metres beneath the house, the only access a steep wooden staircase rotting away to its core. No-one ever went down there, no-one except us. A ferocious wind battered us relentlessly as we stood out of the protection of the jagged rocks near the water's edge, threatening to knock us to the ground. I agreed wholeheartedly with my gut as it churned uncomfortably, perhaps it wasn't the best time to go for a first swimming lesson. I looked back at Chris as he held Isabelle still. His face was decidedly menacing.

"Okay." I said clapping my hands together and sucking up my own doubts. "We are going to swim out to that blue buoy, it's about two hundred metres there, and two hundred metres back, not so bad." I said glaring at the crashing waves, were they calming down? Chris gave Isabelle a push forwards, but she stopped almost instantly as the cold water lapped over her toes.

"It's freezing." She said backing up slightly. I nodded.

"That is true. Faster we're in, faster we're out."

Isabelle looked nervously back at the men, Chris was obviously grow-ing tired of her and without hesitation, he stepped up and shoved her hard into the shallow water.

"There you go, first bits over." He growled. "MOVE."

Spitting the gritty water out of her mouth she struggled to her feet, her eyes sweeping the cliff for any possible sign of rescue. My chest sparked with frustration. Why couldn't she just get in the bloody water? I grabbed her arm and yanked her, forcing her to take some steps into the deeper water.

"I'm not going to tell you again." I snapped. "You can walk the first part."

She relented and finally, we got swimming. I'd been a strong swimmer my whole life and cut through the waves as if they were nothing. Half-way to the buoy I turned and watched Isabelle, to my surprise she was making progress. Her head popped up, and she gasped for breath. When her eyes fell on me, they widened in shock. I spun around with just enough time to dive under the monstrous wave heading into the shore. When I came up, I couldn't see Isabelle anywhere. Shit.

"Isabelle?" I yelled desperately scanning the waves. "Isabelle!"

Rick had his jacket off and was about to dive in when something grabbed my leg and pulled me under, swallowing a mouthful of salty water I forced myself back to the surface dragging the anchor up with me. Head above water, I struggled to wipe my complete comb-over from my eyes.

"Tilly!"

Finally, I scraped back the curtain and saw Isabelle bobbing in the water right in front of me. Without hesitation, I grabbed her around the waist and swam backwards to the buoy where I knew I would be able to stand. Using the blue flotation for support my feet fell down on the sharp uneven ridge as I caught a hand to the face.

"Put your feet down." I groaned letting go of her. With neck and chest out of the water, we were able to take a breather. Isabelle set about trying to wipe the salty water from her mouth, with her wetsuit sleeve. "Bloody Hell." I breathed checking I still had all my body parts. "Are you okay? That was awful."

I gave Chris and Rick a quick wave before turning to Isabelle.

"That's not going to work babe, just stop, we can stop here for a minute." I grabbed her arm and pulled it away from her face, her fingertips had turned a funny sort of blue and she shoved them under her armpits in a vain attempt to install some heat.

"They won't come out here, will they?" She jittered looking back at Chris and Rick. I shook my head.

"Does it look like Captain Red-Beard would come any closer to the water, fat lards." I smirked.

"What the hell is happening?" She cried suddenly. "I want to go home."

"I know... Iz, it's not going to happen; there is no way to get out." I said as she crumpled into a fit of tears. I wondered if I should hug her or whether she would shove me back into the water, thankfully she decided for me and grabbed my arm in despair.

"Please." She cried again. "Why are we doing this?"

"So when we do the jobs you don't die, you don't get killed." I said as Chris's waving caught my eye.

"What? What jobs?" She breathed. "Do you know how crazy you sound?"

Ignoring Chris, I tried to explain.

"These guys, they aren't playing games, they brought you here to help me and if you can't, they'll just get rid of you."

"My parents will come. They're looking for me right now."

I shook my head.

"I used to think that." I said. "They won't find us, Isabelle. There are no clues, there never is."

"You were kidnapped as well?" Isabelle asked shocked. I nodded.

"I've been here for years and years." I said. "It gets better, life changes when you pass training, I promise it won't be like this forever." I said, but Isabelle wasn't listening, she was too busy trying to digest the information.

"You've been here for *years*?" She breathed shaking her head as if she couldn't quite believe what was happening to her.

"Isabelle, I can't get you out of this situation. All I can do is make it easier for you okay? You have to get faster and stronger. If you do what I say they aren't going to do anything to you. This will be over someday. They can't keep us forever." I said desperately thinking of any words that would keep her going. She seemed to settle at this thought. "Okay?"

She nodded taking a few deep breaths and shivering violently.

"We'll get you dry when we get back…It's two hundred metres back to shore. If you jump off here as far as you can and catch a good wave it'll carry you into shore without a lot of effort." I said calmly. She nodded and took a couple more deep breaths preparing herself as I took her hand and shaped it into a cup.

"Cup your hands, it'll propel you forward better."

A deafening bang echoed from the beach. I felt the sound waves hit my chest before I'd even looked up. Chris had his gun pointing up in the air.

"He's got a gun!" Isabelle cried grabbing my arm.

"He's not gonna use it." I reassured her. "He's just bored of waiting for us."

I looked behind me and saw a wave coming,

"In, one, two…"

Just before the wave hit us, we dived forwards. We reached the beach ten minutes later, Isabelle collapsed on the sand utterly exhausted.

"What the hell were you doing out there." Chris snapped, his red cheeks quivering.

"I was explaining to Isabelle how to use the current to her advantage. What were you doing? Trying to alert the whole world to our where-abouts?"

A purple vein popped up on the side of Chris's head as I smirked at him.

"Get up!" Ralph shouted at Isabelle who was laying on the ground, cov-ered in wet, cold sand.

"Leave her alone." I snapped, shoving him away as he attempted to haul her to her feet. "Come on, let's get dry." I said taking her hand and pulling her to her feet.

Chris and Rick shook their heads gravely at each other as we headed back up to the house.

The world atop the cliff was a completely different world from the windswept, wave crashing hell we left behind. The sun had come out

Abigail L. Marsh

and beat down on us as Isabelle and I headed outside for our cardio session. Max lazed on the patio 'on guard' as we started the circuit with a quick warm up.

"We do this in P.E all the time." Isabelle said reaching for her toes.

"What's P.E?"

She stoppedand straightening up stared at me, confusion etched all over her scrunched up face.

"What do you mean what's P.E? It's a class, don't you go to..."

I shook my head.

"No, I don't go anywhere. Talk and stretch, we have a major tonne of stuff to do and if Cain sees you slacking we'll both be dead."

Isabelle grabbed her toes and smiled at me.

"Flexible huh? Let's see if you can do this." I said painlessly dislocating my shoulder and twisting my arm around, so it was facing the opposite direction.

She stepped back in a mix of awe and disgust.

"That's not right."

As she shook her head at me, a rustle in the bushes on the other side of the garden caught my attention.

"What?" Isabelle asked looking.

"Just carry on?" I said pulling her around and pointing at the floor.

"Fifty press ups, then sit ups... And don't turn around."

Abigail L. Marsh

Max grumbled at her as I sprinted across the grass. The bushes shivered as the person hiding in their midst panicked.

"Don't make me call my Alsatian. Come out where I can see you!" I snapped.

A moment later a boys face appeared. He had his hands held up and looked at me with a cocky smile I wanted to wipe off his annoying face.

"I come in peace." He said in an accent I had never heard before.

"Who the hell are you?" I demanded baffled by this scruffy boy's sudden appearance.

"I'm Seth. Who are you?" He asked raising his eyebrows. I narrowed my eyes like a five-year-old attempting to sass her mother for the first time.

"Well, where'd you come from? "I snapped glancing back at the house.

"Cool it. I live in Cromer. I just moved here from Yorkshire and…"

"Cromer is miles from here, why are you here? What made you think you could sneak into our garden?" I interrupted, eager to clean the conversation up and send him on his way before one of The Pack noticed him and held him for ransom.

"I saw you yesterday, out running with a huge guy, is he your boyfriend?"

Well not that I would mind that at all but sadly not.

"No! I, don't have a boyfriend." I said shaking my head in contempt.

"You had better leave; you can't just wander into peoples gardens."

"Good cos he'd probably squish me like a bug…Who's that, she's properly going for it." He laughed pointing over at Isabelle who was still pumping away at the press ups.

"Switch." I yelled over at her. She didn't look over at me but flipped over and began doing sit-ups. "Why would he squash you?" I asked turning back to Seth.

"Who is she?" Seth pressed, ignoring my question with shifty eyes.

"Uh that's…. My sister." I said scrambling for an answer that would involve the least questions.

"You guys are fitness crazy." He said.

"Yeah, we like to stay fit." I shrugged. He laughed and I caught a twinkle in his dark eyes I hadn't seen in anyone before.

"What?" He asked brushing his fringe away from his face awkwardly.

"How old are you?" I asked.

"Sixteen you?" He asked.

"Same." I replied.

A familiar bang came from behind me, the back door. Panic shot into my mouth and I shoved Seth back into the bushes.

"You have to get out of here and you cannot come back." I squealed.

Hidden by the leaves all I saw was the cocky grin he had first appeared with.

"Please, go. If my Dad sees you here, he'll…"

"But I didn't get your name." He persisted holding my wrist. I spun around and dared a glance at Isabelle. No-one was there yet.

"Nellie, my names Nellie, now go, please." I begged slipping my wrist away out of his grasp. He shrunk back into the bushes disappearing from view. Max barked as I ran back to Isabelle.

"Shush!" I whispered patting his head. "On guard."

I re-joined Isabelle just in time; Cain came around the corner not a second later wheeling a brand new bike, he nodded at the pair of us. *Phew.* "You need to work to catch up with Tilly. Look at you drenched, Tilly hasn't even broken a sweat."

Isabelle nodded her head in silence.

"Chris will take you two out for a spin on this across the backs. I want twenty miles on the clock before you step foot in this house." He said leaning the bike against the shed.

"Sure." I said.

Isabelle nodded again. Cain eyed Isabelle.

"You know, if someone brought me a new bike, the first thing I might do was thank him." Cain said crouching down awfully close to Isabelle. With a quick eyebrow raise from me, she managed a squeaky,

"Thank you."

Abigail L. Marsh

"Don't let me down." He growled stepping on her hand as he stood up.

Face red and jaw clenched she managed to stay quiet. He nodded at me

and left, Isabelle immediately cradled her hand, biting her lip.

"You okay?" I asked.

She nodded.

"Thanks for not dropping me in it."

I didn't get a response. She was back at the sit-ups. I joined in. What

else was there left to do?

We cycled just over fifteen miles in an hour, it was fast-paced even for

me, but I kept up with Chris easily. Isabelle fell behind us, Max running

by her side. He was puffing and panting almost as much as she was.

With a mile left to go lunch was almost in sight, but it was just not

meant to be. Isabelle's front wheel hit an unusually big rut in the road

and she careered over her handlebars with a scream. I screeched to a

halt and turned just in time to see her helmeted head plow into the road,

splintering everywhere. Max stopped, looking from me to her his

tongue lolling out of his mouth.

My tyres grazed the dirt roughly, spitting gravel in all directions as I

spun my bike around and threw it onto the grass verge. Isabelle looked

up at me her eyes rolling round in a daze as I ran over.

Abigail L. Marsh

"Are you okay?" I asked dropping down to her level.

Her trousers had a massive rip in them and the cut to her leg was seeping blood onto the tarmac. When her eyes met with the wound blind panic crossed her face, which was quickly superseded by waterworks.

"No, no it's okay, it's just a graze." I said desperately trying to calm her.

"No! I just want to go home." She sobbed reaching down and covering her knee with her hand. I glanced up at Chris for some help. He was still halfway down the road texting someone on his phone. I was only distracted for a second, but it gave Isabelle just enough time to spring up and knock me over. Taken by surprise, I slipped and whacked the back of my helmet on the tarmac, my eyes spun out of focus. As I forced myself into a sitting position my eyes readjusted and I watched Isabelle sprint up the street away from us.

Chris was yelling as Max dropped all responsibilities and laid down on the floor with me and no matter how much Chris yelled at me to go after her, I just couldn't, my feet wouldn't move.

Everything seemed to go in slow motion as Chris whizzed past me on his bike. I struggled off the floor knowing right then and there in the bottom of my heart that I couldn't let him hurt her. As Chris caught up to her in a few seconds, I pulled myself out of my slow-mo moment and felt myself searching my jacket for my gun. It was there tucked away. I marched towards them. Isabelle was on the ground, Chris pinning her to the floor, screaming in her face.

I reached them not a moment later and using the grip of the gun I smashed the barrel skilfully against the back of Chris's skull, hard enough to knock him out. He keeled over, out cold. I rolled him off Isabelle and we stared at each other, shock drowning our features. Then she was on her feet.

"Run!" She cried grabbing my arm and tugging me forward. My heart and my head instantly began fighting. Stay and live my life as Cain's princess or go and get myself put back in the social system. If we even got anywhere without Cain coming after me. It just wasn't worth the risk.

"I can't." I said shakily resting a hand on Max's collar. For a second we stared at each other, my eyes bore into hers and suddenly something clicked, eyes widening to take it in. I knew her. I knew her face, but before I could say anything, she'd let go of my hand and had started running away.

Max barked and was up on his hind legs trying to force his way out of my hold.

"No Max!" I said. "No, she doesn't belong here." I crouched down, patting his head, he whined pitifully at me.

Abigail L. Marsh

"I know, come on. I'll get you some bacon."

His whining stopped at that.

I turned and looked at Chris sprawled out on the floor, three bikes laid out on the road covered in fingerprints and Isabelle running up the street. The police would have a field day.

Hauling Isabelle's bike into a ditch was an effort with a banging head, but the fast pace ride back while trying to come up with a story that made sense was murder. I could barely see by the time I got back to the house. Running through the front door I screamed for Cain.

He came flying into the hallway panic in his eyes. As he scanned me over looking for the bullet hole, he slid the helmet off my head and touched the blood dripping down the back of my neck.

"What's happened? MEL!"

"Isabelle's gone, Chris... There was a bike crash. We fell. Chris is still on the road." I cried as Mel came into the kitchen. She never made a fuss at the sight of blood and checked my head as Cain pressed me for answers.

"Why didn't you stop her, shoot her foot or something?" He asked snatching his keys from the side and pulling me out to his car with Mel following.

Abigail L. Marsh

"She was already gone by the time I had checked Chris was alive." I said.

He looked at me and quickly changed his mind.

"Stay here with Mel, she'll fix your head, call me if the girl comes back, okay?" He said calmly. I nodded. He got in the car and floored it, a plume of dust rising up behind him.

"As if she would do that" I mumbled to myself wiping a fake tear from my cheeks.

"Right, inside." Mel said taking my hand and pulling me towards her medical room, aka the back room where she kept all the medicines and bandages you'd ever possibly need in a zombie apocalypse.

As I was frog-marched back inside my face contorted with confusion, it was still troubling me how all of a sudden her face had changed and I knew it from somewhere. I thought and thought and thought, as Melanie glued the small slice where the helmet had dug in, back together, but no matter how much I ran her face through my brain I just couldn't place her anywhere.

"All done baby, go and lie down. Take it easy for a few hours. Cain will find her." She passed me a lollipop she had for when Tate came in with a wound and rubbed my cheek softly.

Abigail L. Marsh

"Everything okay?" She asked. Nodding I thanked her and left the hospital scented room which made me feel sick every single time I went in. Max was sat by the fridge whining. I dropped a few rashes of bacon into his bowl, he wolfed it down then skeDaddled out of the room as someone outside called his name. Feeling miserable I made myself a sandwich and was sitting down at the kitchen table when my eyes met with a sight that sent shivers down my spine.

Harley, the big, fat Romanian man, with spiked black hair and a ridiculous moustache, that made me think if he ever ended up in prison, he wouldn't make it past the two-week mark. He stood blocking the whole doorway with his stench leaking across the room towards me.

"Where's your pretty friend?" He smirked sauntering over to the table. I clenched my jaw biting my tongue so hard I could taste iron at the back of my throat. I wasn't going to give him the satisfaction of a single word.

"Cain's going to kill her." He joked in a singsong tone sliding out the chair opposite me and breathing his stale breath across the space between us.

"God Harley, do you ever brush your teeth?" I choked, wafting a hand in front of my face. "Did you have fish for breakfast? That's disgusting."

Abigail L. Marsh

His lips quivered with anger but he was good at taunting me, but I'd give him just as good back.

"Your friend is gonna die today, he'll find her and when he does..." He trailed off, a smirk on his face.

"Aww, lost your train of thought, go jump in front of a bus." I spat letting my anger rise up into my chest.

"And then he'll throw her off a cliff, she'll break her neck and her body will wash away to sea... or maybe he'll dig a hole in the mud..." He continued to taunt me. The anger in my chest wouldn't stay put and I lost control. Gripping my cutlery in my hand, I stood abruptly and launched the knife covered in mayonnaise at him. It bounced off his head and landed on the floor with a clatter spraying mayo everywhere.

"You have no idea what you're talking about!" I yelled spraying egg mayonnaise across the table in a complete fit of rage.

Harley looked horrified for a moment before his shock turned to anger; he reared up out of his chair and threw his meaty hands towards me. Thankfully the table separated us and his stubby arms fell short as I dived to avoid them.

"Come here you little shit!" Harley screamed. I backed up against the fridge furious with myself for not being able to ignore him like I always had done. What was different this time, hey? Your stupid little friend? The one that had almost knocked you out?.

"MAX!" I yelled knowing I couldn't beat the man if it came down to a fist fight. Harley grinned.

"Your old pal isn't here, Jamie just taken him for a little walkies on the beach." He knocked a chair out of his way clearing his route to me. "It's just you and me."

Shit!

Some God, somewhere, must have been smiling down on me as the crunch of gravel sounded through the crack in the kitchen door. I risked taking my eyes off Harley and was relieved to see Kurt jogging up the back path to dispose of the rubbish for me.

"Stop you oaf!" He cried as he battered the door out of his way and seeing my predicament. Sighing I watched him come running over as Harley curled his fist into a tight ball ready to pummel me. Kurt, a giant gym god compared to Stubby, grabbed him by the scruff of his collar and chucked his flabby body away from me.

"You know what Cain will do. Do you want a bullet through your head? Just cool it and leave her the hell alone." He snapped. Harley glared at me over Kurt's shoulder as I snuck out of the room. That had been a close one.

I lay in bed that night jumping at every tiny sound that found its way into my bedroom. No-one had returned, not Cain or Chris, not Isabelle.

Abigail L. Marsh

With a spinning head, I pictured her mangled body laying the bottom of a cliff. *Had Cain killed her as Harley had said? Or had she done the impossible and escaped?* A tear rolled down my cheek and soaked into my pillow as the house lay silent and dark. *Who was she?*

Chapter Four: Running

A light flickered across my ceiling, distracting me from fiddling with the frayed label poking out of my pillow. I glanced up at the digital clock sitting on my bedside table. It's red figures burned into my eyes, 02:14 am. Creeping across the floor to the window I peeked through the break in the curtains, sure enough the car was back, stationed right outside the back door fifteen feet below me along with the two men. Cain lit a cigar and sat back against the bonnet, Chris joined him slamming the passenger side door.

Cain waved at him angrily then looked up at my window. I backed up into the shadows hastily. When all had gone quiet, I crawled back up to the window and unlatched it, silently pushing it ajar. The men's voice drifted up to the window, they were quiet, but I caught snippets of their conversation as they talked freely, unaware they had a listener.

Abigail L. Marsh

"Did you see the game?" Chris asked taking a sip from a bottle of water he had in his hand. Cain laughed.

"I know *you* didn't, face down in a ditch." Cain laughed.

"Yeah well, that was compliments of hers truly." he said waving in the direction of my room. I bobbed back and found I could hear just as well from the comforts of kneeling on my bedroom floor, head resting on the windowsill.

"I'll talk to her, but you're a fully grown man."

"So the game… Who won?" Chris asked flipping the subject on its head, clearly embarrassed that we had beat him.

This conversation went on and on as I sat on the floor beneath the window, head starting to lull. My fingers started to go numb from the cold seeping through the open windows when…

"What are we gonna do with her then?" Chris asked. My head jolted and I was up at the window, straining to hear as their voices quietened. Cain sighed and stood up flicking his cigar butt to the ground, scattering its glowing embers across the cobbles.

"Train her. We don't have a choice. But Tilly is no longer in charge. She's proved she can't do it. It's too much for her."

My heart hit the bottom of my chest with a cold thud as I realised she'd been apprehended.

Abigail L. Marsh

"Why'd you make her do it in the first place?" Chris asked. "You know she's not…She's not like us."

Cain scratched the back of his head like he always did when he didn't know how to answer a question. After a puff of air and a shrug he tried to explain,

"I wanted to see her reaction. I knew the girl would make a break for it at some point. I wanted to see how loyal Tilly really was."

"And…"

Cain shrugged.

"She came back didn't she?" He said going around the boot of the car. I watched as he blipped the key and the vehicle acknowledge his request by flickering its lights. Cain and Chris stood at the boot for a few seconds. It was infuriating not being able to see anything from my vantage point .

"Grab her legs." Cain finally said reaching in. I watched, horrified, as Isabelle's body was lifted from the car and tossed over Cains' shoulder like a rag doll. Chris slammed the boot as Cain headed for the back door underneath my room.

"Jesus! Shut up! I do not want to wake Tilly." Cain whispered harshly, Chris raised his hands in mock surrender as they went inside and closed the kitchen door.

The back stairs creaked heavily as I dove back into my bed and yanked the duvet over my head leaving only a tiny gap open to listen.

"She's pretty beat up boss.." Chris whispered. I had purposefully left my bedroom door open the smallest of cracks.

"Nothing that won't heal." Cain whispered back as they tiptoed past my room. "She won't try it again; that's for sure."

And then they were gone. After shutting my window, I laid back down, pulling the duvet around me as tightly as possible, screwing my eyes shut as I tried in vain to expel the image of Isabelle being flung around out of my head.

As I settled down thinking I could maybe get some sleep footsteps came back down the corridor towards my room. I laid like a statue unsure of what to expect. There came a soft knock on my door. I didn't answer. The door opened, the light from the hallway beyond filtered across my room. Squinting, so it looked like I was still asleep, I watched Cain step out of the light and into my room. He didn't hang about, walking straight over to the bedside table he picked up the alarm clock running his fingers all over it.

"Where the hell is the off button." He grumbled quietly. I didn't dare move. I didn't want to give him the slightest inkling I'd been eavesdropping on a private conversation; I'd be strung up for sure.

Abigail L. Marsh

"For God's sake." Cain swore under his breath before yanking the plug out of the wall, catching a pair of sunglasses he'd knocked before they hit the ground. Satisfied with this he turned to leave, but before he could my scrambled duvet caught his eye. Stopping he straightened it out, patting my legs gently once he was done. Then he left, closing the door quietly behind him. I rolled over into a better position and was asleep in moments.

Morning came with new lightness on the situation. I woke up late to the smell of bacon wafting through the cracks around my door. Rubbing the sleep out of my eyes I plodded down the back stairs into the kitchen where Melanie was frying bacon and dancing to some crappy club music playing away on Alexa.

"Morning sleepyhead." She said when she saw me. "Alexa... Down two..."

"The weather today will be partly sunny with some cloud, highs of eighteen..."

Melanie rolled her eyes at the machine and manually turned the volume down.

"Bloody robots..." She grumbled as I took a seat round the back of the table and looked at my trainers muddied up by the door. Mel caught my expression.

Abigail L. Marsh

"I guess you figured out you're not training Isabelle anymore." She said placing another three rashers of bacon in the pan. They sizzled loudly sending up a plume of smoke into the extraction vent.

"I wasn't very good at it, one day and she disappeared." I said laughing half-heartedly.

"Well, they caught her... But I'm guessing that didn't get past you either?" She smiled knowingly.

I shook my head, not giving the game away.

"Is she okay?"

"I didn't see her." Mel said honestly, "But I wouldn't have wanted to be her when those two caught up with her... Would you?"

"No." I shook my head.

"It'll be alright Tilly, not worth fretting about. Here, eat this, then when it's settled why don't you go for a run? That always makes you feel better."

As I bit into my crispy bacon sandwich, I realised she was right. Running was the only real thing I knew. I had always run, since way back when, when my best friend and I would sprint through the woods racing each other until our lungs burst. It was a fond memory, but I kept it buried deep inside of me. It was the gateway to much darker things. If I went through that door, there was no guarantee I would come back. So I

Abigail L. Marsh

would stay focused on my breathing, each step pounding in my head, feeling the beads of sweat trickling down my back and falling to the ground. Thats what kept me grounded.

As I took my last bite and stood up to leave Melanie gasped in horror. I stopped and looked in the same direction. The back door swung open and Isabelle was roughly shoved inside, slipping on the 'un-welcome' mat she ended up splattered across the stone floor groaning in pain. My mouth fell open at the state of her, eyes locked on her face.

She was more purple than she was white, her eyes swollen and black, casting a dark shadow across grazed cheeks to a bust lip.

"What the hell did you do to her?" I cried tearing my eyes away and looking at Cain as he slipped his shoes onto the rack. He glared up at me, his mood evident from the stoney expression that had exploded across his face.

"The job you were supposed to do… Get up!" He said hauling Isabelle to her feet. Yanking a chair across the room and spinning it around to face the brick wall he shoved her into it.

"Do not move." He spat. Turning to me he pointed violently at Isabelle. "That is how you train someone to do as you tell them. That is how you were trained, do you remember? That is what you responded to." He said. Dragging up my past from where it lived in the gutter was not the done thing, not in that house, not anywhere and Cain knew this. I

Abigail L. Marsh

couldn't even formulate a sentence to respond to him; there were no words to honour the fire of pure hatred bubbling up inside my chest. With an explosion of anger, I launched the plate I was holding at the fridge on the other side of the room. It hit it with such force, shards of crockery sprayed like arrows in every direction slicing everything in their path to pieces.

With blood trickling down my arm I strode past Cain and ran up to my room. I was in my running things not two minutes later, feet pounding across the courtyard I left in a maddening frenzy. I must have run ten miles before I ended up back on the beach that backed onto the house. I sat down on the sand dunes breathing heavily. Having left in such a rush, I'd forgotten to take a water bottle, bad move.

"Hey." a boys voice called breaking my train of thought.

I turned around to see a figure striding along the beach towards me.

Chapter Five: A Welcome Distraction

As he got closer I recognised him as the boy from the bushes.

Abigail L. Marsh

"Oh hey." I said trying to brush him off, not in the mood for his cocky grin, but the fact I couldn't breathe clearly wasn't getting the point across.

"Are you okay?" Seth asked reaching me.

"Yeah, just run a long way… I forgot my water." I said.

"I've got some." He said pulling a bottle of water out of his bag and holding it out to me.

"Thanks."

"Do you mind if I sit?" He asked.

I shrugged looking up at him as I downed half the bottle in under five seconds.

"Free country." I breathed finally dropping the bottle and wiping a trail of watery dribble off my chin.

He smiled and sat down, digging his hands into the warm sand and looking awkwardly out across the still blue ocean.

"Where do you run too?" Finally breaking the silence.

"Uhh depends, sometimes just along the beach, sometimes we go north to Blakeney and sometimes south to Bacton." I said.

"Bacton? That's a long way!" He exclaimed flicking a small bug off his arm.

"About ten miles there, ten miles back." I shrugged passing him the bottle back. "Thanks, I thought I was gonna die."

Abigail L. Marsh

"How do you run so far?" He asked awe spreading across his face like wildfire.

I shrugged.

"Someone must have taught you to do it?"

Sighing I gave him an answer.

"No-one taught me." I said. "I can just do it." This didn't satisfy him and he continued to stare into my eyes waiting for me to carry on. I gave up with his intrusiveness and told him. "I had a friend once. We used to run together when we were little."

"Did you fall out?" He asked.

"What?" I asked dismissively.

"You said you used to run with her; why'd you stop, did you fall out?"

Frowning I shook my head.

"No… We just lost touch."

"Why don't you find her? Then you could have her water instead of al-most passing out on the beach." He laughed lightly. I didn't think I would be able to run fast enough or far enough to ever do that. I looked away from him.

"So." He said sucking air between his teeth, "Do you go to school around here? Only I've not seen you at mine."

"You've been looking for me?" I asked, a smirk appearing on my face.

Abigail L. Marsh

"Well no." he blushed. "I just figured since we're in the same year I'd have bumped into you by now... Or do you go to *a private school*?" He asked putting on a preppy, posh boy voice. I laughed at his attempts and shook my head,

"No, I don't go to school! Which school are you at?"

"Cromer Academy...The only school around here for miles." He pointed out to me his tone suggesting I was complete stupid.

"Right." I agreed as if I totally understood what he was talking about. "Cromer Academy...Yes."

"Do you not get out? How come you don't go to school, that's so weird. Does your sister?"

"My sister?" I queried. His face creased in confusion and I clicked. "Oh right, yeah we're both homeschooled." I said covering up nervously. "No school for us."

For a moment he stared at me in complete bewilderment and I thought I'd weirded him out, but suddenly his face fell into a smile and he laughed.

"You're so lucky!" He said looking back out to sea. "But how do you make friends and stuff?"

That was a question I wasn't prepared for,

"I, uh... I have my sister." I lied, knowing full well that girl hated my guts.

Abigail L. Marsh

"She doesn't count."

"Why not?" I demanded.

Seth paused for a second, thinking of a response.

"Exactly, she does count." I said as my phone pinged in my pocket. I pulled it out and looked at the screen.

Alpha:

Where are you? You've been gone hours.

"Who is it? Your boyfriend?" Seth joked.

"I don't have a boyfriend. I've already told you." I said standing up. "I really gotta go, Thanks for the water…Safe walk back, or, whatever." I said stumbling awkwardly as I searched for the appropriate thing to say.

"Hey, Nellie." Seth said sliding down the dune after me.

"Yep." I stopped and waited for him to catch up.

"I was just wondering." He said scratching his head just like Cain sometimes did when he couldn't find the right thing to say.

"What?" I asked nervously.

"Can I have your number?" His face went bright red as I frowned at him perplexed.

"My phone number?" I asked.

"Well, yeah…"

With raised eyebrows I found myself nodding,

"Sure."

He broke into a huge smile, relief flooding his face as he passed me his phone. Once details had been swapped we stood, awkwardly staring at each other.

"Well, I'll text you." He said patting me on the back. I nodded, completely and utterly bemused by him as he strode away back down the beach.

"What the heck?" I muttered to myself as I turned and sprinted back towards the house, a grin on my face I couldn't shift.

"Where have you been?" Cain demanded when I walked back into the kitchen. He was sat at the table, his muddy feet up on the bench, a black cigar between his lips.

"Do you know, one of those a day will send you to an early grave." I said sliding my shoes off an kicking them into the rack.

"You didn't answer my question. Why do you look guilty… I know you Tilly, what have you been doing?"

I gave him a withering look and gestured to my clothes.

"I went for a run Cain, where the hell do you think I've been?" Frustration fringing my voice.

Abigail L. Marsh

He dropped his feet to the floor with a bang, spraying mud across the freshly mopped floor.

"Don't you get gobby with me Tilly." He said. I raised my hands, surrendering.

"I'm going upstairs." He watched me with a grumpy stare as I plodded past him and climbed the stairs, grinning the moment I was out of his eyesight.

A week later I had been talking to Seth nonstop, Melanie had been right all along, it was good to have someone to talk too, someone my age. It couldn't have been Isabelle, we weren't in the right place for that, but Seth, he was a whole different ball game. The only thing that drove me mad was his persistent begging for me to attend school. I just couldn't. Cain would never in a million years allow it.

None the less I hadn't had a proper friend my age in a long, long time and I wasn't about to give that up no matter how precarious it was for my future here. Cain had come close to finding out about Seth more than once. The first time Seth had been running down the beach towards me when Cain had decided to join me on a run. I had bolted in the other direction, away from Seth, explaining to Cain that I didn't like running on the dry sand and Seth had been stood up. After that we had been super careful, only meeting when Cain was out, or where we were far enough away from the house.

I loaded a bunch of addicting games onto my phone, so I could easily bluff my way out if Cain asked why I was on my phone so much, with no-one to text he would have been on to me in minutes, but I had that covered. It made my mundane day to day life exciting. Seth and I met up most days but never for very long, there was always something in the way, he had school and I had told him my Dad, (Cain) wouldn't like me dating so we had to be careful, or he would 'end it.' Seth understood but took that comment figuratively. I let it be, but I knew Cain and Seth would be in danger if he ever found out I had a friend external to his precious pack.

Cain knocked on my bedroom door early one Saturday morning. When he came in something about his depressed expression panicked me. He'd found out.

"What do you want?" I asked keeping up my grouchy facade as I tried desperately to think of a way to get out of it.

"Still mad at me Princess?" He asked sitting down cautiously on the end of my bed.

"Don't call me that." I said moving my phone out of his reach and shoving it under my pillow.

Abigail L. Marsh

"You're avoiding me, I can tell Tilly. You're never here." he lower lip

protruded as he said this in a vein attempt to get to me to laugh.

"I'm avoiding a lot of people." I admitted not giving in to him.

"Don't you like it here?" He asked suddenly forgetting his act as he re-

alised I wasn't going to take his bait I was taken aback at the genuine-

ness in his voice and allowed myself to think maybe it wasn't about

Seth at all.

"Well, not right now. Isabelle... She's dragging up a lot of memories

from when I was brought here and trained. There's just a lot I don't want

to think about. Plus, she wasn't in a care home, was she? I mean, she

cried for her Mum all the time. Don't you know how much that hurts?"

"Tilly, don't make assumptions about her; you have no idea where she's

come from."

I stopped myself from asking the next question lined up in my head and

backtracked,

"What does that mean?"

Cain shook his head,

"You and her, you're very similar."

"So you did take her from a care home?" I asked thinking that at least it

was better than ripping her from her parents.

Cain shook his head, then abruptly changed the subject.

"Next week you and I are going on holiday."

I had been on holiday before with Cain, believe it or not, he was actually a lot of fun, with no work surrounding him and the rest of The Pack at home, he was relaxed and was happy to do whatever I wanted to do.

"Where?" I asked shocked by this sudden turn of events.

"Los Angeles."

"Very specific, any reason why?"

Cain's expressions turned sheepish and I felt there was a condition attached somewhere.

"I have to pick up some kit from an old pal who lives out there. We'll fly business on the way over and then my pal will send us back via his private jet."

As I was about to ask Cain what this ominous 'kit' was, he mentioned the private jet and I got sidetracked.

"Private Jet?" I asked, my excited voice betraying the grouchiness as the fact I was supposed to be spitting in his direction, slipped from my mind.

Cain nodded.

"Alright, so friends?" He asked opening his arms. I gave up on my hate campaign, bought by his holiday and hugged him.

Abigail L. Marsh

"Wait." I said pulling away. He only marginally let go of me, just enough to see my face.

"What?"

"Please promise me you won't hurt Isabelle again. I can't bare it."

Cain pulled me back into a hug not answering my request. "I need a favour." He said instead. Rolling my eyes, I smirked.

"Oh I see, I'll take you on holiday, but you gotta do something for me first."

"No, that's not it. Tommy is back from London, can you please take him on a run, I would do it myself, but I have business to attend to." He said batting his eyelids like a five-year-old asking for sweetie money.

"Sure thing boss." I nodded sliding off the bed.

"Thanks, kiddo."

Grabbing the lead from the chest at the top of the stairs I descended into the kitchen. I didn't have time to turn around and run away as Isabelle came into my sights, she looked straight at me. Tommy, our more vicious Alsatian, was sat in front of her, baring his teeth as Max laid idle in his basket which he'd managed to drag over to the warmth beneath the stove.

"Tommy away!" I snapped stepping off the final step. He gave her a snort and licked his lips before turning to me.

Abigail L. Marsh

"Max. On guard." I commanded looping Tommy's lead around his neck. Max huffed at me and dragged himself out of his bed as if he were an old man, plonking himself in front of Isabelle and defying me with a stony glare.

"I'm taking Tommy; Max's here." I yelled through the open door that led into the rest of the house.

"Okay!" Kurt yelled back. "I'll be there in a second."

I looked back at Isabelle. She was well and truly worn down, sitting at the table, eyes cast down to the floor, not even looking at the open back door; her whole body screamed defeat. Tommy grumbled impatiently at me.

"I know… Kurt, I'm leaving right now." I yelled not wanting to wait with her any longer.

"Alright, alright." Kurt moaned coming out of the living room with a book. "I'm here."

I spun and left. Seth was waiting for me down on the beach, a tennis ball and launcher in hand.

"So you are playing hooky?" I asked as he tried to put his arm around my back. Tommy's hair shot up on the back of his neck and he growled ferociously.

"Woah!" Seth said jumping away. I yanked Tommy's lead hard, he coughed and I immediately felt bad, he was only doing what he had been trained to do.

"He's our friend. Tommy do you hear me. Seth is our friend." Tommy looked up at me, I smiled reassuringly as he turned to Seth, after a a small woof of an apology he obediently sat down and held out his paw. I nodded at Seth's concern face.

"It's alright now. He won't hurt you." I said.

"Unless I double cross you right? Better not do that."

"No, if you double cross me, *I'll* hurt you." I said half-jokingly. Seth laughed as he shook Tommy's paw, unaware I meant it.

"I'm going away next week." I said when Seth took my hand and we began strolling down the beach just out of reach of the rushing water

"What? Where?" He asked stopping in horror.

"Los Angeles." I said tugging him along. "Come on."

"For how long?" He asked as I launched the ball a hundred metres down the beach. I let of of Tommy's lead and he went flying, sending flicks of sand up in his wake.

"I don't know, a couple of weeks maybe…" I said brushing the grit off my jacket. Seth's mouth fell open.

"A couple of weeks?"

"Three weeks tops."

"That's almost a month! We can't even go away for five days before my Mum starts pulling her hair out. Why so long?"

I laughed at the thought of his Mum running around ripping her hair out in anguish.

"I haven't been on holiday in years." I said. "Ca... My Dad decided." I said catching myself before I had a chance to ruin everything.

Seth pouted like a five-year-old, kicking the ball that Tommy had dropped at his feet hard. I watched it skid across the sand smirking at his demeanour.

"I'm not going away forever." I said attempting to mess up his short hair. He pushed me away, his eyes grinning even if his mouth didn't.

"It'll feel like forever." he said going all mushy on me.

I stuck my fingers in my mouth and pretended to gag.

"Why can't we be cute?" He demanded.

"We are cute." I responded pushing him lightly. But being the clumsy fool he was, he slipped on piece of strategically placed seaweed and fell over backward splashing headfirst into the surf. I keeled over onto the sand gasping for breath laughing at his angry face.

He stood up and looked down at himself. He was absolutely drenched. As water dripped from his back his eyes met mine eyebrows knotted

Abigail L. Marsh

ساوئے

(Error)

together in fury, but he too saw the funny side and began laughing, then he suddenly bent down and splashed me.

"Arrrgh!"

"Not so funny now is it?" He giggled splashing me again.

Tuesday morning arrived and two giant suitcases stood at my bedroom door. I dragged them downstairs with much grunting and groaning and when I reached the last step I met Cain, who's eyebrows raised in disgust.

"What?" I asked wiping the sweat from my brow.

He glanced to the side of him where there was a tiny black suitcase packed- carry on style and a backpack slung over his shoulder.

"We can't all wear the same clothes for weeks in a row; some of us have to look fabulous." I declared yanking the heavy case off the last step. It landed awkwardly on my foot and fell on its side as I ripped my toes away in pain. Cain chuckled before turning and picking up his suitcase. Struggling over to him I dropped the second case at his feet defiantly.

"Can you carry that?' I asked striding out of the open front door. Turning back I gave him my best smirk as he grabbed the case with attitude and followed a smear of sass spread over his face.

Abigail L. Marsh

We drove away from the house the sun bouncing off my sunglasses and finally I felt free of Isabelle and all the complications she brought with her, at least for a little while.

Chapter Six: LA Memories

The airport was packed full of grumpy tourists fighting their way through security and kids screaming as their mothers piled gloopy sun-cream on to them prematurely. Cain and I looked dismally around at the scene before striding towards one of the first class lounges and in-dulging in back massages and buffet food until I felt sick.

As our gate announced itself over the tannoy, Cain hauled me off a heated reclining chair where I was munching on a bunch of grapes. To-gether we strolled down to the plane. I glanced around at all the security personnel wandering around in their fluorescent jackets and I couldn't help but think how ridiculous they looked.

Flying first class was still a novelty to me and I played with all the but-tons on my seat, then messed around with the buttons on my TV until Cain told me to pack it in. I ended up curled up under a blanket, head resting on a British Airways pillow watching film after film until I fell into an uncomfortable sleep.

When I woke up, it was to a sharp pain in my neck. I found myself leaning across the partition onto Cain's arm. I couldn't help laughing as I sat up, the 3D glasses he was wearing were two sizes too big for his face he looked like a bug-eyed freak. He paused The Incredibles and turned to me rubbing his eyes.

"Hello, sleepyhead." Cain said taking his headphones off.

"Where are we?" I yawned.

"Flying over Chicago." He replied.

My stomach flipped sharply and I scrambled over him to open the blind, almost knocking his steaming coffee all over his lap.

"Whoa!" He exclaimed. "Watch it." He said steadying me as I looked out of the window. There it was way, way below us, winding its way through the sea of green, The Mississippi River. Tears prickled the edges my eyes stinging them as my stomach turned inside out.

"Hey, what's wrong?" Cain said pulling me back where he could see me. I fought out of his grasp, pushing him away. The plane was moving fast snd I didn't have long before it would be gone.

"Tilly?" Cain pressed. A song played on a loop in my head, one I'd listened to a thousand times when I had first arrived into care. It always

Abigail L. Marsh

reminded me me of the place I had grown up, on the banks of the river Illinois.

"… Home to the banks of the Illinois." I whispered turning my head and pressing it hard again the window as we flew over it.

"What are you talking about?" Cain asked his face creased with ultimate confusion.

"That's where I'm from." I said turning to him.

"Before my Mum died, my Dad started drinking and I got dumped in another state… I lived there." I said pointing back at the river which was fast fading from view. "On the Mississippi"

Cain watched me for a moment, his eyes netted together, pained.

"Do you want to go back?"

Did I want to go back? Hmmm. The question rattled around my brain never really settling on an answer. Finally, I had to speak, the silence was choking my heart.

"No." I shook my head. "My sisters, my Dad, they didn't want me… They left me, all of them. So why would I?" I said pulling the blind down and sitting back in my seat. I switched my television screen on and put my headphones over my ears, ignoring Cain's worried face. The rest of the flight I was silent, I couldn't have spoken if I wanted to, my voice had retreated deep inside of me, not trusting itself to utter a sound. When we landed at LAX I felt sick to my stomach. Cain guided

Abigail L. Marsh

me through the airport by the time we reached the cab my hair was already sticking to my forehead with the heat with the heat.

We whizzed along the freeway to the Ritz-Carlton in Santa Monica, I realised as we pulled up outside that Cain had most definitely splashed on our little holiday, so sucking up the horrific mood that had thrown me into a complete tailspin I did my best to put a smile on my face. The beach outside the hotel sent me back to a fonder time in my childhood. Packed full of people splashing in the water and munching on ice-creams, I remember the holiday we had taken to Daytona beach in the '90s. My Mum had bought us a flamingo floaty, and back when I actually had sisters to fight with, the three of us starred in a hilarious squabble which ended in my victoriously paddling away, ice cream in one hand and flamingo floaty securely situated under my bum.

"Tilly, come on, we can go swimming later. Let's grab a quick nap, and you'll feel better."

I turned away from my memories to see Cain standing on the steps of the hotel, suitcases surrounding him.

"Okay."

Abigail L. Marsh

Something happened to us. I blame the weird tasting water I had been

given on the plane because I completely crashed, and didn't wake up for

fourteen hours — too many memories.

Chapter Seven: Double Take

The first week of the holiday was fantastic. We walked too and from the

beach, doing whatever we wanted every single day, eating ice-creams,

sunbathing, taking the jet-skis out until we were exhausted, and then

we'd head back to the hotel, order room service and pig out in front of

the ridiculously large wide screen television. I was living the life. Seth

text me every day, I made him super jealous of all the stuff I was doing

by sending him photos and videos of the beach. It must have been a

couple days into our second week there when I first saw her.

Cain and I were eating lunch at a sweet little beachfront cafe - Café

Maria, he was distracted by his phone, and I was watching a group of

people pile out of a cab with surfboards. One girl in particular caught

my attention; the surfboard she was carrying as almost twice as big as

her, how she was ever going to surf on that I didn't know. Her brown

frizzy hair cascaded around her shoulders as she struggled to keep the

board upright, it dragged her with it whenever it tipped slightly off balance. I grinned at her battle, but I didn't think much of it until the board

tipped in the direction of the cafe, she spun around to catch it before it

squashed an unsuspecting tourist and I saw her face. Putting my salmon

and cream cheese bagel down on the plate, I stared. Her whole being

looked so familiar, my mind scrambled but to no avail could it place

her anywhere.

I stared at her for a moment until Cain started talking.

"What are you gawping at?" He asked.

"Nothing, just people." I answered casually scooping up my lunch again

and taking a bite, still watching her.

He flicked his gazed over at where I was looking, but the girl had gone

down some steps onto the beach and completely disappeared from

sight.

I stood up.

"Come on, I want to go down to the pier." I said.

"All right, bossy." Cain said, standing up. He left the money on the table

and I dragged him away. We walked side by side down to the pier. The

truth was I wanted to use the telescope to find the girl; it was driving

me mad that I couldn't place her face anywhere, but he didn't need to

know that.

Five minutes later, I was putting a quarter into the machine. I traced the

beach looking for any signs of her, my mind frantically trying to put her

somewhere in my past.

Abigail L. Marsh

I couldn't find her no matter how long I looked, maybe it was just too hot and my head was playing tricks on me. Even if she was from somewhere in my past, it wasn't like I wanted to go looking through that door, I'd left there when I was seven and that was almost ten years ago. If we ever met she'd have just as much trouble remembering me as I was her.

I turned to Cain, and he looked down at me as exhaustion clouded my head.

"Let's go." He said. I nodded and followed him back to the hotel. I spent the rest of the afternoon in front of the television with the air conditioning turned up full blast, an ice cream Sundae on my knee, convinced I had imagined the whole charade.

Unfortunately for me the last day in L.A. swung around in a flash. I found my self sat in the foyer of another hotel in Venice Beach, staring at my peeling arms and feeling sorry for myself as I waited patiently for Cain to collect the 'kit'. The lobby was bustling with people, bell boys ran to and from the desk hauling heavy bags onto gold trolleys and smiling ridiculously fake smiles at the guest as they strode by noses aloft, not taking a blind bit of notice.

I watched as a tall blonde lady carried in the most pathetic looking Chihuahua I had ever seen, its head on one side, tongue lolling out of its

Abigail L. Marsh

mouth swinging as she strutted over to the main desk in heels taller than the top of the empire state building. She clicked at the man standing behind the front desk, getting his attention.

"I want the Presidential Suite, and I want a fruit basket taken up to it along with a packet of Jameson's dog's biscuits put out for Chow-Chow."

The man attending the desk took a second to catch on to what she was saying, he clicked a few buttons on his computer then smiled at the lady.

"I'm so sorry ma'am the presidential suite is booked out for the next four days. Can I suggest we put you in the Royal Suite? It has beautiful views of the ocean. We will compensate you with a complimentary meal in the main dining area tonight."

The woman tutted in utter disgust.

"Again, I must apologise for any inconvenience, we can make you a reservation for when the presidential suite becomes available if you would like?"

"I think this is just appalling." She snapped, looking around to see if anyone else agreed and I laughed when her face fell. No-one was paying her the slightest bit of attention.

Abigail L. Marsh

I could see the poor mans face as he battled not to tell her to go somewhere else if she didn't want to stay in the Royal suite and shove her opinions right up her arse.

"Do you have any idea who my father is?"

Taking a deep breath, the man smiled widely.

"If you'd like to speak to the manager about our policies here at the Ivory Palace, I can ask him to come and talk you through them."

I almost choked on my lemonade as she scrambled for a response.

"Well, uh, I supposed I can make do with the Royal Suite... Put it on here." She placed a black card on the desk.

"Excellent, can I take your name?"

"Miss Eloise Cardinal." The woman sniffed.

After scanning the card through Eloise snatched it back and dropped it into her purse as if it was diseased.

"Please do join us in the dining hall for dinner tonight, won't you." He smiled, passing her a small card which read, *complimentary dinner for two'* in gold letters.

"Just have my bags brought up when they arrive and don't forget my fruit basket and Jameson's biscuits, I want them brought up to the room immediately."

"Of course, Miss Cardinal. Do enjoy your stay with us here at the Ivory Palace." He said as she strutted away. The man looked over at me and

Abigail L. Marsh

shook his head dismally. I smiled back at him, there was no way I could have entertained a conversation like that, I would have knocked her out as soon as she opened her snotty little mouth.

Time ticked on, people came in, and more people went out, but I was still sat like a lemon on the heavily cushioned sofas, so I decided I would get up and go for a walk.

"Any good ice-cream places near here?" I asked, leaning on the front desk. The man who had so expertly dealt with the intolerable woman and her pathetic dog Chow-Chow smiled up at me.

"Yeah, if you go out the main door and hang a right, about a hundred yards down the beachfront you'll see a shop called Poppa J's, very underrated but that there is the best gelato you'll taste in America."

"You must have been to a lot of ice-cream places." I smirked reading his name tag. "Thanks, Marco."

The sun stung my browning shoulders as I wandered down the busy beach front. Thousands of families were sprawled out on the golden sands enjoying the hottest Saturday on record. Dodging a couple of boys skateboarding down the pavement I stepped up to the telescope and slid in a quarter, determined that I would see that girl before I flew back to England, so I could stop doing my nut in about it. I scanned the beach furtively until my four minutes ran out.

Abigail L. Marsh

"Hey, it's our turn." A tubby kid behind me yelled as I dug in my pocket for some more money. I looked back ready to tell him to do one but was met with a rather chunky man with large muscles standing behind him. I could've taken him but Cain would have been furious with me and anyway, my eyes landed on Poppa J's down the street so I smiled sweetly. "There you go, kid." I said, stepping down off the podium. "Knock yourself out." I whispered to myself as I walked away.

Marco had been right, Poppa J's looked severely underrated, its sign in desperate need of a lick of paint and a few screws putting in place, but I suspected the Dairy Queen that had moved in right next door had something to do with it, the queue was out of the door and down the street.

Doing as I promised I stepped into Poppa J's, a little bell attached to the door jingled, I stopped, relishing in the cool air being blown from a vent just above the entrance.
"Hi there." A man said, poking his head out from one of the freezers.
"Hey." I smiled, stepping into the shop. I glanced in each of the five freezers as I made my way over to the till. There were so many flavours I had never heard of before.
"See anything you fancy?" The man said.
I stopped, eyes widening in confusion as my eyes landed on a yellow tub.
Abigail L. Marsh

"What the heck is Goat Cheese Cashew Caramel Gelato?" I asked cringing at the disgusting sounding flavors that had been mixed together.

The man shook his head and laughed heartily as if he'd been asked that question a million times. "Would you like to try it?"

I shook my head and settled on a flavour of ice-cream they never seemed to sell in England.

"No thanks, can I have a scoop of Milk and Cookies?"

"Ahh a personal childhood favourite of mine." He said taking his silver scoop out of the milky residue of water it was sat in. "Cone or tub?"

"Cone please."

He nodded.

"You're a polite kid, and for that you can have a double scoop."

I slipped a couple of dollars out of my pocket and when the cash machine tingled open the man traded me my ice-cream.

"If you don't mind me asking, where are you from? A can hear a twang, but you don't sound like you're from here."

"I live in England." I said as the little bell on the door rang again.

"And before that?" The man asked acknowledging the person behind me with a smile.

"Uhh yeah I lived in Illinois, but that was a long time ago. Sorry, I gotta go, my Dad will be waiting for me." I said feeling an uncomfortable atmosphere settle across the ice cream shop. I turned and stopped dead.

The girl I had seen getting out of the taxi almost a week ago was standing two feet behind me her face twisted into a peculiar shape. I watched her for a second taking her in, her brown eyes, olive skin and the waves in her hair. It was as I noticed the small scar just below her ear-lobe that the dark connection between one of my greatest mysteries was made and it hit me square in the chest. She was staring at me, eyes wide as if I had just arisen from the dead. She knew me too.

"Tilly?" She breathed. For a split second I truly thought about saying yes, about throwing everything away, but I couldn't. My mouth opened but no words dared to leave. I closed it again feeling like a fish out of water.
"Everything alright?" The ice-cream man said prompting me to do something.
"Uhh, no, sorry. I'm Molly." I smiled briefly at the girl and side-stepped her, but that didn't seem to satisfy her. She grabbed my hand and yanked me back round to face her, tears gleaming in her eyes as they searched over my face for any sign of who I was.

Abigail L. Marsh

"Callie, I'm Callie. Come on you remember me don't you? You know who I am?" She begged. Lying came naturally to me, I had done it my whole life, it wasn't hard, I could do it in my sleep, but as I looked into the girls eyes, I couldn't deny it to myself. It was my oldest sister. It was Callie.

She didn't miss this realisation either.

"Yes, see you do know me, right?"

I shook my head, mouth drying as it hung open in shock.

"No, I, I don't. I really have to go." I said wrenching my sweaty hand away from hers, my heart banging in my chest screaming at me to run.

"Please, please, just wait, just wait one second." She cried. The distraught tone in her voice tore through my hard shell and forced me to stop. She breathed hard, shocked.

"Look…" After scrambling through her bag for her purse, and unzipping it hastily she yanked out a photograph, holding it out to me, willing me to look at it. I glanced at the ice-cream man behind her awkwardly; he looked just as awkward as I felt.

"I don't…" I began, looking back at Callie, but the desperation in her eyes clouded my vision, so I took it from her and looked at it.

It was a picture of the front porch of our house in Illinois, there was Callie and I and our younger sister Autumn all sitting in… No wait, the face of my younger sister matched something else packed away in the many box of my mind.

"Do you know where Autumn is? She's gone from..." Callie's voice trailed off as my mind darted back to two weeks ago when I was sitting in the middle of the road staring at a girl who'd just come flying off her bike. I didn't even register my ice-cream as it plummeted to the floor and splattered across my shoes. Stumbling backwards Callie caught my arm as I fell into a chair.

"Are you okay?" Callie asked.

I dared another glance at the creased photograph, piecing everything together as fast as I could, like some sort of horrific jigsaw puzzle, each piece that seemed to fit into place was like a knife through my chest,.

"It is you! Isn't it?" Callie cried.

"I think I'm going to be sick." I whispered dragging my hand through my hair in despair. *What had I done?*

"Tilly who took you? Are they here? Come with me and we'll find Dad." She said tugging my arm.

"Dad?" I stammered shakily getting to my feet and allowing myself to be lead.

"Yeah, he's here, he's better. Tilly you have to see him." We had made it to the door of the shop, the tinkling sound it made as Callie ripped it open was enough to pull me back to reality. I ripped out of her grasp.

Abigail L. Marsh

"NO!" I almost yelled. "I don't want to see *him*."

"Oi, what's going on?" The old man from behind the counter asked, shocked by the sight of his shop floor.

Callie was searching my eyes for an answer to his question.

"I can't... I have to go, I'm gonna be late for the plane." I stuttered.

"No, Tilly, you're safe. We're going to go and see Dad. He's going to sort this out." Callie answered her voice irate with confusion. I found my head shaking as I stepped towards the door.

"I have to go." I said, she caught my arm as I bolted, but my strength outweighed hers ten times over and she lost the fight.

I streaked back along the sea front to the Ivory Palace, terrified I would bump into Robert every step of the way. I did collide with someone. As I took the steps of the hotel three at a time my foot stumbled over a length of rope and I landed face down on the red carpet outside the re-volving doors. I glanced up, groaning as my knee cracked painfully back into place. Wide horrified eyes met mine, casting my own eyes down I realised I had tripped over the lead of Chow Chow, and the dog was tangled up in my legs trembling.

"How dare you! Look where you are..." Eloise started to yell in trauma-tised horror. I didn't hang around to hear the rest and stumbling to my feet I revolved into he building, desperate to find Cain.

Abigail L. Marsh

I didn't have to look far, he was standing by the front desk, anger plastered across his face, briefcase clasped firmly in his hands. Marco's
white face smiled timidly and pointed to me as I walked briskly over to
them. Cain turned.

"Where the hell have you been. I told you to stay here." He snapped
grabbing my arm and pulling me back towards the doors.

"No wait." I said tugging him back, he turned round ready to take my
head off for acting up but something stopped him, perhaps it was the
tears running down my face, or the terrified look in my eyes. He pushed
me into a small nook, out of the hustle and bustle of the lobby and
stared into my eyes.

"Listen, whatever it is can it wait until we're on the plane?" He asked.

"Isabelle… She's my sister isn't she?" I asked with a shaky voice. His
eyebrows flew up his face as he stammered for a response.

"How did you…"

Bile shot up from my stomach, burning the back throat as he admitted
to it. Swallowing it back down painfully I lost all sense of self control.
"Why didn't you tell me!" I spat shoving him in fury. "How could you
not tell me?"

"Tilly. Do not do this here, I will talk to you once were on the plane. Do
you understand me?" He said. I glanced down at the briefcase in his

hand, I had made a decision in the ice-cream shop to go with Cain, and I had to live with it. Clenching my jaw I nodded. He made a move to leave and then second guessed himself, pushing me back into the nook. "How did you find out?" He asked firmly.

"Callie is here, I think my father is too."

"Shit." He swore running a hand through his hair. "That's just what we need.". Grabbing my arm he pulled me back over to the main desk. Marco looked about ready to quit his job as he looked up from the computer and saw Cain's furious eyes.

"I need a cab to take us to LAX." Cain said still gripping my arm. I smiled at Marco, knowing if he thought I was scared we'd never make it out.

"Please." I added forcing a grin.

"Of course."

He dialled a number whilst we stood there, Cains eyes scanning the lobby for any signs of trouble. The bulge in the back of his suit trousers told me any trouble would be met with a sticky end, and an awful lot of commotion.

"You're taxi is waiting outside." Marco said. "Thank-you for visiting the…"

I didn't hear what he said as Cain pulled me away. Going outside was a sketchy business but it was the only way. As we revolved out Cain saw

Abigail L. Marsh

the thousands of people crowding the street, but I saw him. My father. Callie had found him and followed me, or followed me and found him, either way it didn't matter. He was there, standing ten metres away, not even looking at me, yet my blood still turned to ice. I stopped, forcing Cain to stop, my eyes transfixed on the man. His hair had greyed, his face slightly creased and that was all I noticed about him as fear consumed me, until his piercing blue eyes landed on mine and my breath caught in my chest.

"Tilly move." Cain said yanking me down the last few steps. My eyes were transfixed.

Once, a long time ago I was hiding up a tree with a loaded paint-ball gun that weighed more than I had done, part of some stupid exercise Cain had dreamt up. Anyway I'd been up there hours and hours, waiting. Eventually my eyes had closed, I lost my grip and fell ten metres onto the dusty ground landing on my back. The impact had knocked every single ounce of air from my lungs, I couldn't breath, I couldn't do anything.

That was how it felt as I stared at my father. He'd closed the gap, now standing between us and the taxi, a look on his face that told me he wasn't going to be messed with. Cain stopped in the crowd. People kept moving around us, some knocking into us, others moving skilfully around us as if they were used to the hustle and bustle of Venice Beach,

Abigail L. Marsh

they didn't know or care, we were anonymous in the sea of foreign faces.

I glanced up at Cain, he was red with anger, my Dad didn't stand a chance as we stepped up to the taxi.

"Tilly?" Roberts voice entered my ears, the same voice that he had used to call me in for tea all those years ago. I bit the inside of my cheek until it bled, desperate to keep my expression anonymous.

"This is our taxi, back off before someone get's hurt." Cain started, giving him a chance . I glanced at the seemingly empty taxi rank, forcing my mind away from the confrontation. If I looked at him my churning stomach would give me only one option.

"Tilly." My father persisted. "Tilly is that really you?"

"I'm only going to give you one more chance to back off. If you don't I'm going to put a bullet through your daughters stomach." Cain growled quietly. My heart skipped, what did he mean put a bullet through my…. I turned back and saw Callie standing next to our father, her face pale and tear stained face.

"I don't know who you are." I said desperately trying to defuse the situation. Cain put his hand up to stop me as Callie interjected

"She's lying, she wants to be with him." Callie sobbed.

"I just…" I didn't get to finish my sentence Cain threw a punch and Robert dropped to the floor with a thud. I stared shocked.

Abigail L. Marsh

"Oi man, what's going on?" A man yelled breaking from the moving crowd. Cain wrenched the taxi door open and pushed me in.

"I told him I didn't want to buy any drugs, blokes off his head." Cain said sliding into the taxi as Robert lay unconscious on the ground, Callie crouched by his side sobbing.

"Airport."

"Everything alright?" The driver ask turning his neck slightly to look at us.

"Yeah, just extremely late for a flight."

"Right, better get going then." The driver said as I forced a smile.

"Yeah, please." Cain said before slamming the compartment doors between the front and the back of the taxi shut.

"What about my stuff?" I asked as Cain pulled out his phone and began dialling a foreign number.

"We'll get you new stuff."

Cain talked on the phone the whole way there. When we reached the turn off Cain directed the driver around to the private jet terminal. I hadn't flown on a private jet before, many of Cain's 'friends' owned them and leant them out, but Cain had never seemed that interested.

There was no time to look around the terminal and all it's luxurious, Cain was paranoid Robert was only minutes behind us. I desperately wanted to go home and allowed myself be tugged out of the taxi and over to the plane parked on the runaway as the sun dipped low on the horizon. A tall butler looking man, with a wisp of hair flickering around in the wind on the top of his head stood at the bottom of a flight of stairs. Cain whispered something in his ear and the man bowed. Baffled by this strange behaviour I followed Cain up the steps.

He tossed the briefcase into an overhead locker and pointed to a chair. "Sit down, buckle up." He said, his tone fraught. I sat down, buckled up and let my head bash against the window in exhaustion. Cain disappeared, then came back, then sat down, got up again and then sat down again the engines revved up. His leg jiggled in complete anxiety until we were soaring above the parched field of East California where he got up and disappeared into a back room. I didn't see him come back, my eyes closed, all adrenaline gone.

Chapter Eight: No Home

Opening my eyes indignantly at the intrusive light shining in them, I was momentarily stunned by my surroundings. I didn't recognise them at all. I sat up cautiously and rubbed my eyes into a whole new dimen-

Abigail L. Marsh

sion. When I could see straight again I squinted around the unfamiliar room I had found myself in. The curtains were drawn but they were so thin they were about as much use as a chocolate fire-guard. There was a writing desk by the wall and a wardrobe adjacent to it, with the door opposite. It was simple, but told me nothing about where I was.

Still wearing the same clothes from the day before I stumbled sleepily over to the window wondering if the outside world would let me know where I was. Pushing back the blue curtains revealed a cold, wet, windy beach. Yeah, we were back in England. My ice-cold hands snaked their way into the pockets of my jacket, my fingers grazing the photograph Callie had given me. I pulled it out and turned it over.

"Oh." I sighed as nostalgia rose up in my chest. It was the picture our Mum and Dad had taken of us, the three of us sat on the porch steps of our house one summer. I looked about six, Autumn must have been four and Callie seven. Our lives had been perfect. We had a lovely house and garden, an amazing Mum and Dad who loved us, great friends that we always got into trouble with for having muddy clothes and scraped knees. *What had happened?*

Putting the photo back in my pocket I padded downstairs, managing to find the living room on my second attempt at a door. Cain was sat in

Abigail L. Marsh

there with the television on. No surprise my face was all over it. I sat down on the floor in front of it after acknowledging Cain with a soft nod, preparing myself for what I was about to hear.

The reporter droned on about how I had been kidnapped over nine years ago and this was the first time I had resurfaced. Then Robert came on the screen startling me.

"Tilly wherever you are, wherever that man has taken you, I will find you.... I promise you I won't let you slip through my fingers again." He said. "I want you to know that I never wanted to let them take you away, but when your mom died I couldn't cope. I let drink take over our lives and I have never forgiven myself for that." He broke down in tears. "I'm better now and I will find you."

I grabbed the remote and switched the television off. I couldn't look at him anymore, all I saw was a stranger. The things that happened when he was drunk... He would never remember and I would never forget. Cain sat down on the floor next to me and spoke softly,

"Don't torture yourself." He pulled me into a hug and I no energy to protest.

We sat there for a little while before I pulled away and looked up at him.

Abigail L. Marsh

"What?" He asked.

"You said we would talk, that you would explain." I said. "I want to hear it all... Who am I?"

He sighed and scratched his head as he always did. I had never really had the time to sit down with Cain and get the answers for the questions swimming around in my head. Sometimes I hated them, I didn't want the answers, I didn't care for anything before England, but now, after everything, after seeing my sister, I had never craved anything so much.
"You're Tilly."
"Tilly who?"
 He sucked air noisily between his teeth before responding.
"Well you don't have a last name, mainly because you couldn't have mine and you couldn't keep your old one." He began. "I kidnapped you from the orphanage when you were seven years old and brought you here."
"Why did you kidnap me?" I asked sliding backward and sitting against the wall underneath the window.
"You know why we do what we do." Cain said. "I was in New York at the time, I heard about you on the news, your story went far and wide in the US, did you know that?"
I shook my head.
"I don't remember." I said.
Abigail L. Marsh

"You had a traumatic childhood." Cain said. "Your Dad abused you, he became an alcoholic after your Mum died. So the social worker took you into care."

"Yes, I remember that part." I said with a tireless edge to my voice.

"You were taken to New York and then I came and brought you here. What else is there?" He asked.

"Autumn, and why you never told me who she was." I said looking up at him darkly, a hatred inside me sparking up. "She is *my* sister, I had a right to know."

"You have a right to nothing, if you want something, you earn it." Cain's tone took a sharp turn.

"Yeah." I laughed sarcastically. "I'm starting to think you make up all these life rules yourself."

"I needed another you." Cain said through gritted teeth. "She was the closest one... And I didn't tell you because I didn't want you to know, end of story." He said standing up and leaving the room in frustration.

"All my life has been one big pile of shit." I snapped following him off the floor. "Can you at least tell me what I did to deserve any of it?"

"You love it here and you damn well know it!" Cain snapped slamming the door into the kitchen. I followed him through, not faltering in my pace. Cain was routing around in the fridge.

"But it will never be my home." I breathed, "And I want to know why?"

Abigail L. Marsh

"Because you're Dad was an alcoholic and refused to take care of you, and being a decent human being." Cain growled turning around with a can of beer in his hand. "I fixed you. So be grateful I didn't leave you to rot."

He opened it and downed half of it in five seconds, not once taking his eyes off me.

"Do you think it's true?" I asked. He wiped his mouth on the back of his sleeve and nodded at me.

"What?"

"Do you think he's stopped drinking?"

Cain scoffed.

"Don't even go there Tilly. He's an addict. He will never stop drinking."

Cain necked the rest of his can, slammed it down on the grimy kitchen counter and stepping around me left the room. My reflection in the mossy green windows was shaking from head to toe in utter rage.

"What the hell would you know?" I said, reaching out and whacking the can to the floor.

With Cain paranoid about the police after our hasty exit from America, he wouldn't let us leave the bounds of the safe house. That's what he called it, a safe house, off the grid, protected by the dunes that sur-rounded it, anonymous in the wild. With nothing to do all week and absolutely not phone signal, I paced the house until Cain got frustrated and told me we would have to pay for new carpets if I walked on them anymore, so then I paced the garden and then the beach until even they were starting to look muddy. I knew I needed to get home so I could finally talk to my sister. Over and over into those long nights I rehearsed what I was going to say to her, until my brain switched off and I drifted into a fitful sleep, never sure where my dreams would take me.

I wanted to go back to Illinois, I knew that much. Just to talk, to hear what my father had to say, to get some answers. I had no idea how that was going to happen.

Early on the eighth morning at the house Cain relented and pulled me into the kitchen to talk. Looking dismally around at the tens of discarded cigar stubs and cans off ale piled up in the bin that I myself had started to add to, I waited patiently for another round of drunken charades, the only game either one of us knew how to play.

"We're leaving in an hour get your stuff." Cain said, ripping a bin bag out of the cupboard under the sink.
"We are?" I asked an excited smile appearing on my face.

Abigail L. Marsh

"What did I just say?" He snapped his temper everlasting. Ignoring it, I sped out of the room and banged up the stairs. Since leaving all my things in LA had Cain snuck into the local town and had got me a few clothes, but nothing was especially nice. I chucked a floral dress into a plastic bag and rolled up a few jeans and t-shirts before clattering back down to an increasingly impatient Cain.

"Stop banging around… Keys. I'll be there in a minute." He said lobbing single black key at me. I hadn't seen the briefcase since it had been tossed into the overhead locker on the plane. Cain had been cagey about letting me into his room, the only one with a sea facing balcony and when I asked about it he'd shut me down. I hadn't pressed the matter, living in such confined spaces with him hadn't done his temper the world of good. Sat in the passenger seat of a black Mercedes that had mysteriously appeared in the drive in the night, I watched through the driver's mirror as he slipped out of the house, crept across the driveway and slam it safely in the boot.

"What was all that about?" I asked, tossing him the key as he slipped into the driver's seat.

"Never you mind."

Putting the car into drive we were on the motorway not fifteen minutes later, the mix of excitement and terrifying dread churned around in my stomach.

Chapter Nine: Different

My bum grew more and more numb as we drove without stopping. Seven hours! I had to put up with seven whole hours of Cains classical music and clench jaw until I saw the signs for Cromer and eased up.

"I don't want you getting any silly idea's Tilly, do you understand me?" Cain spoke. After seven hours of silence I struggled to find my voice. "What do you mean?" I croaked.

"I don't want you putting crazy ideas in Isabelle's head. Your father is an abusive alcoholic, if you were to leave here and go back to him, heed my warnings you will find exactly what you left. Addicts don't ever recover. You will be beaten again and again, just like when you were little."

Cain's soft words sent a shiver down my spine as I stared at the winding road ahead. Cain turned to me. "And you will not find me here when you get back ."

The last ten minutes of the ride was somehow more silent than it had been for the majority. Cains words echoed around my mind, the week coming may very well be the last I spent in the house of Black.

My knee's cracked satisfyingly when I stepped out of the low car. The front porch light flicked on in the dying sunshine as I made my way over to the oak door that would lead me to Isabelle, or Autumn as I now knew her. Standing back on the porch of the house I felt the sudden feeling in my churning stomach that things were different. Cains hand landed on my shoulder giving it a tight squeeze. I looked back at his smiling face in confusion.

"It'll be alright." He said. Somehow I knew his words were empty, things had changed in the three weeks we'd been away, but I didn't know how to change with them. As he opened the door and left me standing on the porch I wondered if I would ever feel the same again.

The house had a lingering smell of takeaway and I wondered how Mel had let the boys get away with is as I slid my shoes off and followed the smell into the living room. The television blared as the whole Pack sat around eating pizza out of the blue boxes that seemed to pepper the room. I spied Melanie sitting amongst the rabble drinking a large glass of wine whilst the others had beer bottles strapped to their hands. The

Abigail L. Marsh

football was on so no one was paying me the slightest bit of attention. I got the shock of my life when my eyes fell on Isabelle. She was sat on the floor at the end of the coffee table, pizza box on her knee and a beer can in her hand.

The whole 'trainee' physique had disappeared. She didn't looked scared or weak, the muscles on her arms bulged and her newly chiselled jaw-line turned me green-eyes. How was it I worked out everyday, swam in the freezing sea and could run 10k without breaking a sweat, but nothing I did, ever made a difference to my chubby cheeks? It wasn't fair.

I was proud of Isabelle, sitting bold as brass amongst the lads, not an obvious care in the world. She looked almost at home.

"Fast work Iz." I mumbled.

Although she looked better than when I had left, a scar running ten centimetres down her right shoulder looked painful, and her whole body was covered with scratches and nicks. Her new look was enough to make me think that no-one on the street would want to start a fight with her on purpose.

Cain, now with a new suit on and a pair of shiny shoes came up behind me and pushed me into the room, he too looked surprised at Isabelle. Shaking off his sudden smile he spoke up,

"Pass us a beer then."

Abigail L. Marsh

Heads turned and a cheer went up. I could only just pull a half-hearted smile, still focused on Isabelle.

"We weren't sure you were coming back." Kurt said standing up and shaking Cains hand sturdily.

"We had to lay low." Cain explained reaching for the keg of beer sitting on the counter behind the sofa and cracking it open.

My heartbeat shot into overdrive as I watched Isabelle turn around and look over at me. Now I knew who she was, my mind chastised me for being so stupid. Of course it was Autumn, her slightly off kilter nose, eyes with a hundred different flecks of colour exploding in them, the small diamonds shaped birthmark on the bottom of her left ear lobe. It was her and she was going to *hate* me for what I had done to her.

"Tilly, come and tell me all about your trip." Melanie said dragging both Isabelle and I out of our stare. Moving pizza boxes from my path I sank into the sofa next to Mel, feeling dizzy at the prospect of the conversation I knew I would have to have with Isabelle. I kept a wary eye on her as I filled Mel in on the excitement of my holiday, leaving out the bombshell that erupted at the end changing my whole aspect on my life. The drive had knocked me out and at half past nine I was yawning widely. Knowing full well Kurt would be sending Isabelle up to bed shortly I made my excuses and left.

Abigail L. Marsh

99

As I walked the length of the kitchen to the back stairs the back door opened and I heard a sound I had been longing to hear since I'd left, excited whining.

"Max!" I cried as the dog flung himself against me in completely overwhelming happiness.

"Hello you! He's been crying for you since you got on that plane." Tate said dumping his lead in the wicker basket by the door. I smiled at Tate gratefully as Max leapt up putting his paws on my chest, stumbling slightly I tousled his head kissing his cold wet nose.

"Come on, bedtime." I said pushing Max off me and racing him up the stairs. He bolted across the room and leapt onto his spot at the foot of the bed. I was about to follow in his maddening footsteps, but was halted in shock to see a a second single bed pushed into the alcove adjacent to the door.

"What the hell?" I demand to no-one in particular as I strode over to it. I stared at the offending object waiting for a response when the door creaked behind me. Spinning around expecting to see Cain, or even Mel standing there laughing at my reaction to their weird prank, I was even more baffled to see Isabelle there.

"What are *you* doing?" I asked as she stepped into the room and closed the door behind her.

Abigail L. Marsh

"I sleep in here." She said softly sidestepping my accidental attitude and lifting the top pillow up to reveal a pair of spotty pyjamas.

"Since when?" I asked doing my best not snap at her, it wasn't like she was in control of things like that.

"The roof leaked, so…" She shrugged. I watched as tossed her pyjamas over her arm and walked towards the en-suite, closed the door and locked it.

"What the hell?" I asked looking at Max. He raised on eyebrow and dropped his head to his paws as if to say 'three words girl…Not my problem.'

Descending the stairs in a fit of rage I stepped into the living room.

"I told you." Chris laughed.

Cain glanced over at me, now with a pizza box on his knee, beer attached to one hand and Melanie wrapped up in other. It didn't look to me like I would be getting anything from him tonight but it didn't hurt to try.

"Why is Isabelle in my room?" I snapped.

"The roof leaked." Kurt said grabbing the remote and turning the TV down a few notches. "We didn't have anywhere else to put her."

"Well how long until its fixed?" I demanded hand on hip.

Kurt shrugged nonchalantly.

"The boys are working on it, maybe a few weeks?"

"Well…" I grumbled in frustration.

"I would have thought you were happy about the new arrangements."
Cain said an edge to his voice that told me he we sick of the sight of me
and wanted me to get lost so he could watch the football, and other
things I won't go into.

"Well, she better not touch any of my stuff." I said with as much sass as
I could muster before turning and flouncing back up to my room.

Isabelle was still in the shower, so I quickly changed into my pyjamas
and brushed my teeth in the big bathroom, there wasn't time to have a
long soak as much as I needed to. I needed to talk to my sister, before I
bottled it. I was in bed scrolling through my phone, grumbling at all the
missed phone calls I'd had from Seth after being in the middle of
nowhere with no signal for a week, when the latch on the bathroom for
clicked. Steam from the shower flooded into the bedroom and Isabelle
stepped out in her pyjamas, hair tied back in a plait.

She didn't speak to me as she went sorting her bed out and going
through her new night stand which used to be my makeup draws. I
couldn't blame her for the silence; I hadn't really been much of a friend
to her before I had left. I flicked the occasional glance over the top of
my phone as she finally climbed into her bed and pulled the duvet over
her lap. My heart skipped a beat as I went to open my mouth.

Abigail L. Marsh

No. I couldn't could I?

My mouth shut, all the lines I had rehearsed as I ruined the carpets had deserted my head. As she reached for the lamp on the nightstand I took my chance.

"Autumn?"

Chapter Ten: Confessions

Autumn's head snapped around, her eyes wide with complete shock as she stared at me.

"How do you know that?" She whispered, and my heart flooded with relief.

"I knew it. It is you."

Looking me up and down to make sure I hadn't completely lost my marbles Autumn's eyebrows knitted together in utter confusion.

"What are you talking about?" She asked, baffled. My head spun like a merry-go-round as I tried to decide the best way to tell her without sounding like a complete loony bin.

"It's me, Tilly." I said, throwing the duvet off me and sliding to the floor, much to my dogs annoyance.

"Yeah… I know your name."

The frustration etched across her face was evident, but even after practicing this moment over and over and over again I still didn't know how to tell her. She shook her head, impatiently.

"You're so weird." She said, pulling the duvet up and turning to face the wall.

"I used to have a last name." The words fell out of my mouth instantly, and she turned back sighing heavily as if I was acting extremely annoying on purpose. While I had her attention I plowed on. "Once a very, very long time ago I was Tilly Carmichael, and I didn't always live here, I'm American, I'm from Illinois." I paused; it was a lot to take in.

"What?" Autumn breathed.

Autumn sat up as I stepped up to the bed, feeling that if she could see me, really truly properly, it might click.

"My Mum's name was Lilly Carmichael, she died in a car crash when I was seven. I have an older sister called Callie Carmichael, I have an alcoholic father called Robert Carmichael, and I have a younger sister called Autumn- Rose Carmichael… Only that's not her name anymore, and I don't know how I didn't recognise her all those weeks ago and I am so, so sorry that I didn't." I said my speech mirroring that of a ball rolling down a hill, picking up speed until I ran out of breath and gasped for air.

Abigail L. Marsh

"No, how could you be? Tilly's dead." She said, confused.

"I'm not dead." I said, suddenly moving from the spot I had been stuck to, and sitting down on the edge of her bed.

"My parents, they said you didn't exist anymore… They told me you'd died."

First of all, *rude.* Second of all- "I didn't die, Autumn, I'm right here, I've been here for so long." I said, desperate for her to see.

"But the people that took me and my sister Tilly, they told Pat…"

"The people that took us were corrupt; they lied to us, they lied to many people, they shouldn't have taken us like that. They didn't follow the rules Autumn." I said. She went quiet, I could see she was trying to organise her thoughts.

"I don't understand." She said suddenly. "If you *really* are my sister… How could you let them do this to me?"

"I didn't know any of this! How could I possibly have known? You were four, and it's been nearly *ten years.*" I paused for a breath, knowing she had every right to be upset. "The day they took you away, I fought for you so hard, but they weren't bringing you back." I said bunching her duvet so tightly in my hands my knuckles turned white.

"They said you could have seen me, but you didn't want too." She said spitefully as if all this was somehow my fault. "And then, then you died in a car crash."

Original, I thought.

Abigail L. Marsh

"I didn't die in a car crash, don't you see?" I said, my voice breaking. "I tried to see you as soon as you were gone and every day since, but eventually I had to stop. I couldn't take the rejection, it hurt me more and more. Eventually I burnt out."

"But..."

"You'd gone. Everything I knew, everything I loved had been taken away. My life... It didn't exist anymore." I said softly.

"But still..." She persisted. "*You've* changed. I know I was only little when Dad sent us away, but you weren't... *You* should have known me!" She shouted as she finally accepted the truth and it all dawned on her.

"Shh!" I snapped, not forgetting where we were.

"You should have known me." She cried softly.

"But I didn't. I've been here for *ten years*; I don't see anyone. I don't talk to anyone; my old life stopped the day I got here. I'm surprised I remember anything that happened back in Illinois."

"I will never forget what he did." She spoke quietly, her voice turning dark.

"You were four when Mum died... You had *no* idea what was going on."

"I still have the scars."

"Scars? He didn't touch you we made sure of that."

Abigail L. Marsh

"Not all scars are visible; surely you know that." Acid flooded her eyes at this remark. She was right, I did know that, probably better than anyone in the world. There was a long pause where I didn't know what to say. Autumn sat back against her pillow, and we both sat in a stunned silence.

"So you said you'd been here for ten years?" She said taking a sharp breath which startled me. "Prove you're Tilly."
"Prove it?" She nodded.
"How?"
Autumn shrugged.
"Any weirdo could know all this information; it's all out there on the internet."

I thought about this for a moment; then it came to me. I got up and went over to the denim jacket I had been wearing for a solid week, tucked away in the pocket was the photo Callie had given me.
I took it back over to Autumn. After looking down at our smiling faces, I passed it over to her.

"Me, you and Callie and our cat Belle, named after my favourite Disney princess when I was seven. I had the Belle blanket, Callie and I used to fight over it until we ripped it down the middle and then Mum sewed it back together and gave it to you…" I said." The photo is how I figured it out."

Autumn smiled at it, glassy-eyed.

"Where'd you get this?"

"I bumped into Callie in LA. That's why we have been gone so long. We ran into Callie and Robert."

"You saw Dad?"

I nodded.

"What did he say?"

Clenching my jaw, I thought about what he had said, about what Cain had said.

"What?" Autumn asked.

"He said he wasn't an alcoholic anymore, that he came looking for us."

The photograph fluttered down to the bed; Autumn shook her head dismally.

"I know you've been stuck here, but I haven't. He never came looking for us. Someone would have told me. He's a drunk Tilly; he won't *ever* get better, you shouldn't believe anything he says." She said voicing Cain like she was a pro.

"But what if he has? How did you go from Autumn-Rose to Isabelle? I mean, he was looking for an Autumn and a Tilly. I was kidnapped, and

Abigail L. Marsh

your name isn't the same."

"Mum and Dad didn't like it." She shrugged. "But that doesn't prove anything. It was all legalised, written down on paper- if he looked, it wasn't very hard."

"Who are they to change your name?"

"My parents, the ones who have loved me and taken care of me since I was four."

I took a deep breath realising I was defending the very person who had ripped our life to shreds.

"He told me he didn't drink anymore." I sighed.

"Oh yes because when an alcoholic tells you, they aren't an alcoholic anymore they must be telling the truth." She said rolling her eyes.

"Callie's with him, he must be doing something right."

Autumn shook her head, taking several deep breaths.

"What are you saying, Tilly?"

"I'm saying look where we are. We can't live like this; this isn't how normal people live Autumn."

"You've been fine for ten years."

"But now I know."

"Know what? That Roberts been looking for you? That he's stopped drinking and wants you back? Do you even hear yourself?"

Abigail L. Marsh

"I have to go. And you have to come with me."

"What? Are you kidding? No way! I'm not going back to Illinois." She said. "Not ever."

"What? Why?"

"I'm not going to go on some wild goose chase and risk getting my butt kicked again. You don't know how horrible that is. They are starting to like me." She said. "I'm getting good."

Anger erupted from my lips in a fiery sigh; only a few weeks ago this was all she had wanted.

"Of course I know how bad it is. I thought you wanted to go home?" I said.

"Not the one you're talking about, I already told you I'm not going back to Illinois."

"But we can do this together." She shook her head.

Why not?" I demanded.

"This changes nothing Tilly. I don't even know you." She snapped, yanking the duvet back over her. Although what she said was the truth, it still hurt my already heavy heart.

"This changes everything Autumn. Don't you see now, we can get away from all this." I said pleading with her.

"You don't really want that though, do you Tilly? You like it here. This is some wild fantasy you have cooked up in your head whilst you've been shut-up in a shitty house in Cornwall, alone. It's a knee-jerk reaction. I'm not leaving." She shouted loudly.

"Oh they've completely brainwashed you." I spat angrily.

"Go to bed."

"Why won't you help me?" I shouted back, not caring about Cain or Kurt or anyone else hearing anymore.

"Because he sent us away Tilly. He didn't want us. He *abused* us. Now leave me the hell alone and let me sleep, I have to get up at half four in the morning, you don't!" She hissed, turning her bedside light off, laying down and pulling the duvet over her head.

That marked the end of the conversation. Frustration coursed through my veins as I yelled a string of swear words aimed at the world, and when I stood up, I took a discarded trainer that was lying on the floor and launched it across the room like a shot-put thrower in the Olympics. It hit the wall above my bed with a bang, doing absolutely nothing to release my fury. Max sat up, growling at me.

"Shut up, mutt!" I barked falling onto my bed and burying my face in my pillow. It was nice to be back in my own bed I guessed, but now I was feeling homesick, homesick for somewhere that maybe no longer existed. I just knew in the depths of my heart that there was no other choice but to find out.

Abigail L. Marsh

Chapter Eleven: Who are you?

When the sun blasting through the open curtains which I had regrettably forgotten to close in my fury the night before, finally grew to much for me to bare, I grumbled in annoyance and opened my bleary eyes. My little alarm clock told me it was almost ten' o clock, the empty bed across the room told me I hadn't dreamt the disaster the night before had turned into and the smell of pancakes that wafted in through my door told me if I didn't get out of bed quick I'd miss out.

As I went around my room getting dressed and complaining to nobody about how bloody cold it was in England, Max slid off the bed like a serpent and landed ungracefully on his face, squashing is sideways. I couldn't help but chuckle.

"I know." I said tossing on a jumper and pulling the cords tight around my chin. "Lighten up, right? Because what could be worse than messing up a seriously important conversation and potentially ruining our lives?" I laughed again, watching Max as he jumped off the floor and bounded over to the door, snout in the air.

Abigail L. Marsh

"Mel's cooking my breakfast mate, not yours." I said, ruffling his head and opening the door. He flounced off, not taking any notice of me in the slightest.

The kitchen was completely desolate as I plodded down the stairs, I panicked that I had missed breakfast altogether until I heard a rustling in the back room and Mel came out with a big bag of chocolate chips in her hand.

"Don't look so worried. I saved some for you." She smiled.

"I wasn't worried." I grinned perching on the rather cold countertop.

"Tables are for rissoles, not..."

"Arseholes, I know. But I'm tired, and I don't think I can make it over to the chair." I waved my hand pathetically in the direction of it.

Mel rolled her eyes as she mixed the batter with the chocolate chips.

"You're turning into one of those wolves." She said shaking her head in utter contempt.

"You say that like it's a bad thing Mel." I said laughing at her comment, but when her eyes met with mine I could see the concern etched in them.

"What?" I asked.

"Do you want to be one of them?" She asked, finally looking away from me and pouring the batter into the pan.

Abigail L. Marsh

"I don't understand your question. A wolf is strong, reliable, loyal. They're not afraid. Why wouldn't I want to be a wolf? Why wouldn't I want to be able to take down anyone I wanted?"

Mel stopped watching the batter crisp and bubble, giving me her full attention.

"What *are* you afraid of?" She asked, suddenly intrigued. My brow furrowed at the thought. I hated how our conversations always turned around to bite me.

What was I afraid of? That question was tricky. I feared many things, nothing I'd admit to of course. The waves scared me when they crashed over my head, swirled and swelled. Fire, fire frightened me, the thought of being trapped, unable to breathe. I often had terrifying dreams about not being able to slow the car down, my inexperience jeopardising lives as I plowed through my family and friends. However, the one thing that scared me the most, the one fear I could never chase away was the one where I was back in the house, the one in Illinois. The hallway stretched on and on forever, doors locked on either side. One end was me, seven years old, the other the tall black shadow of my father. I swallowed hard.

"Nothing. I told you, I'm a wolf."

Mel didn't buy it, but the pancake batter spat at her hand distracting her. Holding it with a tea-towel she groaned in pain. Taking my chance I

Abigail L. Marsh

hopped off the counter and grabbed my shoes.

"I'm not that hungry anymore. I'll go for a run. See you." I said, slamming the back door closed as I bolted off in the direction of Seth's house.

I puffed and panted as I rounded the final corner on the windswept south end of Cromer where his semi-detached was. A smiled creased my face as I saw him sat on the gatepost, legs swinging as he waited patiently for me.

"I missed you." I said as he jumped down and collided with me, pulling me into the tightest hug his muscly arms could muster.

"I missed you too." He said planting a wet sticky kiss on my forehead that had me pushing him away from me.

We linked arms and walked the rest of the way into the town centre at a relatively relaxed pace, although the peace shattered every single time Seth asked me about the trip. He had so many awkward questions about why I had been gone so long, what I had been up to. I desperately shoved them all away as unsuspiciously as I could, until he stumbled upon a question I could answer and my heart lifted.

"Why do you need a disposable phone?" He asked as we walked into the EE shop situated on a little cobbled backstreet, away from the seafront.

"In case I drop it in the sea when I'm out on runs and stuff. I almost dropped my iPhone in LA and I then I wouldn't have been able to talk to you." I said, laying it on thick as I scanned the shelves for the cheapest, crappiest little mobile I could find, thanking my research for knowing full well the police's GPS systems wouldn't pick it up.

"Oh, well get a Nokia then, they're perfect." Seth laughed, picking up the phone I had been staring at and tossing it to me. "Indestructible."

"Untraceable too." I mumbled to myself walking over to the counter and smiling innocently at the spotty faced assistant trainee. While he figured out the till I scooped up a huge international mobile directory hidden at the back of the shop. This earned me a quizzical look from Seth.

"Prank calls." I said like he was stupid. He smiled at me and nodded.

We spent the rest of the morning getting chocolate and fizzy drinks from W H Smiths and hanging out at the park near the school. Normal stuff, that normal kids did. It was almost refreshing.

"Ugh, its Monday tomorrow." He moaned using his feet to rock the swing gently. I looked over at him in contempt.

"That sucks for you!"

"I wish you came."

I shook my head defiantly.

Abigail L. Marsh

"I'm glad I don't... Hey, can I try that monster thing?" I replied, holding my arm out to snatch it from him.

He passed me his canned drink, and I took a huge gulp and then another.

"What is it?" I asked downing half the can, its fuzziness burning my throat satisfyingly.

"It's an energy drink. You are going to be so hyper later." He laughed swiping the can off me.

"So, please come to school?" He said his voice changing from the one I knew to a whiny five-year-old

"No, Seth, I don't want too." I replied.

He pouted at me.

"But you don't know anyone. You don't have any friends…"

"Seth I don't want to talk about this." I pressed feeling annoyance spark up in my chest. I hated how he went on and on and on about school like it was the be all and end all.

"You can't live like you do."

"You have no idea how I live." I said fighting the wolf within me as it barked ferociously at his stupid comment.

"That's because you don't let me in."

"I can't." I growled. *Oops.*

"Why not? What are you hiding?" He demanded stopping the swing dramatically and facing me off.

"Nothing. I, I'm not hiding anything." I shrugged breaking a square off the Cadbury Milk bar and cramming it into my mouth so the wolf was distracted.

"Oh well now I feel confident. What is going on? You hide up there in your big house with all those men, you say your Dad doesn't like me, but he's never met me. You leave for a month and hardly text me at all. You don't go to school. Somethings wrong and you're not telling me."

"Nothing is going on. I just like my own space and if you can't accept that then maybe we shouldn't... Be with each other all the time."

"Together Nellie, we're together. You are my girlfriend... God, you can't even say it can you?"

I cringed, hating it whenever he mentioned the name, Nellie. It was a horrible reminder how it was going to end.

"Seth, I... I'm sorry. I just, I can't explain... Where are you going?" I cried in despair as he got to his feet, grabbed his bag and marched away.

"Home."

My heart sank as he stormed across the park and slammed the metal gate shut. Tears pricked my eyes as a strange feeling sank to the bottom of my stomach like a boulder.

Abigail L. Marsh

'Fight Song' suddenly blared out of my phone sitting on the warm bark chippings, I wouldn't have answered it, but the name Alpha popped up on the screen and I didn't want to enrage Cain.

"What?" I said, biting my lip hard as I fought to keep any emotion out of my voice.

"What do you mean what? Where are you?" Cains voice tinged with anger came through the speaker.

"I'm in Cromer." I sighed, getting a grip on myself.

"Cromer?" He asked, confused.

"Yeah, but I'm coming home now. What do you want?"

"I called you for lunch, and you weren't here." He grumbled.

"Aw were you scared?"

"Just let me know when you go out, all right!"

I sighed.

"Yeah, I'll be back soon, save me some food."

The run back was not pleasant. The clouds rolled in and torrential rain splatted down on the sand, making it almost impossible to run. The white bag from the phone shop kept getting tangled around my legs and I couldn't shake the depressing feeling clawing its way around my heart. I couldn't believe Seth had flown off the handle so badly and the fact that it bothered me so much, bothered me more and more.

Abigail L. Marsh

The living room seemed like the place to be, the noise filtering out suggested The Pack was over so I was extra careful as I crept up the main stairs. Dumping my bag at the back of my wardrobe I tossed a bunch of dirty laundry on top of it for special measures. Max padded down to the kitchen beside me, probably hoping to get in on whatever was cooking.

"Are you all right, Tilly?" Mel asked as I sat down at the table, turning my nose up at the oaf sat opposite me.

"Yeah?" I said brightly picking up my knife and fork to slice the thickly cut cooked ham that had been waiting for me on the table.

"Why are your eyes all red?" Harley said in his usual tactful voice as he sprayed egg and chips in my face. I glanced at my reflection in my knife and cursed my ever growing lousy luck. I had hardly shed a tear and they were angry tears, not sad, so why had they made me looked like a fool?

"It's raining out, close your damn mouth when you eat." I said indignantly.

"Have you been crying?" Harley smiled sickeningly as he showed his gold teeth covered in egg yolk and ketchup

"Shut up." I growled. "You're a massive…"

"Tilly stop it!" Mel snapped over my voice. I shut my mouth clenching my jaw painfully to stop my emotions getting the better of me, again. "Harley leave her be, don't make me tell you again." Mel said the savage tone she only ever used when she was about to lose her cool. "If you two can't behave then I don't want to see either of you down here for dinner. I don't know why…"

"Stop talking Mel." I growled the fire from the swings igniting again tenfold.

"Excuse me?" Mel said.

"Ohh, someones touchy." Harley jested.

Then that flame inside of me shot up through my chest and came out as hot as any dragon had ever flamed. "Shut up. Shut. UP. Both of you." In flaming fury I jumped up, sending my chair clattering tot he stone floor.

Looking down at my plate, there seemed only one logical thing to do. With one swift motion I threw the burning egg, ham and chips directly into Harley's smirking face. Screaming in pain, he swiped the slimy yolk with his sausage fingers and shot to his feet. Max growled warningly from his bowl of ham at the other and of the kitchen.

"Stop it! Both of you." I heard Mel yell over the sound of ringing in my ears, but the pair of us were far too riled up to pay any attention.

"Come on then fatty." I shouted, egging him on as he stumbled around the table to where a tea-towel was lying. His red eyes locked on mine as I stood in the middle of the room, making myself an easy target on purpose.

"What are you going to do?" I taunted as he wiped egg from his pink cheeks.

"Nothing! Harley, get out." Mel said stepping between us, but like hell was Harley about to do nothing. Aggressively throwing the dirtied tea-towel to the floor he knocked Mel aside and made a bee-line for me. Max who'd been monitoring the situation carefully was by my side in an instant snapping wildly at the man who dared threaten his beloved girl.

Kicking out angrily was Harley's worst mistake that day. With a quick snap of the head, Max's teeth sunk deep into the fat man's flesh. Harley went down like a sack of potatoes, howling pitifully.

"Don't you ever try play games with me!" I yelled, acid spewing from my mouth. "Don't ever, *ever* think you are able to do that."

"What the hell is going on?"

I spun around to see Cain standing in the kitchen doorway black suit on, tie perfectly in place and a scowl plastered across his face that told me he wasn't pleased about being interrupted.

"Where the hell have you been?" I demanded, putting on the complete pretence that I wasn't intimidated by his sudden disconcerting presence.

"What happened in here?" He asked, not answering my question as a sign of dominance.

"That dog bit me! Get it away from me." Harley groaned rolling around on the floor like a child.

"You were going to kill me." I spat back taking Max's collar and pulling him away from the incongruent man-child.

"Whatever the hell is going on here, get it sorted. Carnaby Hanson is due to arrive within the hour. I do not want him to walk into this circus." Cain snapped, his tone sharp and cold. Max's teeth were all on show as I dragged him past Stubby still sat on the floor a bloody rag wrapped around his leg as Melanie went about tidying up the mess we had made, a stone cold glare and clenched jaw accompanying her.

The next three hours were spent locked in my room pouring over the telephone directory and crossing names off the Robert list. Painstakingly there were thousands upon thousands of Roberts in the world. Carnaby's black saloon car came and went, the rain stopped and started as my back grew more and more twisted out of shape. Eventually, with no fruits of my labor, I gave up, going downstairs and grumbling about my back like a crippled old man as I went. Autumn was doing less compact days of training as it was coming to an end. I found her and Wes in the kitchen-drinking smoothies. Autumn turned abruptly away from me as I wandered over to them and perched on the edge of the oak table as I scanned the garden beyond for signs of trouble.

"Has anyone seen Mel or Harley?" I asked. Wes smirked.

"I don't know what you did kid, but I don't think you'll be eating for a few days."

"It wasn't my fault."

Wes shrugged.

"Mel's gone to town, and I haven't seen Harley."

Nodding absentmindedly my interests moved on to my sister, who was staring at the white paint on the walls as if it were the most interesting thing she had ever seen.

"How's the training going?" I asked, directing my question at Wes .

"Fine, Isabelle's gotten so much better, she can show you when we go for our run later."

Without hesitation, even with Autumn turning and glaring at me as if I was about to tell her deepest secret, I nodded.

"Yeah, I have nothing better to do."

Chapter Twelve: Good Luck, Bad Luck

Much to my annoyance that afternoon, I realised there were thousands Mr. Carmichaels in the world. It was the most demoralising process I had ever gone through as I sat thumbing through the international directory, crossing them off one by one when their first initial wasn't R. My vision started to go blurry around half five, so tossing on my running clothes I left the house to check out Autumn's progress.

I was out of breath by the time we ran up the sandy path at the back of the house, my face red and hot. Autumn had made leaps and bounds since the last disastrous run I had been on with her. When we reached the back door Wes sent Autumn up the stairs to get changed, sweat trailing behind her she went, me following suit. The moment my bedroom door was closed, she turned on me, a burning rage of annoyance ignited in her eyes.

"What the hell was all that about?" She demanded furiously.

"All what?" I asked yanking my damp top over my head and launching it at the washing basket next to the wardrobe door.

"Why did you want to come running with us?" She asked, striding into the bathroom and turning on the taps. "What's suddenly so interesting to you?"

"It gets boring running alone after a while." I shrugged. "Plus I've just found you again, is it that wrong to want to hang out?" I asked. The half sarcastic laugh she gave next shocked me.

"He abandoned us Tilly and then you abandoned me. You don't get to just wander back when you feel like it, it's not..." She stopped, shaking her head. "Anyway, why don't you go running with your boyfriend?" She retorted.

I almost swallowed my tongue.

"My who now?" I choked, feeling the blood draining from my face as if someone had pulled the plug.

"You know- short black hair, tanned skin...Yeah, I've seen you two walking along the beach, hand in hand...." She said her expression descending into smug territory.

I stared at her for a second, horrified.

"He's pretty cute, how did..."

"You can't tell Cain." I almost burst.

"Don't worry." She interrupted. "I distracted Wes, I won't tell your secret." Her mouth creased, smiling slightly. Exhaling a breath I didn't even know I'd been holding, my shoulders dropped, a warm unfamiliar feeling settling in my chest. I didn't like it one bit.

"Thanks." I said, turning away from her abruptly and tucking a pair of black jeans pocking out of my drawers back into its rightful place. "And I didn't abandon you if you remember, you left me in that hell hole."

"That wasn't really my fault."

"And it was mine?" I said, turning back to her. Eventually, her tense shoulders dropped.

"No." She replied.

The door to the en-suite was shut with a soft bang. Alone in my room I rubbed my suddenly pounding head.

"Why do all our conversations end like this?" I whispered to myself.

Feeling suddenly cold I grabbed a new towel from my wardrobe so I could have a shower in the big bathroom across the hall before anyone else wanted one. My eyes fell on the chocolate bar laying half open on the bed. A thought occurred to me and feeling a pang of remorse I grabbed a pen and scribbled a note for Autumn.

I won't tell.

I left the rest of the chocolate bar on her bed with the note on top of it. I didn't get chocolate when I was training, it wouldn't have surprised me if she hadn't had any either and what's life without a bit of sugar? Taking a long leisurely shower was just about my favourite thing to do, with the room filled with steam, ears filled with music I could have been absolutely anywhere, anywhere I wanted to be. The chocolate was gone by the time I got back, bedroom empty. I smiled, maybe this could be the start of something for her and I.

Abigail L. Marsh

Tea was a quiet affair, just Jamie and I, and he wasn't even in the room, his mind in Rio at the World cup as he stared unrelentingly at the flatscreen TV hanging on the wall. I gave up trying to pique his attention and collapsed into bed, ready for a little downtime. I watched Eastenders catch up for about an hour before a breaking news update interrupted my show.

Autumns face popped up on BBC news and then suddenly to my great shock my seven-year-old faced joined it. Heart hammering I whacked up the volume of the broadcast. A short fuzzy video clip of me pacing the beach in Cornwall appeared.

'Is this Tilly Carmichael? Has she resurfaced almost a decade after being kidnapped from her home in New York? Local fisherman Clemance Trenowden spotted the girl in the video pacing a hidden cove just off Lantic Bay, on the Polperro Heritage coast. The video is blurry, but locals say they recognised a girl matching the newly released photos of what Tilly Carmichael would look now, around the area just last week."

The ugly photo they had photoshopped my cute little kids face onto in an attempt to resemble what I might have looked like now, was terrible. I glanced in the mirror, they'd messed up my nose big time.

"I do not look like that… And eww what *have* they got me wearing? They are not gonna find me wearing plaid." I said faking a small laugh

Abigail L. Marsh

as I tried to push thoughts of being found back into their chest and clamp the padlock shut. As the broadcaster let the clip play out my mind wandered back to the beach; I hadn't thought there was anyone around for miles and miles.

"Further to this investigation, police are looking into the possibility that Tilly Carmichael's biological sister, formally known as Autumn-Rose Carmichael has been abducted by the same group of people. The footage here, taken from a hidden security camera shows a young girl wearing the same clothes Autumn was last seen in being roughly tossed into a white van by a man wearing all black in a derelict warehouse, in Hammersmith. The warehouse owner has been questioned in connection to the activity but is not a suspect in the kidnapping. Autumn-Rose now goes by the name Isabelle Parker. If anybody has any information regarding this on-going investigation, please call, one, one, one and give the reference code 456UHA8JK."

The clip that played wasn't one I had seen before. I didn't recognise the van or the warehouse in the slightest. I had never asked too many details on where Cain had found Autumn, or how he had managed to get her to the house without a whiff of suspicion, it had never been of interest to me, but now…

When the clip ended, I was expecting Danny Dyer to pop back on arguing about a pint of beer with his cockney accent, but I was wrong. The

Abigail L. Marsh

live broadcast came back and my Dad's face appeared. Swallowing hard as my chest constricted with shock I stared unblinking. The mans lips were moving, but none of the words spoken entered my head. There he was, my Dad. *Breathe Tilly.*

"...If you're watching, please call me, please let me know you're both alive." Roberts voice finally registered in my brain. Routing in his pocket he yanked out a crumpled piece of paper with a number on it. Scrambling for the TV remote which agonisingly slipped off the edge of the bed as I lunged for it, I paused the television, grabbed a pen and paper and wrote the number down.

In a daze, finally having what I'd been searching for I clicked the play button and watched as Robert was pulled from the screen. Then Danny Dyer appeared, necking a whole pint of beer. Usually I would have been impressed, but I couldn't stop staring at the number Eastenders didn't even enter my brain. That is until the creak of the third floorboard from the top of the back stairs buckled under the weight of someone, and I screwed the paper up, tossing it down the back of my headboard. The door swung open with no regard to what I might have been doing. It was Autumn. My heart beat again.

"What?" She asked, staring at me bemused.

Abigail L. Marsh

"Nothing..." I replied, choking suspiciously on my own words as I re-verted my shifty eyes back to Eastenders.

"I won't tell... Come on, we've established this already."

I watched her as she walked the length of her room to get her pyjamas and came back over to my bed eyebrows rasied.

"Why are you still living in my room? Has Jamie not fixed the water leak?" I demand sitting up and reaching for my water bottle, my mouth suddenly dry.

"Don't change the subject."

"Alright ... Bossy..." I breathed after chugging half the bottle. I could see she wasn't going to let it lie and sighing heavily I told her. "I just saw Robert on TV and I thought you were Cain." I explained. "He, uh, he wouldn't be so happy if he saw me watching stuff like that."

Autumns eyes creased in what I could only see to be concern.

I pulled the duvet up to my chin self-consciously. "Don't look at me like I'm a lost puppy."

"You're lying to me." She huffed taking a step towards the bathroom

I was shocked, one for the bratty tone she evidently thought she could speak to me in and two, how did she know I wasn't telling her the whole truth?

"I'm not lying." I snapped. "And what gives you the right to come waltzing into my room and start mouthing off." Autumn was taken

Abigail L. Marsh

aback at my sudden venom, she took a step towards the bathroom ready to slam the door if I decided to get out of bed and do something, but I wouldn't, I couldn't do that to her, not again.

"Go and have a shower for God's sake, you smell like garbage." I sighed, turning over and resting my head on the paw of my giant teddy bear.

"I saw the news broadcast." Autumn soft voice stabbed straight through my wall of anger. As guilt fell into my stomach I turned slightly so I could see her silhouetted in the bathroom door.

"Tilly, if you took that number, swear you'll get rid of it. Don't waste your time, don't let him break your heart again."

She stepped into the bathroom and closed the door leaving me with the only coherent thought I had left. *If you want answers Tilly, you don't have a choice.*

The next day of my tumultuous life proved to be catastrophic for me. Sneaking out to see Seth had been easy as pie up to that point. Cain was busy, Isabelle kept Wes distracted when she could, no-one really cared where I went or what I did, as long as I was back for tea. I assumed Cain didn't have time to worry about Robert, with his new plans to take our 'business' abroad he always seemed to be away from the house. I hadn't said anything about it, he knew Isabelle and I had fallen out so he'd taken his eye off the ball and that was just where I wanted him.

I opened my eyes to a text from Seth, frowning at his name I opened it distastefully.

Seth: I'm sorry for what I said yesterday. I shouldn't have been so hard on you. How about I skip school an we can spend the day sunbathing in the dunes, far away from everybody? I'll make it up to you x

A smile crept onto my face as I replied.

Nellie: I don't know. You were a pretty big jerk yesterday.

Seth: I know :(Please let me make it up to you?

Nellie: Fine... But I want a bunch of roses.

Seth: Errr okay... But why roses?

Nellie: It's what all the boys do in the movies when they screw up.

Seth: You watch too many movies ;) ... See you at Fox Point in an hour?

Nellie: Sure.

My phone beeped aggravatingly as the screen turned black.

"Bloody iPhones." I grumbled grabbing the charger and shoving the phone on charge into my desk drawer.

Abigail L. Marsh

I left the house an hour later claiming to go for a run and choosing to be fashionably late, just to make him sweat a little.

There he was, stood at the edge of the cliffs facing out to the blue sea.

"You know I should just shove you off here." I said placing a hand on his back. Jumping out of his skin he spun around and walloped me in the head with a bunch of ruby red roses.

"Jesus!" He cried. "Sorry I thought you were a murderer."

Biting my lip, nervous by how uncomfortably close he was to the truth. I snatched the roses from him taking a long sniff.

"Beautiful." I grinned.

"Am I forgiven?" He asked.

"Hmmmmm…" I speculated tapping my cheek with my index finger and smiling cruelly.

"I'm really sorry. Do you want me to beg? I can beg." To my horror he got down on his knees and looked up at me, hands together as if I was god.

"You're forgiven! Get up!" I said looking around at the empty clifftop almost as red as the roses. "Come on, I want to get some sunbathing in before I get dragged back to the house."

The sun beat down on us as I sipped the cool orange juice Seth had brought in his flask. We'd been lounging around in the dunes letting the

Abigail L. Marsh

heat bronze our shoulders and watching the deep blue sea rush up the sand for hours.

"Shall we go for a swim?" I asked pulling my t-shirt over my head to reveal the bikini I had begged Cain to buy for me last time we'd been out in Norwich. He'd looked so disapprovingly at it as we'd stood in the ladies section of TopShop, I thought I'd never be allowed to wear one again, but my tactical whining had driven him crazy and the poor man had relented.

"What?" I asked as Seth's eyes traveled up my torso. "Do you want my fist in your face?" I demand.

"What? No. Sorry… It's just, I really like you Nellie." He said an twinkle in his eyes that confused my already jumbled brain.

"What? Don't you like me?" His voice was soft, like gossamer and silk. I nodded suddenly unsure of where the conversation was going.

"Of course I like you." I smiled looking down and flicking an imaginary piece of dirt off the back of my hand.

"Then what's wrong?" He asked reaching out tentatively and sweeping a strand of my wild hair out of my eyes. There were so many things wrong, so many that it hurt to think about. I'd tried in vain to push them out of my mind, to enjoy the time that we had.

"Can we just go for a swim?" I asked my tone almost sharp as I battled to cut away from what I realised he was sailing for.

Abigail L. Marsh

"Nellie, please stop pushing me away."

I cringed hard, closing my eyes in pain as he mentioned the name I had grown to resent with all my heart.

"What is it?" Seth asked. I looked into his concerned eyes.

"You don't even know my real name." The words slipped out of me before I could stop them.

"Huh?" Seth said pulling away from me, confusion etched into his soft concerned expression. Stunned by my own confession I struggled desperately to backtrack.

"I…" I was suddenly caught of guard as a dark shadow covered Seth's face. Turning to see what was blocking the sun from keeping it's comforting arm around my back, I practically leapt away from Seth as if he had turned into a giant fire ant. Standing on top of the dune was Cain. A dirty look on his face that told me to run.

"Dad." I spluttered. Seth sat up in a flash.

"Hi *darling*." Cain said in a deadly tone. "Who's your friend?"

"This is Seth, we, uhh, we were just sunbathing." I explained as Cain walked down the dune not sliding once, it was like the sand was saying 'do not anger him on pain of death.'

"Hi Sir." Seth said scrambling to his feet and holding his hand out. Cain admired a man who had balls, but not Seth, he grabbed the boys hand and twisted it painfully.

Abigail L. Marsh

"Dad." I cried as Seth winced. "Please stop, we were just sunbathing, nothing else." Cain turned to me, Seth groaning as he twisted his arm backwards. I looked pleadingly into Cains face but there was nothing there, his eyes were narrowed, rigid, cold. I shrunk away, a coward. Cain's attention was drawn back to the almost crying boy.

"WHO ARE YOU? WHO ARE YOU WORKING FOR?" Cain shook him hard. I was confused by his questions.

"I'm Seth, I'm just Seth. I'm go to Cromer Academy, I don't work for anyone." Seth groaned bracing his arms against Cains chest attempting damage control.

Cain's eyes flickered as something registered in his brain and his shoulders lowered.

"This is the last time you are going to come anywhere near her, do I make myself clear." Cain growled dangerously.

"But sir…" Seth dared. My heart fell as he tried to plead our case. "We aren't doing anything wrong." Seth protested.

There was a pop as Cain yanked Seth's arm from it's socket, dragging my only friend in the whole world off his feet. Blood pumping and heart beating erratically I opened my mouth to interject but stopped short of a single sound. I had never been terrified of the Alpha's anger when it came out as fire, scared, yes, but not terrified. This was different. His eyes hard, sharp, cold. I had always been silenced, petrified of the ice that could erupt from his soul.

Abigail L. Marsh

"If I have to tell you again, I am going to put a bullet between you mother's eyes." Cain growled. I watched my macho boyfriend's lip tremble and held my breath, my body wouldn't move. After the longest second of my life Cain threw Seth roughly to the ground. The boy stumbled to his feet, glanced at me and raised his hands.

"Alright, alright." He said face red with bottled emotion as he backed away.

"Wait." My meek voice came drifting across the space between us. He couldn't just leave, this couldn't be it but my voice, no matter it's purpose was the last nail in his coffin. Seth looked over at me his hands still held up in some sort of surrender as I registered Cain's clench jaw and white knuckles.

"Are you going to be okay?" He stammered taking a dangerous step in my direction.

"LEAVE." Cain erupted, spit flying from his mouth as he made a few rapid steps towards Seth.

My always happy boy ran, skidding on the sand as he fled; I flicked a glance up at Cain he was looking at me with pure disgust, his face screwed up and red, his eyes narrowing dangerously. He reached out grabbing my arm painfully, yanking me with him as he strode past.

"Move." He spat.

Abigail L. Marsh

138

I slipped and skidded down the final dune as he forced me to move faster. We marched across the beach stopping just shy of the waves. I watched him unsure of what the hell we were doing.

"Cain?" I breathed as he routed around in his pocket, was it a gun? Was he going to shoot me? The funny thing was although that was horrifying, I was more shocked at what he actually did. Finally dragging whatever it was out of his pocket he turned and showed it to me.

"I thought I could trust you Tilly." He said holding out my iPhone, the tone of disappointment in his voice making me baulk.

"Y, you can." I stammered tears welling up behind my eyes. "You can. I won't see him again, but please, please let me say goodbye."

Cain laughed sadistically shaking his head.

"Not a chance."

With one hand still wrapped tightly around my wrist he used the other one to launch my phone with all our messages, his number, and our photos clear across the ocean. I stared after it, watching it splash insignificantly into the blue, my heart choking. As it sunk from view Cain nodded, satisfied he'd done the best thing. With a clenched jaw I saw a flash of red. He'd ruined everything, spinning around I screamed in his face.

"GET OFF ME." Hurling a couple of poorly aimed punches at him. Brushing them away he caught my flailing arm and pulled me around so

Abigail L. MarshAbigail L. Marsh

we were face to face. Tears blurred my vision as I stared at him, unreadable, no fear, no irritating smirk, nothing.

"Tilly, you won't see him again, you won't talk to him again, you won't go near his house. Do not make me end this! Let this be the last word." He said. My lip quivered, I knew what he meant. Seth and I were done. For the sake of his life, not mine.

Dropping one arm Cain walked past me dragging me along with him. I followed silently, hating him with the fire of a thousand suns as tears trickled down my cheeks and found their way into my mouth. It had been years since I had shed an actual tear, a sad tear and this man, the man I thought I could trust had finally managed to crack me.

Before we left the beach I glanced back. A small figure at the far end of the sand stood watching us. I knew it was Seth, and that this would be the last time I ever saw him.

Cain frogmarched me into the courtyard at the house and slammed the gate so hard several slats of wood splintered under the pressure. After cursing loudly Cain bolted it and closed the coded padlock, scrambling the numbers.

"You can't keep me locked up in here!" I spat, trying again to yank my arm away from him with absolutely no success.

"How long?" He demanded, eyes ablaze. I knew arguing with him was like duelling with a hand grenade but I'd reached my limit.

"I don't want to live like this!" I erupted.

"What?" He said anger and confusion mixing in his voice as if it were two shirts in a washing machine, one red, one white, it was bound to end badly.

"I don't want to live like this, I want to eat ice-cream on the beach! I want to complain about homework with my friends! I want you to teach me how to make pancakes! I want to embarrass my little sister on her first date! I want a normal life Cain… Anything but this." I said my voice breaking in half as the wolf in me revved up for its next attack.

"What are you talking about?" He demanded. I looked up at him stomach flipping painfully, he didn't get it, he didn't understand. I ripped my arms away from him and finally, he let go.

"HOW LONG TILLY?" He barked as I stumbled away from him.

"A VERY VERY LONG TIME! And you, you ruined everything!" The wolf inside me rearing its ugly head and taking a chunk out of the Alpha.

"You're not going to see him again Tilly." The Alpha growled not taking the slightest bit of notice as I circled him like prey.

"Why? Jealous that I don't totally rely on you anymore? Worried that I'm not your little girl anymore? NEWSFLASH I NEVER WAS!" I screamed furiously going in for another bite, swinging my fist which bounced harmlessly off his shoulder.

"Stop acting like a child!" Cain yelled.

"A child?" A laugh exploded from my chest. "I have never, ever been a child."

"Go to your room!" The Alpha finally snapped at me, fists balling up tightly ready to attack. I couldn't hear my own brain yelling over the wolf inside me. The screeching ravens covering every inch of the court-yard, perched on the house, the fences, the cars, were all screeching in my ears, egging me on.

I slammed my hands into Cains chest ramming him back against the wall. Taken off guard by my sudden strength Cain was momentarily reduced to shock.

"You can't push me around anymore Cain. Y*ou* made me this monster." I growled. Snapping out of his he pushed me back, I obliged, moving away into a fighting stance, ready to take him on.

"Do not forget who taught you!" He said fiercely, clearly refusing to entertain the idea that I could take him down. I laughed pitifully, the wolf in me now totally in charge.

"Don't make me the enemy Cain, I'm not a little girl anymore." I said sarcastically, attacking him from the weakest point I could think of. He gritted his teeth, darkness shrouding his dangerous eyes.

"GET OUT OF MY SIGHT." He barked.

Abigail L. Marsh

"OR WHAT?" Blood tore through my veins in utter fury, my sanity on the verge of non-existence. I couldn't wrap my head around it. He loved me. Cain, loved me. So how could he treat me like this?

Without warning Cain made a lunge for me, training kicked in and I dodged it, slamming my palms hard against his chest and without a wall to stop him this time he fell over, smashing his head on the floor with a dull thud. I swallowed hard, staring down at my palms as if they coursed with fire.

"OI!" Chris's yell broke my trance. Steeling myself for another fight I turned and eyeballed the man as he marched across the courtyard, pulled his gun out of the waistband of his trousers and pointed it at me. I scoffed, fuelled by my first success I dove right into the second. A lone raven soar down from the sky landing metres shy of me and plucked a worm from the ground.

"You think I'm scared of you? You're pathetic." I laughed. "Go on. I'm right here, shoot me!" I sneered waving my arms around in the air. Chris's growl turned into a snarling his arms shot forward. Before I had time to spin around and protect myself, his sharp fist grabbed me, and tossed me to the floor. I lay there winded for a second, regretting my cockiness before he yanked me to my feet.

"Get the hell off me Chris." I snapped struggling to breathe in his grasp as I was frog-marched towards the back door, away from Cain.

Abigail L. Marsh

"After what you've done to the boss."

"Do you know what he did to *me*." I screeched bringing the heel of my trainer down hard on his toes.

"Steal-cap." He smirked as I groaned in pain feeling all the power drain from my body, my lungs still shocked at the sudden impact couldn't seem to take enough air in. Behind me Cain had only just pulled himself off the floor and was sitting up rubbing his head in bewilderment.

Sucking in a lungful of air I battled with my pride before screaming for Cain. As panic overtook me I stopped dead using Chris's momentum and buckle my own legs, so he'd topple over. I almost managed it, for a split second I thought he was going to flip over the top of me and land flat on his back, but he regained his balance and gave me a vicious shake.

"Stop it."

"Cain!" I shrieked.

Cain looked up and regained some sort of composure; he got up and followed us across the courtyard and into the kitchen. Chris had me shoved up against a wall, arm up ready to take a swing when Cain finally came through and yanked him away.

Abigail L. Marsh

"What the hell are you doing?" He demanded pulling the stout man around. "Don't hit her!" He snarled shoving Chris hard away from me. Chris looked from me to Cain, baffled.

"But, she…" He stuttered,

"Don't you *ever* hit her."

Gathering my wits and taking a lungful of much needed air, I strode quickly into Chris's space and swinging my leg back gave him an almighty kick in the nuts.

"ARSEHOLE!" I shouted. "Don't you ever, EVER touch me like tha…" I was rudely interrupted by Cain as he grabbed my arm tightly, forcing me out of the room. We didn't stop there, up the stairs I was lead, a iron grip wrapped around my forearm. I could still hear Chris balling around on the ground as Cain pushed me into my bedroom.

"Do not leave this room. Do you understand me?" He said and not waiting for an answer he slammed the door.

I sat down on my bed. The only thing keeping me sane in this place had been taken away from me. Tears rolled down my face as I battled with my next move. I ended up laying on my bed, staring out of the window to the trees blowing in the wind beyond. Suddenly my life seemed awful… I felt like one of those china dolls, something to look at but never to play with. What kind of existence was that?

Abigail L. Marsh

Chapter Thirteen: A Call

Something was awry all through the night. Alone in my room as Autumn had opted for the easy life on the sofa downstairs, away from my wrath, I watched as cars came and went with lights trailing across the ceiling. Shouts and angry voices found their way through the floor-boards into my room. I didn't understand why it was such a drama, Seth was just a boy, what harm could he do? These questions trouble me as I struggled to block the world out. By half two, I'd tossed and turned a thousand times, my duvet was tangled and sheets rumpled, and my patience fast coming to an end.

"Fine." I snapped into the darkness. "If you're not going to sleep, then you're going to call that stupid number."

Shaken by my own sudden words of motivation I reached down the back of my bed, into the dust and empty sweet wrappers, finding the scrunched up number and Nokia on my second attempt, after shaking off a disgustingly sticky packet of half-eaten honeycomb squares in complete horror. Using the light of the moon, so as not to attract any unwanted attention from the unusually busy courtyard below, I stared at the scribbled number in my jittering hands,

What are you doing? Why? What's this going to prove? He's a liar. He abused you. He gave you away. Don't do it. But what if he's changed?

Don't you want to… No. You can't risk it. You need answers. You have them. No. You don't. You owe it to yourself to find out. What do you actually want from this? DIAL THE NUMBER. THROW IT AWAY. DO IT NOW.

The noise inside my head grew louder and louder and louder. The fighting was unbearable, there was no right answer and I knew it. The screaming ceased as I punched in the numbers. BEEP, BEEP, BEEP. The international ringtone began, and I waited. Six beeps, seven beeps, eight beeps, nine; for one horrifying moment I thought it was going to answer machine. Crackling, the sound of someone breathing

"Hello?" I froze, it was his voice, the voice I had heard at The Ivy, the voice from the house on the Illinois River. The voice of the man that caused my world to crumble around me.

"Hello!" His voice snapped impatiently. "If this is another hoax call I will report you to…"

"It's not!" The words erupted form my chest as if a firework had been lit underneath them, scaring me. "It's Tilly, really."

Not knowing what else to say I listened to the breathing coming from halfway across the world, the fire eruption in my stomach burned painfully as I pleaded silently for him to talk before I snapped, and cut him off.

Abigail L. Marsh

"How do I know it's you?" Robert said.

Thrown off by his question I faltered, what was I supposed to say,' You have a birthmark in the shape of a sausage dog on your left bum cheek?'

"What restaurant did we go to on Tilly's sixth birthday?"

Jesus! Casting my mind back and fighting through the dense fog that had conjured itself over the years, I had to use all my tongue sticking out concentration skills to remember.

"Chucky Cheese?" I asked airily- a real stab in the dark. I missed.

"No. Don't ever call this line again."

"Wait!" I said my heart lighting with anger. This was a man who had put me through complete hell, who had destroyed all traces of my childhood in one foul swoop, he was not going to hang up the phone on me. Not a chance.

"When I was little, I was terrified of thunder, I would hide under my bed with that stuffed monkey and cry. One time you pulled me out, you sat me on your lap and you told me you would never let anything hurt me... You promised. After that, I wasn't afraid of thunder. And I'm not now either."

There was a short pause where I thought I had made that whole speech to an ended call, but then a gush of noise and his voice returned.

"Oh my god. Tilly, is it really you? Where are you? Hold on, I need

Abigail L. Marsh

to...CALLIE! Tilly sweetheart can you tell me where you are? I'll write it down and..."

"Whoah, slow down!" I said tensing at this sudden action. "I, Robert, I need you to listen to me." I said.

"Yeah, of course, I'm sorry. Talk to me. I'm listening. I just think I need to call the cops so they can..."

"No! No cops. Robert if you call the police I swear I'll hang up, I won't ever call back."

"Alright, no cops." His breaking voice croaked. "Just please don't hang up, please, please."

Caught off guard by the sheer desperation in his voice, as if I was talking to a terrified child, I shuddered.

"Okay." I breathed. "Okay."

"Just, where are you baby?" He asked. "No, no it's fine, just go." his voice came again, but this time it was muffled. "Callie's gone, okay, no-one knows."

"Are you sober?" I asked, coming out with the most important question I could possibly think of.

"Yes." Came the response. "I've been sober for eight years now. I go to weekly AA meeting's, Callie lives with me, she's been back with me for five years. Everything is perfect... Except we're missing you and Autumn of course."

Shaking my head alone in my dark room, I cringed at his words 'perfect'. How could it be perfect? The bad blood between us all, the memories had tarnished 'perfect' forever.

"I want answers to everything." I said bluntly flipping the subject on its head, not wanting to think about a world where everything was 'perfect.'

"Okay... I want to know where you are." Robert said. "Why don't we trade some information?" He gave a nervous, half-laugh. This was an interesting proposition, something I knew I would never give away, but...

A crash from the landing beyond my room had me jumping out of my skin.

"What was that?" Robert asked his voice flying from jittery to damn straight through the roof irate. I took the phone away from my ear and shined the tiny screen across the dark room, lighting up absolutely nothing.

"TILLY!" The tiny voice yelled out of the microphone on the Nokia.

"It was nothing." I said, putting the phone back to my ear.

"Did someone hurt you?" He asked.

150

"No." I shook my head, "There's no-one in here."

"They lock you up by yourself?" He demanded, the calmness of our conversation taking a flying jump out of the window.

"They don't keep me locked up." I retorted. "Now I want answers, and if you won't tell me, I guess I'll just have to ..." I said stopping short of what I was about to say as Robert interrupted again.

"Yeah, so tell me where you are, and the police will come and rescue you."

"I don't need rescuing." I said as another crash came from beyond the door. Panicking that someone would break their way into my room next, I had no choice but to speed the conversations along. "*I* will come to you, but I swear I am trained. If I see a policeman, or car, or get a whiff off the fact you have spoken to them and I will if you have, I will run and never, ever get in contact again. Do you hear me?"

Robert didn't have much of choice, I had him bound and a tied, with a little bow on his head for special measures.

"Yes but how..." He stammered. "When are you..."

"I don't know when I can get away. Don't think I don't mean what I say."

"Okay."

Another crash outside the door had me cursing,

Abigail L. Marsh

"I have to go." I said, cutting him off halfway through his plea for me to wait. Leaping off my bed, I rammed my palm against the closed door. "Who the hell is banging out there? I swear to god if I come out there you're going to wish you'd never been born." I growled with a barrel load of ferocity. Whoever it was disappeared down the back stairs not fancying my wrath. I sighed, my heart racing.

Chapter Fourteen: The Gang War

No-one disturbed me the rest of that night, mainly because I had hauled Autumn's bed out of its place in the alcove and with a chest of drawers I managed to wedge the door shut, but also because they knew my fury and didn't dare. My mind played tricks on me, trying to convince me it had to have been Autumn who'd sold me out, because who else was there? Several times that night I pulled out the little Nokia, trying in vain to remember Seth's number, it had three eights and a zero, but no amount of blind anger would bring the rest back to me. With a mix of overwhelming fury and sadness that I couldn't control anymore, I launched the Nokia brick at the wall, where it fell to the carpet, still very much intact. I attempted the whole 'woe is me' Disney Princess,

Abigail L. Marsh

throw yourself on your bed and weep tactic, where I actually drifted off to sleep.

Banging. Unrelenting, intolerable banging woke me up the next morning. When my exhausted eyes focused on the alarm clock I cursed under my breath. They were going to torture me now were they? A metallic clang came next jolting me with a start. Struggling out of the top blanket I had managed to entangle myself in, I turned over to where the sun blared through the curtains that I had forgotten to shut the day before. A face appeared at the window, another angry looking face. Jamie. When his eyes landed on me, he pointed to the latch on the inside of the glass, furiously gesturing me to move my bum and open it.

I did, mainly out of complete bewilderment.

"What are you doing?" I demanded throwing the windows outwards missing Jamie's dodging head by a millimetre.

"Move that shit out of the way, pack a bag and get your sorry arse down to the kitchen." He snapped, knocking the left window with his arm as it's momentum caused it to come flying back and threaten to clout him round the back of the head. "And sort yourself out, you're a mess."

"Pardon?" I growled grasping the top prongs of the ladder ready to haul him off.

"Don't you dare, runt." Jamie said, grabbing the frame of my window to steady himself.

Oh we were playing that game now were we? I didn't know where I found the strength from, but that knackered wolf hiding, defeated in it's den, inside my soul picked up its sorry butt and fixed a cold hard stare into Jamie's eyes. Most of the time my hard set stare would send anyone running for cover, but today Jamie didn't follow those rules, he didn't run, or climb through the window and beat me to a pulp. He saw the pain the little wolf was in and he stopped. His eyes, although didn't move away from mine softened.

"Get dressed, we're leaving in half an hour." And with that, he let go of the frame and started down the ladder, heading back into the kitchen, as I stood alone in my bedroom, still holding the ladder.

Tossing the Nokia and number deep into the pits of my bag where no-one would go looking I packed the essentials, not sure what was actually going on, and found myself moping down the desolate corridor to the back stairs.

In the kitchen I found pretty much everyone standing around drinking cups of coffee, bags by their feet. Eyes drifted over to me as I reached the bottom step, rucksack slung over my shoulder, face washed, so no

Abigail L. Marsh

154

traces of the night before lingered. Max whined at me from inside his cage across the room, shaking his tail, the only one happy to see me. Nobody spoke, either Cain had threatened them into silence, or they just had nothing to say about the behaviour that had put them all at risk. I preferred the former explanation, it meant Cain was still on my side. The Alpha strode into the kitchen, his eyes skipped over me as if I was a ghost- not there at all.

"Tate with Jamie, Kurt and I in the merc. Lucas, you drive Mel, the dogs and the two girls in the cruiser, when we hit the Cambridge road, Lucas, you take that. We'll see you up there this afternoon." He said tossing Jamie the keys for the land cruiser and turning abruptly on his heel. *'Well if he didn't want me in his car then fine,'* my mind grumbled to itself. I caught Autumn watching me closely from her chair at the table and furiously berated my falling features that gave away the ache in the pit of my stomach.

"Come on then." Lucas said. Shaking it off, I followed behind the man looking at his muscles as they strained with the weight of his suitcase. *Seth. Seth. Seth.* He had muscles too.

Up to the point of passing the signs for Peterborough, I had assumed we were going back to the safe house in Cornwall. From time to time we would go on these little trips always heading south away from the big cities, sometimes it was for a few days, others a few weeks. This time I

Abigail L. Marsh

assumed it was all down to my not-so-secret boyfriend and I. If Seth decided to tell anyone what Cain had said the day before, no doubt about it the social workers would decided to pop round and have a little chat. We didn't need that, as anyone could imagine. Going North however, wasn't something we did. With rival crime gangs and turf wars occurring in Manchester, Leeds and Newcastle all the time, Cain preferred the peaceful life, away from that, choosing his allies in London.

"Where are we going?" I finally asked, the burning question proving too much for my curiosity.

"The Yorkshire Dales." Melanie said, sliding her feet off the dashboard and turning to me, a small smile on her face. I watched it for a second, unsure if she meant to smile at me or whether she'd forgotten Cain had locked me in the dog house.

"That's a bit extreme, Seth's not going to say anything. Cain scared him stupid."

"It's not about Seth."

"Then what's it about?"

Jamie turned slightly in his seat.

"You might as well tell her, it's not like anyone else is going to."

"Tell me what?" I said, pushing Mel as she gave Jamie a disapproving swat.

"I didn't want to scare you."

"Just say it, Mel, I'm not the scared little runt everyone around here seems to think I am."

Mel sighed heavily.

"Have you ever heard of a man named Henry Giannaville?"

I shook my head.

"No, who is he?"

"He used to be very close friends with Cain and Carnaby, but years and years ago they fell out big time, all three of them. Cain and Carnaby are back on speaking terms but Henry, he held on to all that hate. He's been up north, underground for a long time but word is he's back with a vengeance."

"That's why Cain's been gone?" I asked.

Melanie tilted her head. "Yes and no. He's been planning a heist abroad, you know that part, but he and Carnaby they've been in negotiations, doing everything they can to get Henry to back down. He's built an alliance with people all over the county. So Cain wants us to take a little break while Carnaby takes the helm. "Henry plays dirty, Seth got in the crossfire. When Cain found your phone and saw you talking to a boy he knew nothing about…." Mel left the rest to my imagination.

"He thought Seth was working for Henry… That's why he's so angry." I said, piecing it all together. "Well he isn't, Seth's my age, my only friend in the whole entire world, how could he possibly be a fucking spy for some crusty old gangster? So why…"

"Because even though he isn't a spy or anything to do with this world, he poses a threat to us."

"He wasn't a threat." I groaned feeling the newly familiar feeling of my emotions creeping up my throat.

"Tilly, you can't see Seth anymore. Cain said…"

"I *know* what Cain said." I snapped biting the inside of my cheeks so hard blood trickled down the back of my throat leaving a sickly iron taste, anything to stop the weakness threatening to fall from my eyes show I kept them cold and unmoving as Mel watched me.

"Then you know you'll only put Seth in danger if you see him again. I'm sorry, Tilly." Mel said, turning back around to face the front.

I wasn't an easy person to read. Concealing my emotions was something I had learned to do from a very early age, something I had learned quickly, something I did to protect myself from a world that threatened me at every breath. So it startled me as I swallowed them back into their box and slammed the lid shut when a hand tentatively placed itself on

Abigail L. Marsh

my leg. I'd forgotten Isabelle was in the car, she'd been silent, melting into the shadows as a trainee was taught to. My expression holding onto its blankness my eyes traced the arms to her eyes. Not the usual eyes full of bitter betrayal, but soft, almost apologetic eyes and a small smile to go with it. Without a flicker of hesitation, I offered her a smile back. An instant later, her hand slipped away, and I turned back to the window, my mind in a fog.

The journey was long, the dogs whined for ninety percent of it. They didn't usually travel in the land cruiser which had worse suspension than a home-made go-kart. When Lucas couldn't handle their racket anymore he flung the car off the motorway and slammed the breaks hard as we pulled into one of the many random service stations peppered along the A1. This happened four times. I cottoned on eventually and braced myself against the chair in front, concerned I would get whiplash from his erratic driving.

Finally the grey tarmac and run down council houses that sat right on the edge of the noisy motorway turned into small winding roads, rolling hills and greenery. Lucas who was downright fed up called for the car to be silent as he navigated the last few miles, manoeuvring around tractors and unsuspecting horses until we found ourselves on a dirt track

Abigail L. Marsh

leading around the side of a desolate hill, that seems to reach up into the clouds.

"This is it." Mel said. Leaning over so I could see through the front window. I wasn't especially excited by the stone building that could only be described as a hut shrouded in moss, as it stood before us.

"Is it?" I asked grimacing at the thought of spending weeks hold up in there; and then just to spite me even more, the moment I stepped out into the mud the heavens opened up. I was soaked to the skin before I had even stepped foot in the foul-smelling porch.

Unfortunately, I was in no place to complain, no-one would hang around in my presence long enough to hear it. So for the next nine days, I spent my life feeling miserably sorry for myself. Mel made me break-fast, lunch and tea, but aside from that I wasn't allowed down from my room where I began to wallow in my own pity and dog hair. Sharing a room with Isabelle and the two dogs was my only saving grace, al-though she didn't have a great deal to say to me when she wasn't out training somewhere amongst the hills, at least I wasn't alone.

The signal at the house was patchy at best, my room inconveniently had absolutely none, so I was forced to wait days before I could contact Robert again. As painstaking as every single day became, something

Abigail L. Marsh

good did come out of that trip. On the eighth day of being held up, Isabelle came back from training completely exhausted, covered from head to toe in thick mud, she took herself off for a shower and that had been the end of her that night. She fell into her bed and was asleep before I could even say goodnight. Thankfully exhaustion wasn't specific to her, everyone seemed knackered. The house fell silent by half-past nine. In the pitch-black that night, I crept out of the room gripping the Nokia tightly in my hands, only stopping to silence my suddenly excited dog as he wagged his tail gleefully at the sudden night excursion.

The house was exceedingly old, and I cringed, stopping frozen to the spot every single time the floorboards creaked. Holding my phone up like I was Rafiki introducing Simba to the world, I snuck around the top floor praying I would find one bar, just enough to text him, to tell him I wasn't having second thoughts. Cursing at the universes apparent lack of biased towards me I found the top of the stairs and descended, holding my breath as I pressed my back to the wall.

The kitchen was oddly creepy, illuminated only by the small light in the fish tank. Standing on top of the island with one leg out sideways, the phone held aloft and my tongue out, I desperately tried to keep my balance. How could that spot be the only place in the goddamn house my phone registered? With one hand and predictive text, I began typing a message.

"What the hell are you doing?" A voice came from behind me. Stifling a scream and with limbs flailing, I half fell, half jumped off the island, landing awkwardly on my ankle. I glanced over at the silhouette of my little sister.

"You're supposed to be asleep." I groaned hobbling back to the island, using my arms to leaver my bum onto it.

No signal. I groaned holding it back out.

"Are you trying to text Seth?" The sudden excitement in her voice caught me off guard as her whole demeanour picked up. I glanced at her face as she stepped closer, into the half-light.

"Why do you care?" I asked.

"Because." She shrugged. "It's the only bit of excitement around here." Hopping onto the counter next to me like a newly born bunny rabbit she pulled the phone down.

"You live in a crime ring… There are a hundred more exciting things to care about." I said as she turned my hand to face her.

"You haven't written anything?" She said, eyebrows knitting together in puzzlement.

"Yeah well, I haven't got any signal."

"You don't need signal to write the message idiot. Write it, then get on

Abigail L. Marsh

the bloody table."

I saw her point, but wasn't going to show it.

"Yeah, well I was just seeing if I could find the signal first." I sneered.

Isabelle nodded sitting back and twiddling her thumbs.

"Umm… You don't have to stay here." I said a frustration bubble in my stomach bursting.

"Do you want some help?"

"With texting? I may have been hidden away for a long time, but I know how to text." I found myself giggling at her naiveness.

"I know that. But I'm guessing Seth is your first boyfriend, I can help you with that…If you'll let me." She said, holding out her hand. Feeling genuinely touched by her offer to help me I felt inclined to tell her I had no intention of texting Seth at all, but that meant telling her the truth and I wasn't sure if that was such a great idea either.

"He's gone Isabelle, I can't put him in danger."

"I'm sorry." She whispered

"Why? Did *you* tell Cain?"

"No, he went into your room. Your phone pinged. I couldn't stop him." She spoke softly.

I nodded.

"Then it's not your fault, is it?"

"I know, I just…"

"It's weird." I started. I didn't want to hear how sorry she was, or how bad she felt about where we were. "It's weird how someone can just walk in, and touch every single thing in your world, no matter how hard you fight to keep them away from it."

"Did he know who you were?" Isabelle asked softly.

"No." I replied, shaking my head. "No, and that's why I have to forget about him and move on, I couldn't even tell him my real name, so what chance did we have…Iz?" I said finding the strength to ask the question burning in my chest and knowing that by telling someone the plan it would be a little more set in stone.

"Yeah?" She said.

"I'm am going to go to Illinois. Do you want to come with me?" There was a dreadful pause where I didn't know which way she was going to flip.

"No." came her quiet response.

"Are you sure? This could be a way out. Away from a war-zone."

Isabelle shook her head.

"It's a way out of the saucepan and into the flames. I'm not going back to Illinois ever and you shouldn't either. When I get out of here, I am going back to Pat and John. Robert, he's not safe." She said.

"You can't possibly know that. You were a kid, the only information you have is second hand. I know taking this risk is scary, it's horrible, but if we don't, if we just assume that he'll beat the crap out of us if we go near him, then we'll be stuck here forever."

"You're only saying that because you're unhappy right now, but Tilly, come on. I've seen you, here is where you're supposed to be. Everything that has happened up to you up to this point was supposed to happen." There was a defiant edge to her voice that told me not to push her. "Maybe not in the way you'd expect, but you have it all here Tilly, why throw it away on a whim?"

"Callie, she couldn't be back with him if he was still drinking, could she? Don't you remember life, I know you were so little, but you must remember something, what about Mum?"

"But Mum's not there. Is she?" Isabelle asked softly. "I'm not going to stop you from leaving, but if Mum is what you're going back for, then don't Tilly, she's not there."

Isabelle was entitled to her own decision, and if I pushed her, the secret wouldn't stay a secret, so there was nothing left to do but nod and agree. "You won't miss me?" I asked.

Isabelle smiled,

Abigail L. Marsh

"I reckon you'll be back."

"You won't tell?"

"Cross my heart."

With that settled, I slipped the phone into my dressing gown pocket and together we climbed the stairs back to our room and I fell into the most comfortable slumber I had had in a long time.

Chapter Fifteen: Plan In Action

Cain was the only person sitting in the kitchen when I came down early the next morning. With a plan forming for my escape it seemed pointless to avoid him, he'd been there for me for longer than my real Dad had done, when I was sick, when I was sad, in danger, he had always saved the day, no matter how angry he had been after. Time was fleeting and it was later than we all realised. So sucking up any pride I had been holding onto I pulled the wooden chair opposite him and sat down.

"I know you're angry." I began when he didn't look up from his newspaper. "I know you think I've betrayed you by seeing someone outside The Pack, but I didn't mean to. It happened so fast. I've been on my own for so long, I think I got carried away."

Cain's face didn't move a single muscle, his eyes focused solely on his paper. Swallowing hard, I was beginning to think it was all over. I would leave in a few days and not have anything to come back to if I was wrong.

"He's gone now." I said desperately, the sinking feeling in my chest beaming out of my face. "I promise I won't contact him, I won't see him ever again, please Cain, let's not waste any more time fighting. In this profession who knows what will happen tomorrow." I said pleading with the absent man across the table. My heart cracked he left a deafening silence. Then all of a sudden, that stoney face I had been staring at for the past two weeks lifted, eyes softening, lips relaxing from their pursed position, a small smile crossed his face. The paper fell to the table as he got up and came around to me. Then he said something so out of character I had to play it back in my head.

"You're very right." He said as he crouched down and pulled me into a hug, arms closing around me tightly, safely.

Not long after our reconciliation, I was sat in the front of the BMW, windows down as we headed out of the terribly assigned weather of North Yorkshire back to the windy east coast where my plan would be put into action.

Abigail L. Marsh

Cain wasn't going to be a problem. Thanks to a lucky coincidence I didn't question, he was going on an undercover recon trip with Jamie and Chris to Manchester for the best part of the week, meaning there was no-one keeping tabs on me, and no-one to wonder where I had been if my solo mission ended in disaster. Thanks to the credit card with a more than generous credit limit that Cain had given Mel, I was able to book a return flight on her card with no-one any of the wiser. Cain usually paid her bills off without question, this resulted in many, many handbags cluttering up her room, but if she was happy and doing her job, Cain didn't bat an eyelid.

My name was Nellie Watson whenever I left the county; aged sixteen. The name still hurt me and as I typed the passports number into the computer, I felt the sting of my recent heartbreak. Shoving it to the back of my mind I rummaged through my draws to find the old piggy bank Cain would push money into when he stumbled home drunk, claiming it wasn't him that had been drinking it was the earth, and that's why it lurched out from underneath his feet every step he took. Inside was a fortune, shoving the wad of fifties into jeans pockets and hidden sections in the lightly packed rucksack hiding at the back of my wardrobe I sat back, satisfied I was ready.

Abigail L. Marsh

That Wednesday evening after getting Melanie absolutely slaughtered-
one of my many talents, I crept up the back stairs to my room. Most of
The Pack lived elsewhere, hidden in other nooks and crannies of the
Norfolk coast, so the only other person around was Isabelle. She'd been
asleep since half five. Exhausted by the training exercise Rick had
pushed her to do, there was no point waking her, saying goodbye was
going to hurt even if I was going to come back for her when I'd proved
my point.

The last thing I tucked into my pocket before the short run to Cromer to
catch a taxi was my crappy pay as you go.
Cromer now reminded me of Seth, the park where we hung out, the
shops where we bought chocolate and laughed at the spotty teenagers
on shift, even the school held memories of the arguments I had fought
to win.

 "Everything okay?" The bald grungy looking taxi driver had asked me
when I asked him to take me to Heathrow airport.
"Yeah, going to see Granny, she'll be waiting for me in the morning." I
lied shrugging him off as I thumbed the phone in my pocket. I knew I
should call Robert, but I wanted him to be surprised when he saw me.

Not a single person questioned me as I sauntered through security and
picked up a double espresso in the extortionately overpriced airport

Abigail L. Marsh

Costa. Flying had never agreed with me very much, which was a pain because I did it more and more frequently, so I was pleased when I managed to sleep the whole eight and a half hours, only being woken by the air hostess as she informed me we had landed at O'Hare International Airport. I didn't need to go through baggage and thank god for that, the queue was absolutely horrendous and packed full of grouchy tourists battling through bleary early-morning eyes to get to the front of the conveyer belt.

Dodging that nightmare I rummaged through my jacket pocket for my phone, debating whether or not to send Robert a message now I was on home turf, but before I had the chance I'd reached the main entrance where I became acutely aware of the fact, there were only two taxi's sitting in the bay.

 I pocketed my phone and hopped in one.

"Where too?" the man said as I slammed the door on a young couple who looked as if they were set to go backpacking through the Amazon rainforest.

"However close you can get me to Thomson." I said. He turned to me looking shocked.

"Thomson by the Mississippi?" He exclaimed his thick Chicago accent piercing a hole straight through my heart as it brought back a horrible mix of feelings.

Abigail L. Marsh

"Yeah, that's where my Grandma lives." I said with my jaw clenched, desperate not to back out over a stupid voice as I searched through my bag for cash. "I'll give you a down payment."

"You have that kind of money?" The man asked, turning in his seat so he could get a proper look at me.

"I have a Saturday job." I lied finally releasing a couple of twenty dollar bills recalling the slightly disgruntled feeling I had encountered at the exchange rate at Heathrow airport. The diver sucked in a deep breath where for a moment I thought he might kick me out, or even call the police, but then shrugged and waved a hand at me.

"Whatever, if you've got the money I can get you to Fulton." he said, holding out his palm.

"Fulton?" I asked, looking at him unamused at the distance I would have to walk after that.

"Yeah, it's about eight miles to Thomson from there." he said

"7.6, actually." I said, "Why can't you take me to Thomson?" I demand-ed, holding back the air of annoyance in case he changed his mind.

"Because that's where I'm going to. We'll call it $100 because you didn't call in advance." Chewing my lip, I thought about it for a second. "Take it or leave it, kid."

I was wasting time, and I knew it, so rather than fight until he tossed me to the curb, I agreed and handed him half the money.

Abigail L. Marsh

Sitting back in my seat, I watched the brightly lit airport vanish from view and swallowed hard. I never in a million years thought I would be going back to the old house on the Illinois.

Alive from my long nap on the plane, I watched the sun rise on the horizon, shedding light on a land once forgotten lost deep in my memory. I smiled at memories of the fair at Rochelle, where Callie had bought a candy floss the size of her face and devoured it in seconds. The theatre at Dixon where we had gone to watch Matilda the musical and Dad had fallen asleep, snoring over the singing and embarrassing us all so much we'd had to leave early. The memories only grew stronger as we approached Fulton, the town of my school, and my friends.

"Are you going to be okay out here?" The Taxi diver said, pulling up to the curb. I resisted telling him I wanted to be in Thomson, not seven miles away and nodded.

"Yeah, this is home." I replied, pulling out the rest of the money I owed him and hopping out of the coolness of the taxi into the warmth of the morning.

I watched the taxi drive off as I spun around getting my bearings. The guy had dropped me outside the towns old peoples home, evidently thinking my Grandma lived there. All I had to do was run in a straight line north and I'd be there in no time.

Abigail L. Marsh

Chapter Sixteen: Museum

Sweat beaded on my forehead as I ran, trickling down my back uncomfortably, my stomach churned, flipping over and over as I passed my old primary school, the laughter of years gone by echoing across the empty schoolyard

"Tilly, Tilly look at me, look. See what I can do." Four-year-old Autumn cried as she hung upside down on a low branch of the old oak tree, tummy button on show, a massive smile on her little face.

Shaking it off, I forced the words of Cain into my aching mind, 'Nostalgia is a filthy liar, only showing you the good bits and not the bad.' Determined not to get dragged into a dream, I yanked my attention back and focused on my breathing, each step hitting the concrete and the noise it made pounding in my brain.

Thomson, Illinois. A small, community-driven village where everybody knew everybody and that meant one thing- gossip. The rumour mill had always been in constant flow. As I ran up the deserted main street, I wondered if that was still true. I'd left in such an ungracious way I was certain the story would have been spun around and around until… The monster of a story that mill would have created wasn't worth thinking

Abigail L. Marsh

about. The world around me was bathed in a warm orangey glow as I slowed to a jog, as if the whole place was happy to see me. I wasn't feeling it .

An old derelict barn standing dilapidated in the corner of an overgrown field stopped me in my tracks. *Huh.*
"Still standing?"
Fighting through a half gap in the thorny hedge I stood before it, the building at the end of the race, the finish line of the weekly marathon my best friend and I ran, come rain or shine.

Realising without a doubt that I was distracting myself form the inveigle I turned away from the barn. Glancing up and down the street for any odd speeding truck my eyes fell on it. Standing tall hidden behind a low branch of a nearby tree was the signpost for Turtle Road, the next on the list of objects I came across that had my heart hammering and brain second-guessing itself. Number one Turtle Road, the only house on Turtle Road, my house.

A quarter of a mile down the lane I walked, trailing my feet heavily along the road that could pass for a dirt track, until I caught my first glimpse. In the now cold light of dawn the house looked only different by the fading colour of white. Nothing else was out of place. The gravel

Abigail L. Marsh

crunched under my feet as I took the first step onto the long driveway peppered with leaves, whispers that autumn was on its way.

A creak had me turning to my left, I paused. The swing that had once brought me so much joy stood abandoned in a lonely corner amongst the weeds, crippled by rust, it's only movement now enabled by the gentle wind that rocked it on occasion. That wind now wrapping its arms around me, and creeping up my spine. Shivering involuntarily I shrugged as much of the uneasy feelings off as I could and staying as hidden under the trees as possible, I walked slowly towards the house, a house that seemed as if it had been fading away from existence for years, and years, and years.

A wilted sunflower leaned heavily against the dirty window of the old living room, it's petals sporadically dropping off and fluttering to the ground where they lay in a rotting pile. Cupping my hands around my eyes I peered through the grime into the house hoping to catch sight of Robert, but it was early morning, and the only sign that anyone was in was a light flickering in the back room.

The back door was going to be my best bet, as a kid it was never locked, even at night, it didn't need to be. Hugging the house and keeping the minor threat of police in the back of my mind, I made my way around to the back door, stepping over broken plant pots and abandoned gardening tools.

The screen door smothered in suicidal bugs opened with an excruciatingly loud creak. Adrenaline shot through my veins, heart rate skyrocketing as I stood there completely frozen, staring at the closed door that led into the kitchen.

Nothing happened. Nobody came.

"Breathe, Tilly!" I chastised myself harshly. My hand shook as it reached out for the brass handle of the wooden door. "You didn't come all this way to give up at the last moment."

With that being said, I couldn't shake the gnawing feeling that I was walking back into my darkest nightmare with my eyes wide open. Stealing any courage I had swimming around my body, I reached forward and pushed the handle down. Without a squeak I stepped right into the kitchen, breath held fast.

Nothing had changed. Nothing! I let my eyes drift over the space where years had passed but everything was the same. Magnets on the fridge holding photo's of our holidays to California and Florida, the flowery apron still hung on the back of the kitchen door reminding me of the times our Mum would make us chocolate chip pancakes, the chicken clock stuck to the wall, that cockadoodled off-key on a stupidly irregu-

Abigail L. Marsh

lar basis for something that gave notice of the time. Even the smell was the same. I could never put my finger on what it was, most houses had their own kind, it was just my smell and standing there alone in my kitchen, inhaling as deeply as my lungs would allow I realised how much I had been craving it.

Eventually tearing my own thoughts away from days gone by I padded quickly through to the hallway. Although the frames were drowning in the dust, not one was crooked or out of place. Much like when I walked around a museum marking down security cameras and guards, the eyes of the people in the photos, in this case me and my two sisters over the years I was there, followed me.

As I approached the bottom of the stairs I came to an abrupt stop, eyes glued tightly to the desk by the front door where stood a photograph of all five members of my family in a tarnished silver frame. The glass was cold as I picked it up. I swiped my palm across it removing the thick layer of dust and tears flooded to my eyes as my Mum's sparkling eyes met with mine. When I'd left I hadn't been given a chance to pick up anything close to me, just my clothes shoved into a tiny suitcase without a single care in the world for any of my prized possessions. Her face had always remained in my mind after that horrible car crash, but to see it in front of me, eyes locking with hers, it sent a warm fuzzy feeling around my body that I never wanted to lose.

"God, what you've missed." I whispered.

Chapter Seventeen: A Repetitious History

A scraping sound from upstairs broke my train of thought, yanking me back to the cold hard reality of what I was here to do. I turned to the staircase, daunting and dark.

"Hello?" Came my hoarse voice at no more than a loud whisper.

When no answer came to my pathetic attempt at announcing my arrival, I moved across the floor, manoeuvring around the squeaky floorboard I knew was waiting at the bottom of the stairs ready to pounce on an un-suspecting burglar, or alert an adult to your secret hunt for biscuits in the middle of the night and padded quietly up the stairs.

The hallway at the top resembled the hallway at the bottom, dusty but pretty much the same as it had been. My bedroom had been strategically placed the furthest from my parents, the wild child that I was meant I was up at the crack of dawn and paid little regard to the rest of the sleeping house. So there it stood opposite me, name in little pink wooden blocks stuck to it fast. The day they had arrived in the FedEx van I had begged my Dad to sick them on. DIY was not his strongest suit, but he'd given it a go. The end of that day resulted in all five of us taking a trip to the ER to get his fingers removed from each other, absolutely howling with laughter.

I glance around the silent hallway cautiously before stepping across the landing and placing my hand on the cool door knob. *Don't do it.* It was a bad idea, of course it was, but the curiosity churning around and around in my stomach forced me forwards, and I just couldn't help myself. *Just a peek.*

The handle was stiff and when it finally became unstuck and the door opened I realise why. My room had not been touched in ten years. No-one had moved anything. I wasn't even sure if anyone had been in there since I'd left. The door had been shut and Tilly Carmichael had been preserved, stuck in time. Stepping in I pushed the door softly behind me, taking in every single corner.

Mickey Mouse wallpaper peeled from the ceiling, pyjamas lay strewn across the floor, my Sleeping Beauty duvet still screwed up on the bed from the day they came. The Jasmine clock hanging on the wall had long ago run out of battery and read the completely wrong time.

Abigail L. Marsh

"I loved Disney." I murmured to myself.

A plastic Arial cup stood on my bedside table and next to it, open on page 48 was the book I had been halfway through. Scarlett the Garnet Fairy. Licking a salty tear off my lip I stared around my room completely taken aback by its state; while I had been gone, my life there had stopped.

BANG. A door somewhere outside my room opened and feet walked toward the stairs. I stood completely still, afraid the slightest movement would bring somebody in and I wasn't sure I was ready yet.

"Dad, I told you not to go in there, what are you doing?" Callie's voiced sighed loudly. I turned to face it as the door was pushed open and our eyes locked. She froze. I froze. Neither of us could utter a single word as she took me in.

In LA I hadn't had half a chance to really properly look at her, now I noticed her. Her hair dark and frizzy as can be, a complete contrast of my own. Her eyes tired but shining with life, she was beautiful and I finally felt the pain of the years I'd spent without her.

"You came." Callie breathed, corners of her mouth turning up into a smile as she threw her arms around me.

I let my bag drop to the floor as we embraced each other. Tears welled in my eyes. I hadn't thought about Callie much since I was a kid. We

Abigail L. Marsh

had been close way back when and when I was in care I often told people how she was going to come and rescue us one day, they would laugh
and jest and say only the stupidest kids thought someone was going to
come and save them, but I knew deep down everybody wanted somebody to come and save them. Callie pulled away first and wiping a few
tears from her cheeks, I followed suit not even realising I had been crying.

"I've really missed you too." I said, smiling at her through my blurry
eyes. There was a short pause where we stared at each other, not quite
believing the scene before us. "I'm sorry about, um, LA. I didn't…"
Callie was shaking her head.

"That doesn't matter."

Drying my eyes I nodded and attempted to return to the job at hand.
"Where's Robert?" I asked.

A sudden vale of sheepishness crossed Callie's face, I faltered misread-
ing it.

"Wait, I want to ask you about Autumn first!" Callie said. "Have you
seen her? She went, missing…"

Sighing mentally as the only reason I had come all the way across the
world was to get the answers, not talk about my little sister. I saw Autumn every day and she was actually quite annoying, but Callie didn't
know any of this.

Abigail L. Marsh

"I know that you live in… I just wondered if maybe she was…" I looked at the pleading stare radiating from Callie. I didn't think I could lie to her.

"Yeah, okay." I said.

We sat down on the bed, as I did, I managed to sit on top of something. Standing back up I folded my duvet over. I had accidentally sat on my very best friend, my stuffed monkey, Monkey. I picked him up.

"I forgot how fast they took us away." I said, running my fingers over his plastic eyes and furry face before hugging him to my chest. A scent wafted from his head up to my face and sent my mind casting back to the days my mother wore her famous homemade rose-hip perfume, al-most choking us when we walked into the greenhouse on the day she would concoct it.

"The house was a museum when I first got back." Callie said as I finally sat down, Monkey sitting on my knee comfortably.

"It looks like one now." I said.

"Dad was in denial, he wasn't drinking but he didn't want to move any-thing, it was… Difficult to breathe sometimes."

My heart clenched, I didn't want to talk about that, I didn't have time to talk about things like that.

"So Autumn." I said changing the subject and thankfully the tone quite abruptly. "I can't remember much about any of this, but we got split up after a months or so of being in care. She got adopted by a couple in

Abigail L. Marsh

Maryland an I got pulled deeper into the social system, her parents didn't like her name, so it got changed to Isabelle."

I paused for breath, wondering if I should tell Callie that I was living with our little sister, that I saw her every single day, that she knew I was here and refused point-blank to come with me.

"A month or so later I got kidnapped… I was there on my own for a long, long time."

"Did they hurt you?" Callie breathed.

"Yes and no, I'm well protected now. I live in relative comfort, I don't do something if I don't want too." I said refraining from indulging myself any further down that lie. "I'm happy there."

"Happy? How can you be happy?" Callie gasped.

"I just am. Life is different than it was here, but it's better… Anyway." I shook my head determined to get back on track. "Last October time, they brought this girl back to the house."

"Autumn?" Callie interjected jaw clenching in concern. My eyes drifted across my bedroom, the lies had to stop.

"Yes." I said. "It was Autumn, well Isabelle- but I didn't recognise her you know? More than nine years had gone by, we had both changed so much. It wasn't even that I just didn't recognise her, I didn't know her." Callie nodded.

"That was until I saw you, then everything came back."

Abigail L. Marsh

Callie's face twisted into confusion.

"Where is she now? Did you leave her there?" Her accusatory tone sparked a fleck of anger in my chest.

"It's complicated. She couldn't come with me." I said, trying my best to explain without telling Callie Isabelle outright didn't want to come.

"Why, why could you escape and not her?"

"I'm not, I'm not escaping." I stammered. "It's different for me. I'm higher up in the hierarchy, I can do and go wherever I want to within reason. The man in charge, the boss, he's acted as my father for years and years, we have a trust." I said. *'One I'm evidently breaking right now.'* I thought.

"Tilly, he kidnapped you. That's illegal, that's…" Callie said her face reddening in anger.

"I told you, it's complicated. I don't know how I can explain it so you will understand. It's weird."

After this revelation there was a break in the tension. Callie didn't have anything to say to me and I felt drained. Hop skipping and jumping around the truth was hard work. Then something than had been playing on my mind for a longtime re-entered my brain. I looked over at Callie, her tired eyes seeming more sunken than they had done when I'd arrived.

"Why didn't you come and rescue me?" I asked quietly. Her eyes met mine in a flash, pain creasing her eyebrows.

"I wanted too." She said. "I even tried to a few times, but I was eight Tilly, I barely made it out of the front gate before one care assistant or another dragged me back."

"You could have tried again! That day, when I was locked in the car you said you would come and save me. I've waited my whole life for you to come back for me because you promised you would."

"I'm sorry." She whispered, pulling me back into a hug.

"Everyone's always sorry." I said swallowing the lump in my throat and allowing myself to be hugged.

"Tilly, what's his name?"

I pulled away, shaking my head; there was a line I wasn't willing to cross. I stood up, catching Monkey as he fell to the floor.

"I need to see Robert now."

Panic flooded her expression.

"What?" I asked, looking towards the closed bedroom door. "He is here, isn't he?"

I opened the door and bypassed Autumn's old room as I followed the familiar route to my parent's bedroom, a journey I had made so often as a child after a nightmare, or for cuddles in the morning.

"Tilly stop!" Callie cried running after me in haste. I reached for the handle but missed it as she swatted me away.

"What?" I demanded exasperatedly, my nerves getting the better of my me as they flew around my brain in a whirlwind of fear. The last time I had properly seen this man he had thrown me against a sink, I could take him this time no problem, but the pain in my chest reignited.

"You need to know something. Dad has been stressed recently. After seeing you in LA, your phone call and waiting for you every day since, he kind of... He had a..."

"Had a what Callie?" I pressed. My mind raced with fury until it landed on an answer to her whitening face and it finally dawned on me. I threw her hand away from the door and shoved it open.

The smell hit me first, a mixture of vodka and sweat. Across the room Robert lay asleep, tangled up in his duvet. A bottle of vodka lay knocked over on the ground a reminder of its contents a puddle on the wooden floor.

My heart stopped, and all the nervous butterflies that had been fluttering in my stomach died. After all this man had put me through, after everything that had happened to me, after I had travelled over four thousand miles to do what he had pleaded with me to do, to hear him out, a hungover drunk was what stared me in the face.

Abigail L. Marsh

"I don't really know what I was expecting." Was all I could muster as I turned to Callie feeling physically sick.

"Tilly he's been really worried about you, and Autumn." Callie defended.

"Why, Callie? Why are you still making excuses for him? He's ruined everything for us! No wonder you look so tired, looking after this…" I said tears trickling down my face.

"This is the first time in years!"

"Did he hurt you?" I said, grabbing her arm and yanking up the sleeve- there was nothing to see.

"No!" Callie snapped yanking it back.

"Why are you still here?" I cried. She tried desperately to come up with something, but I had had enough, I wanted to go home. I didn't wait for an answer, not even looking back at him I disappeared down the corridor to my room.

"Wait!" Callie called charging after me. "Where are you going?"

"Home Callie, I'm going home." I said slinging my bag over my shoulder. When I turned back to the doorway Callie was blocking it, tears streaming down her face.

"I never should have come here. Please, get out of my way."

"You can't leave us."

"I *can* and you should. Leave Callie, leave while you still can. Don't let him do to you what he did to us, he's not worth it." I said walking over to her and surveying the little girl inside me's room one last time before glancing down at Monkey who was still clutched in my hand. His black plastic eyes stared up at me fearfully. Swallowing hard I passed him to Callie.

"I'm sorry." I couldn't take him with me, the memories were too strong. Pushing her easily out of my way, I went down the stairs, crossed the creaky floorboard and headed towards the door. I paused in the kitchen, wanting to take something back for Isabelle. My eyes landed on the fridge magnet with our Mums face on. Shoving it in my pocket, I spun to leave.

"Tilly! TILLY!" My Dad's voice bellowed through the house; heart rate spiking I found myself unable to take a step. The last time he had yelled that loud I'd taken a crack to the ribs. As I stood there barely able to breathe the kitchen seemed to double in size, and I was seven again scrambling for cover. I stumbled forward to the door grasping at the handle.

"NO!" I yelled as corridor behind me stretched and Robert appeared at the end of it. I kicked the door hard.

"Open!" The noise attracted his eyes. He'd seen me.

Abigail L. Marsh

"No!" I screamed yanking the door hard. As the rusted hinges buckled and I felt the cold air filtering through the gaps I allowed a spark of hope in me. This was crushed instantaneously as the man was almost on top of me, tossing me headlong into my worst nightmare as his hands slammed the door shut. I backed up, mind scrambled as I searched desperately through the boxes in my mind for the skills I'd learned since I'd been gone. Usually they came so readily but it seemed if someone had sealed all the lids.

"It's alright." Robert said, his voice softening as he saw my blind fear. "It's alright, I'm not going to hurt you, I just need you to stay for a moment." He said still keeping one foot against the door, but holding his hands up to show he meant no harm. I took a breath and holding tightly to the back of a chair I knew I could toss in front of me to gain a few seconds if he changed his mind, I forced myself to tune Cain's words into my mind- 'Fear is not real. It does *not* control you.'

With Cain in my mind my body allowed a brief lapse in adrenaline. Fear wasn't real. This man could do no more harm. As my eyes re-focused on Robert he smiled, a rarity since my Mum had died.

"You look so much like your mom." He said, his American twang and the mention of my Mum setting off another round of nostalgia in me. I didn't speak.

"Where are you going?" He asked as Callie entered the room. I threw

Abigail L. Marsh

her a dirty look and opened my mouth to speak.

"Home." I said shaking the lazy wolf in my soul to see if it had remembered who this man was and what he had done.

"No, please don't go, not yet. Can we talk first?" He asked.

"What comes after that? A bottle of vodka? Or a round of beating? I don't quite remember." I snarled the wolf finally bearing its teeth. Robert didn't falter but Callie's voice interrupted before he could apologise.

"You have to understand Tilly, he's been so stressed out. If you'd just stayed with us back in LA none of this would have happened."

My head snapped around to see her standing meekly in the doorway.

"Don't you dare turn this around on me. I am not seven years old, you cannot manipulate me anymore."

"No-ones trying to do that." Robert said, his voice a calm interjection. "Callie, Tilly is right to be cautious, I had a relapse, it's happened a few times in the last decade, but I have it under control now."

"Under control?" I scoffed not buying any of it. "You're an alcoholic, the very definition of that means you don't have control. Don't *lie* to me Robert."

"I do have control. Out of the 3,439 days since you've been gone, I have been sober 3,398 of them." He said his voice still gentle and calm.

Abigail L. Marsh

"What about the other... Days?" I asked, not being able to do the maths in my head.

"The first thirty I was working on it, I went through some intense treatments, then the other 12...They were relapse days, the first one lasted a week, the second three days, the third two days and then yesterday." He said the shame in his eyes penetrating my hard shell. "Every single time it happens, I go back to therapy, back to my doctors. I have a social worker. Callie has a social worker. They check in on us all the time. It will not defeat me again."

"He surprised everyone." Callie said sticking in her defence. "He's a survivor."

"I get it, you're getting better." I said refraining from telling Callie where to stick her two pennies worth. "You're trying."

"Very trying." Robert said, smiling slightly at his joke as a few tears rolled down his cheek. I didn't.

"But that doesn't excuse all the damage you did, all the pain you caused. We were all grieving and you, you promised you wouldn't let anything hurt me, do you even remember?" I said fresh anger and tears gushing back into me.

"I remember, that thunderstorm..." Robert said fighting to hold onto his emotion.

"I was so scared." I sobbed.

"I know, I remember."

I shook my head drying my eyes with the sleeve of my top and dragging that wolf back out of its hole. Standing it firmly in front of me where it where it finally did it's job.

"No I'm not talking about a thunder storm. *You* terrified me. I was scared of you, because you promised me nothing would hurt me. And you lied!"

"I'm sorry." Robert choked on a sob as he took his foot away from the door and stepped closer to me.

"It was *you* all along! You hit me you hurt me, you made me afraid in my own home." I shouted, fire shooting from my soul as I dragged the chair in front of me. "Don't!" I warned. "Don't touch me."

The three of us stood there as Robert sobbed loudly. I hadn't seen him sob since my Mum died and it caught me off guard.

"Tilly please." Callie begged yanking my brain back from its rapid descent into feeling something other than pure, red hot anger.

"No." I shook my head. "I shouldn't have come here, it was a mistake. I'm really glad you getting better and that you found your way back." I said looking from one to the other as tears streamed down all three of our faces. "But you are not my father, you lied to me to get me here and I can see now how gullible I have been." I said as I backed up. "I don't want to be here and you can't stop me leaving. You don't hold the power anymore."

Now armed with a plan I had been working on ever since I'd been cornered I jumped into action. Bending down, I used all my upper body strength to launch the chair I'd hauled in-between me and my father. He backed up as it collided with him, giving me the space to slide across the table where I faced off Callie. I didn't want to hurt either of them, my spite was gone, I just wanted to get out. I gave her a reasonably feeble (for myself) two-handed shove and hooked my ankle around her's. Grabbing her hand, I lowered her to the floor swiftly, winding her only slightly and leapt over her. The front door was straight ahead, with little regard for whether it was locked or not I collided with it, the rusted old locks creaked heavily, and I was bursting through the screen door not a millisecond later.

Chapter Eighteen: I'm So Sorry

In true Tilly style, my feet got tangled in a section of reeds that seemed to have grown up through the wooden decking and I stumbled clumsily down the porch steps.

"Tilly!" Robert yelled. Throwing a glance behind me as I raced up the driveway I realised both Callie and Robert were after me. I could outrun them for sure but a strikingly horrifying thought occurred to me, if they called the police I would never make it back, roadblocks, security cameras and all sorts would be all over the place, not to mention the travesty the airport would be.

I started to slow, breathing heavily to make it seem as if I had spent all my energy. I knew what I was going to do next would haunt me for the rest of my life but I couldn't risk the past repeating itself any more than it had done, not for me.

As I reached the gatepost at the top of the driveway, I pretended to keel over, doubling up. Not five seconds later, Robert's hand landed on my back. With no time to hesitate, I quickly whipped around, curling my hand into a fist, smashing it skilfully into his jaw. The forc knocked him onto the grass by the side of the drive, out cold. Power surged through my veins as I towered over the man who'd caused me so much pain.

I looked back at Callie who had seen the whole thing while running after us. She had always been the slowest, couldn't run for toffee, wouldn't run for a bus. It had been a damn good thing Cain hadn't gone for her instead of Autumn. Callie stopped short of the gate, hands covering her mouth in complete shock.

Abigail L. Marsh

"Shit!" I said forcing a panicked look onto my face. "Shit! Callie! Callie I didn't mean to!" I cried laying on the theatrics thickly as I fell to my knees beside Robert. Using my body to shield him I tipped his head to the left so he wouldn't swallow his tongue. Callie arrived on the scene and crouched down placing a hand on his forehead.

"Dad, oh my God! What have you done?" She cried in anguish.

"I'm going to get some ice!" I said scrambling away from him and racing back towards the house with only one thing in mind.

"Call an ambulance! I don't get a signal on my phone!" Callie yelled after me.

"Okay!" I yelled back allowing myself to feel relieved. Robert was fine, the force had knocked him out that was all, he'd come round in a little bit with a cracking headache, but it gave me some much needed time to escape. The landline socket was in the cupboard under the stairs. I pulled it out and cut the wire so there was no way they could call out until they'd been seen by an electrician.

The freezer was just feet away and feeling somewhat ashamed of my actions, I grabbed a bag of ice and wrapped it up in a tea-towel as I jogged back over to the pair.

"Did you call them, are they coming?" Callie whined as I dropped the ice next to her. I scratched the back of my head as she placed it onto his chin.

"No, he doesn't need an ambulance." I said, crouching down and rolling my floppy father into the recovery position.

"What?" Callie asked, clearly confused. I watched her as she dried her red eyes.

"He'll come around in an hour or so, but you need to stay next to him in case he rolls over and swallows his tongue." I said standing up and shrugging my bag which was digging painfully into my neck, into a more comfortable position.

"Where are you going?" She choked watching me. I gave her a withering look as if to say, 'come on you're not seriously that stupid.'

I saw it dawn on her as her eyes flicked between Robert and me and her concerned face switched to fury.

"You did that on purpose! You tricked me!" She shouted.

"Wow, you catch on real quick." I said sarcastically. "I'm going home Callie, goodbye."

"You! You bitch!" She yelled, glaring at me.

"Don't start on me Callie." I growled and turned to leave. "And don't follow me, he'll roll over and choke." I added taking a few paces before I had a slight change of heart and looked back at her with a little more sympathy.

"Or leave him and go and live your life, either way."

Abigail L. Marsh

"What the hell happened to you?" Callie asked, her voice packed full of betrayal and hurt, her head shaking.

"Life happened." I replied bluntly before turning to walk away. As I stepped out onto the road, I remembered one last thing.

"Oh and here." I said, fishing around in my pocket and pulling out a crinkled up piece of paper. "I don't know the people in this picture, they don't exist anymore." I dropped the picture of Autumn, Callie and I to the floor. I had come to realise that photos were a way to hold onto nostalgia, it was true the moments they showed would never change, but the people in them did. It was sad but I didn't want to be reminded of the memories or the people, they were all gone. Callie burst into tears as she picked the photo up with a shaking hand.

"I'm so sorry Callie. Goodbye." I croaked with as much voice I could muster before turning and running.

I ran into town as fast and as recklessly as my body would allow, by the time I got there my breathing was laboured and I keeled over for real this time, desperately trying to suck some air into my lungs. Falling to my knees my fist collided with the concrete several times before I registered any pain. Why had I been so stupid? How could I possibly have thought that this man had changed?

Eventually, I forced myself into a reasonable composure and hailed a taxi, that for a completely overpriced fair, would take me all the way to

Abigail L. Marsh

O' Hare International. When I demanded to know why it was so expensive the driver explained that O' Hare International was out of his driving range, whatever the hell that meant. The drive was silent, thank god. I didn't need a chatty driver the way I was feeling. I might have killed him. It was almost four o'clock in the afternoon when I boarded my flight and collapsed into the uncomfortable budget airline seats.

With the time difference I arrived back into Cromer in the backseat of yet another taxi at four am. Emotionally and physically exhausted, I couldn't have run if I'd wanted to. Settling for a slow jog I crashed into my bed, body aching, wolf defeated a little after half five. Isabelle was gone but I didn't notice, my eyes shut and I was out.

Nothing and no-one disturbed me until half-past two that afternoon. Feeling like death I was rudely startled when my bedroom door was flung open and a person yelled in excitement.

"I'M DONE!"

I groaned, rolling over to catch the end of a ridiculous dance Isabelle was performing in the middle of the room. She let out an ear-piercing scream when she saw me, quickly covered up by her hands.

"Oh my god! You scared me." She choked, falling over herself to close the door. I grumbled pitifully in response.

Abigail L. Marsh

"How'd it go?" She asked, sitting down on the edge of the bed and patting the lump under the duvet that was me. "Mate you stink."

I rolled over and squinted at her angrily before my brain suddenly couldn't cope with being angry anymore and I sighed emotionally.

"What happened?" Iz asked taken aback by my show of feelings.

"I swear to god if you say I told you so." I warned.

Iz smiled a little.

"Iz, he was drunk." I said. "You were so right."

Isabelle nodded gently.

"But it's okay, cos we're here and we're together and I'm done with training. Life's not that…"

"Bad?" I prompted. She shrugged. Although our life wasn't perfect, we had each other and we had a life that we could live, a plan to follow. If only for the time being.

Isabelle laid down next to me.

"Are you okay?" She asked, wrapping her arms around me.

"Yeah." I smiled turning into her embrace. After a few seconds, she laughed.

"What?"

"You really really need a shower."

Abigail L. Marsh

<u>Part 2</u>

Six months later.

Chapter Nineteen: The Robbery

New York... JPMorgan Chase... 0100 Hours.

I stood with my back planted to the wall of New Yorks biggest bank. The temperature had dropped below freezing hours ago and my numb fingers kept nervously checking the bullets in my handgun. I knew they were there. I had loaded them myself in the car on the way to the airport early the morning before but that didn't stop me feeling somewhat para- noid. There was next to no wind that night, so the snowflakes drifted down gently shimmering in the light shining from the streetlamp across the road. I shrugged my jacket over my shoulders more and zipped it right up to the top shivering inside it. The street was completely dead, a couple of people had wandered along in the hour I had been standing there and I had had to dive back into the darkest shadows to avoid being seen, but now I was alone.

Jamie and Tate weren't far away, parked in the cars a street over waiting just as nervously as I was. This job was tremendously risky, I didn't know how it was going to play out.

I'd managed to bag the worst job going, The Lookout. Radio clutched in my hand with an earpiece attached, ready to warn the team inside if

Abigail L. Marsh

anything went awry. I'd been there going on seventy minutes already, every few minutes taking a walk up and down the block in case anyone took a peek at the outside world. It would look ridiculously suspicious if I were standing rigid outside a bank at one am.

"We're in." A crackly voice spoke in my ear making me jump out of my skin. The voice was referring to the safe where the big bucks were stored. I turned and watched as Tate drove around the street corner past me and down the ramp to an underground carpark, which was now very noisily beeping as it opened. My breath hitched. I glanced around, hoping no-one had heard. The night was still dead, silent... Eerie.

I waited and waited, then waited some more, cold creeping through my bones as if it meant to consume me. Nothing happened for ages, the longer I stood there the more I was sure that we were going to get caught. Fiddling with the gun in my pocket I took to breathing deeply, clenching and unclenching my toes to the point were it became painful and focusing solely on that pain. This technique had gotten me through many many nights like this.

"Just a few more minutes." I kept telling myself. They were going to come out in just a few more minutes, Isabelle and Cain would be fine, and we could all go home... As I turned and began walking back up the block, my own head laughed at me. Who was I kidding? We were at-

Abigail L. Marsh

tempting to rob the biggest bank in America, in the Big Apple, with police that had guns! *So* many things could have gone wrong.

"Chill out will you!" A voice came through the radio. It was Jamie. He was laid flat on the roof of the apartment buildings opposite with a sniper aimed at anyone who threatened the heist. I hated the sniper, it was dangerous and hard to control, meaning it was a risk and the more risks we took, the higher the chance of being apprehended and then what? Jail for them, but what would become of me? I glanced up.

"You're going to wear the soles off your shoes, just take a breath, we've got this under control." He laughed lightly. Not agreeing with him I turned away and looked to the open gate, willing them to drive out and pick me up right that second.

"Tilly he trained you for this." James spoke again. I wanted so badly to turn and flip him off, but that would risk alerting someone looking to his whereabouts, or just make them think a crazy person was swearing at at the sky.

The weather got colder and colder as the snowfall started to settle on the ground, my fingers had long ago gone numb. I had zoned out my eyes tracing the snow as it fell, mind only awake for the distant sounds of

Abigail L. Marsh

police cars as they darted across the city. Then all of a sudden I was drawn to a wail that had penetrated the barrier and my eyes re-focused on the street, heart-stopping.

"Jamie! Jamie, do you hear that?" I said desperately into the radio.

"It's okay, don't panic, crimes happen all over New York. It's the city that never sleeps, just get out of sight." He said. Spinning around I looked for anywhere to hide. There was a little garden shrubbery type area just over the road that would work. Jumping into action I scrambled across the street, dove into the bushes headfirst and laid flat in the cold snow. I felt sick, but Jamie's was right, the police cars flew right past and disappeared into the night. I laid on the ground a few more moments just to make absolutely sure, then groaning as my body objected I hauled myself off the ground. Dusting myself off was a bad idea I only succeeded in getting my hands wetter and colder than they had been before.

"What the hell was that?!" Cain screamed through the radio making me wince as I shoved my blue hands under my armpits.

"What? They've gone." Jamie asked.

"Not you!" Cain shouted, and then the radio went silent. I rolled my eyes, he could be such an arsehole sometimes.

After a few silent moments the radio crackled back into life.

Abigail L. Marsh

"Uhh boss, we've got a bit of a situation." Chris's voice spoke.

"I don't want to hear about it, get it sorted and meet us at the door in five minutes." Cain snapped.

"Right." Chris replied.

Thank-god five minutes, we could do that.

"See, no problem." Jamie said to me. I groaned inwardly, had I known how those words would screw us all over I would have put a bullet in that man there and then.

True to his word as the clock stuck to the front of Grand Central Station chimed half-past one, Tate's car came flying out of the underground carpark. Coming to a halt for a split second in front of me the door was shoved open and wasting no time I bailed in. We were moving again before I managed to pull myself into an upright position. Struggling gains the G-force I managed to sit myself down in the seat between Cain and Isabelle facing the back of the car where Wes, Kurt and Chris were sitting all looking tense.

"You're freezing!" Isabelle said, breaking the silence and clasping her warm hands over mine.

Abigail L. Marsh

"Yeah, I've been outside for hours." I said flatly, silently appreciating Isabelle's warmth if only slightly green-eyed about it. My wandering eyes crossed the car and landed on Cains thunderous face.

"What's your problem?" I asked bitterly. His features softened as his eyes fell on mine.

"I'm sorry…" He said, resting a hand on my arm. "You *are* cold."

"What went wrong?" I squinted refusing to let him squander any information. Cain pointed at Chris with an angry finger.

"What? What was the situation?"

"Look in the back." Cain said. Wes and Kurt moved their heads apart as I slid across the space between the seats. With one knee on the seat in the middle of them, I moved a panel across and peered into the dimly lit boot. My breathing faltered as I saw an unconscious man laid on his stomach, trust up like a turkey with a 15-centimetre gash across the back of his head dripping blood onto the cold plastic floor.

"What the hell did you do?" I exclaimed glancing back at Chris. Chris wasn't looking, his eyes and mind desperately trying to be anywhere but with us in the car.

"He opened a door he wasn't supposed to. That guy was working the night shift, Isabelle had it under control and that idiot." Cain spat leaning back in his chair. "Ignored months of thorough investigations and waltzed into the wrong room!"

Abigail L. Marsh

Chris didn't even turn to defend himself and love me or hate me for it, I didn't feel the need to protect him.

"What are we going to do with him? Someones going to miss him surely?" I questioned, staring back at the huge man lying unconscious on the floor.

"We can't let him go." Wes said, sticking in an oar where it wasn't wanted.

"So what?" I asked, looking around the little cab at all the frustrated faces. "Kill him?" I demanded as the car was flung around a sharp corner. I would have fallen head over heels if Kurt hadn't reached out and steadied me.

"We don't have another choice, so sit in your bloody seat and deal with it." Chris said, turning in his seat and taking my head off.

"Enough!" Cain raised his voice. "Tilly, please sit down before crack you're head."

I was taken off guard by his fatherly tone, but there was nothing more to be said on the matter so I sat back down, yanking the seatbelt across my chest with fury.

The drive was fast and if I might add a little reckless, my stomach churned with car sickness as we pulled up at an abandoned airstrip just over the Philadelphia state border. I ran to some bushes the moment the car stopped and waited holding my own hair back. Nothing happened, the cold fresh air filled my lungs and I started to feel better. Then-

BANG! A gunshot pierced the night air reverberating around my head

as bile shot up the back of my throat.

"You okay?" Isabelle asked as I stumbled over to the jet Cain had

grimly agreed to purchase, when he realised any heists abroad needed a

quick continental exit. It sat in the dark at the far end of the strip ready

to fly. I nodded as an orange light to my right ignited the cars we had

been traveling in.

"Come on, get in." Iz said, grabbing my hand and pulling me away from

the flames. The jet was simple but I paid it no attention as I crashed

onto a sofa at the back of the cabin and closed my eyes. I was cold, tired

and angry. The roar of the engines put us in the air not five minutes lat-

er. I was quickly fast asleep, the noise of the cabin drifting to the back

of my mind.

Chapter Twenty: An Impromptu Holiday

My eyes fluttered open to the irritating feeling of ears popping. We

were descending slowly. I battled with gravity to pull myself into an

upright sitting position and fasten my seatbelt tightly around my waist.

Abigail L. Marsh

Someone had laid a blanket over me which got tossed to the floor as I became aware of how stiflingly hot the cabin was. Most of the guys were still sleeping, mouths hanging open as they snored. Isabelle looked over at me from her curled up position on the seat opposite with a book open on her lap, she smiled.

"Morning sleepy head." She grinned.

A pang of guilt ran through me, we had called ourselves the private jet pair- cringe name I know, but we were supposed to keep each other company on flights home from jobs. It was designed to take our minds off the things we had seen, but I had been so exhausted.

"Sorry Iz." I smiled apologetically. She smirked

"It's okay, last night was rough on you. I'm sorry we left you outside for so long." I shrugged.

"I mean, that's kind of what a lookout is supposed to do."

The captain's voice (A friendly man called Jimmy who had recently joined The Pack) came over the tannoy letting us know we would be landing shortly and for everyone to buckle up.

There was movement in the cabin, and soon I felt the familiar bump of the wheels hitting the runway and screeching to a halt.

As I stepped off the plane, a wall of warm air hit me. I squinted around the sun-drenched airstrip noting two big black Range Rovers parked in the dust, where the hell were we?

Abigail L. Marsh

"Uhh, Cain?" I said as I reached the ground. He looked over from the luggage hold compartment.

"One sec Till!" He shouted as he reached up and flipped a catch above his head.

Behind me, Harley stepped off the plane wearing an almost fluorescent t-shirt, and some seriously tight shorts for such a chubby man. Isabelle and I stifled laughter and moved out of his way as he clumped down the steps. He gave us a death glare as he strode past us.

"What are you looking at?" He snapped, reaching out to give me a push. I dived out of his reach frowning, he was touchy today.

"Harley get over here!" Cain yelled. I watched as he stomped away from us, Cain passed him the suitcases down from the hold and the man tossed them into the back of the Range Rovers.

"Come on, I call shotgun!" Isabelle said thumping me on the back as she ran past. I raced after her, getting the second best seat in the car. The driver's seat.

Unfortunately as my luck would have it Cain would not let me drive, even though I had aced it in training. So I was forced into the back with Tate and Jamie, holding my tongue at my smug sister sitting all high an mighty in the front.

Abigail L. Marsh

I soon discovered that we were in the south of France, lost in the Pyrenees, way off the radar and going to be staying that way for a few weeks at least. *Sweet.*

"There's no point in risking going back to Cromer just yet." Jamie explained. According to the radio, the police were hot on our heels as we left America, it was best to leave Mel and the two dogs home in case anything traced back to there. A single woman home alone looking after some animals wouldn't, under normal circumstances arouse suspicion. As soon as we were sure nothing was awry, we would drive back.
The thought of a holiday with Isabelle had me settled so I didn't complain about the fact my dog had been left behind in Cromer.
The drive along the winding country roads was long; we didn't reach the little villa, rented under a pretence name until mid-afternoon.

It was sweet to start with; a white villa nestled under the hood of a vast hill, miles from anywhere. The birds were singing and the cool breeze that swept through the air as we unloaded the cars sent an excited chill down my spine, this was my first proper holiday with my little sister in years and even Harley's glares couldn't put me down… Although I wasn't amused when he attempted to slam the car door on my fingers.

Abigail L. Marsh

"What the hell are you playing at?" I snapped, furiously ripping my hand out of the way. He glanced around and then threw me a murderous look and quite suddenly, I became acutely aware that while I was faffing around looking for a bottle of water to quench my thirst, everyone else had gone inside and I was alone with the monster. I don't think Harley had missed that fact either. He sidled over to me his beefy arms grabbing me around the rim of my collar.

"Lay off!" I snapped wildly, throwing a punch at him. He gave me a quick shake.

"I don't like you." He spat, his repugnant breath and spit sprayed all over my face.

"Ew gross." I whined, struggling to turn my face away from him so I could breathe the fresh french air.

"Shut up!" He snapped dangerously, shaking me violently. My head snapped around, and I looked him dead in the eyes. Something was wrong; up to now, things had never gotten passed the verbal stage, this was a new side to him. I realised in that moment that I did not want to be the centre of the mans attention.

"Harley get off me!" I shouted, risking a quick knee in the balls. He flinched, blocking me with his leg and I found myself being shoved up against the boot of the car.

Abigail L. Marsh

"WHAT IS WRONG WITH YOU?" I shouted, slamming my hands into his face trying desperately to cause some sort of pain, but he seemed untouchable in that moment.

"I don't like you Tilly, I never have." He growled his prickly moustache inches from my face.

"Okay I know! I get that, just let me go." I pleaded. The training I had had wasn't matching Harley's obvious weight and height and I could feel my chest constricting. I scrambled around behind me with my left hand, reaching for anything I could use to smash over his head.

"I was here long before you came here and I'll be here long after you've gone." He breathed over me. His breath was stale and fishy, I could see practically all the black filling amongst his yellow teeth. Holding my breath so I wouldn't vomit I wriggled for all I was worth.

"What do you want from me?" I yelled, kicking up a dust storm. I could feel tears forming in my eyes, my pride was fast diminishing.

"Go." He spat. "Leave The Pack."

"Are you crazy?" I demanded.

"GO!"

"OI!" A voice shouted behind me.

Cain came out of nowhere. Harley's crushing weight was ripped away from me and I watched stunned as the men clattered to the ground, Cain on top, relentlessly smashing Harley round the face with clenched fists. I stumbled away from them frantically, choking up.

"Tilly?" Isabelle's voice rang out as I watched Harley's blood spray across the cobbles.

"Tilly." Isabelle said again, her voice panicked. I felt her hands around my waist as I spun away from the brawl.

"It's fine." I managed to say. "Just go inside." I forced her backward as Kurt and Jamie burst out of the door and went running to help. I didn't see what they did next, I didn't want too. Isabelle led me up to our room where I slammed the door shut and pulled an antique wooden chest of drawers in front of it. No one was getting in.

"What happened?" She asked as I sat down on a single bed that creaked loudly. I took a moment to breathe deeply; otherwise, I think I would have passed out.

"Harley flipped his shit." I began. "He said I had to leave, he had me around the throat." I stuttered holding my hands out to see how badly I was shaking.

"Oh my god. Do you want some water?" Iz asked springing into action. She rushed to open her bag on the opposite bed and unscrewed the cap before handing me it. I nodded in thanks and took a shaky sip of the lukewarm liquid.

"Cain won't let him get away with it, don't worry." She said, sitting down next to me and rubbing my back gently. But I did, I worried for a

Abigail L. Marsh

good fifteen minutes until there was a knock on our door. We both looked at our barricade.

"Tilly it's okay now, you can come out." Kurt's voice came, sounding muffled by the wooden door.

"Where's Cain?" Isabelle asked.

"He's in the kitchen, want me to get him?" I nodded at the floor.

"Yeah." Isabelle answered for me.

A minute later Cain knocked on the door.

"It's alright now Tilly, I sorted it, come on, come out." He said trying to open the door.

"Is he gone?" I asked.

"He is outside in the barn. He is not getting out, I promise." Cain said.

"Are you sure?" I asked, creaking off the bed and going over to the door.

"I'm sure. Come here." He said gently.

Isabelle helped me push the chest of drawers back to its place and I opened the door. Cain pulled me into a tight embrace. His black suit was covered in dust from the fight and it smelt like it could do with a wash but I clung to him anyway, anything to stop myself shaking so badly.

"He won't ever do anything like that again Tilly, I promise." Cain said stroking the back of my head.

"I was so scared." I whispered, pressing my face into his shoulder as the attacked played over in my mind.

"I know, I don't know what's gotten into him." He said before pulling me away slightly. "But remember allowing yourself to be afraid is a choice. Fear isn't real, so it does not control you." He spoke softly looking into my eyes, with big soft chestnut eyes. "And Harley, he's the slug of the wolf world, don't let a slug control how you think and how you feel, understand me? It's not worth it."

I nodded, but couldn't bring myself to smile at the uncanny resemblance of Harley and a a slimy green slug.

"He's tied up for now, you're safe."

"What are you going to do with him?" Isabelle asked as I buried my face back in Cain's shoulder. He didn't reply, but I felt his body go tense. He was furious.

Isabelle and I spent the rest of the afternoon exploring the grounds of the villa. The air was humid and heavy as we wandered through the orange groves and of the thousands of crickets chirping away in the long grass, I reckon at least a hundred leaped out at us. I don't like bugs at the best of times, so you can imagine me shrieking and diving behind Isabelle for cover. She found it hilarious and suggested I should have brought my gun along for protection.

Abigail L. Marsh

The night was long, hot and sticky. I tossed and turned wrapping my sheets around me as the springs squeaked away loudly. Isabelle lost it with me and hissed at me to stop moving or she'd give me something to cry about. I was trying to come up with some sort of clue as to why Harley was acting so violently towards me. He'd hated me for a long time I knew that, but why did he flip so severely. Was it finally because I had been left alone with him? Maybe he was having a mid-life crisis? Or maybe my Alsatian wasn't there to rip him to shreds... That must have been it. During the early hours of the morning, I fell into a dreamless sleep only to be woken by a bloody rooster at half-past six.

Feeling the weight of only two hours sleep, I put on some shorts and plodded downstairs with my new semi-automatic pistol clutched in my hand. Cain had bought it for me for the job; if Harley came within ten metres of me I would have him. I made myself a cup of black coffee and a slice of my favourite French bread before switching the television on and sinking into the sofa opposite it. Flicked through the channels was depressing... Everything was in French or Spanish. I barely knew a word in either except for random parts of phatic exchange, so I had to settle for Jeremy Kyle, at least I could guess who was sleeping with whose mother, and whether or not Chantelle's baby was actually Ryan's or in fact belonged to Lewis. When the boys came down at half-past eight I was engrossed in my third episode.

Abigail L. Marsh

"What is this filth you are watching?" Lucas asked, plonking himself down next to me.

"Its Jeremy Kyle." I said in my 'are you stupid' voice.

"Do you speak French?" He asked shocked.

I shook my head not tearing my eyes away from the screen.

"Weird." Lucas mumbled, shaking his own head. He got up back again up to get some breakfast almost knocking my cold cup of coffee over as he went.

Nothing much was done about Harley. He stayed out in the barn for another night then was let back into the house on the condition that if he laid a hand on me, he would be shot. I never did understand why he stayed with The Pack, maybe out of some loyalty to Cain or the fact that he didn't really have anywhere else to go.

The day he came back inside I took a first proper look at his face, it was covered in dry blood, he had two evil black eyes that seemed to cast a shadow over his whole face and his nose looked decidedly wonky. I was sitting at the kitchen table with Kurt, Isabelle, and Tate playing a game of Pack Snap, which is a slightly more violent version than the normal snap, when he lumbered in followed by Cain and Lucas. He dark eyes cast over me. I couldn't read the expression on his face, that didn't really matter. I rested a hand firmly on my gun.

Abigail L. Marsh

"Touch me again, and you'll die." I hissed across the room. A few glances were thrown at me, but no-one said anything as Harley left the room and that seemed to be the end of it.

Chapter Twenty-One: All Alone

Cain got bored of France within a week of being there. The lads did everything from taking cheap shots at beer bottles lined up on a fence to hurtling around the countryside in what can only be described as a reckless driving spree. There was no one out there. The nearest shop over fifteen kilometres away. It was perfect in one sense but horribly isolated in another. None of us really spoke the language so television was out of the window. We were bored stupid and Cain said he wanted to get back to the crappy weather, he didn't like the heat like I did. So we were back in England far sooner than we should have been. What a mistake, a mistake that cost us everything.

It was three o'clock in the morning when we touched down on an airstrip just outside Great Yarmouth in the middle of nowhere. It was dark outside and I'd thrown a hoodie on expecting it to be freezing. We'd dropped out of the news weeks ago, it wasn't supposed to have been a problem, but as I followed the group out into the cold night air and made my way down to the ground, a small red light appeared on my chest. The hairs on the nape of my neck bristled, I knew exactly what it was but it took me a second to process and scream the words. "Get back!" I cried as several blinding lights came on.

"Stay where you are you are under arrest." A crackly voice rang out through a microphone over the deathly silence. I glanced around too shocked to move. There must have been at least seven police cars parked across the airstrip and I could hear more in the distance, The world seemed to stop around me, or at least run in slow motion as I looked over at Cain for some sort of sign. He looked back at me and shouted,

"RUN."

Everyone dispersed. People took off in all sorts of directions some diving under the plane and scrambling out the other side, some running to the left, others to the right. I got caught in the decision of a direction. I dived away from the red laser praying I wasn't about to get shot to pieces and tried to follow Cain. He'd tore off to the left and was making a sprint for the woods, but Tate got in my way and as I collided with him we stumbling backward and crashed hard into Rick both falling down.

Abigail L. Marsh

"Stay where you are!" I heard yelled as police began the chase. I gripped my gun tightly and forced myself off the ground, whirling around I caught sight of Isabelle. Her mind in a fight of what to do. I made the decision for her.

"Iz run!" I screamed charging towards her and grabbing her hand as I flew past. We followed Lucas and Jamie under the belly of the plane and made a frantic dash for the tree line. Gunfire erupted behind us, and I risked a glance around. There was a black van hurtling down the centre of the airstrip, it's side doors sliding open and men inside with bulletproof vests and pointing *ginormous* guns at us. Giving a massive push as more adrenaline flooded my veins I reached the woods relatively unscathed. Once we had made it past the first few lines of trees, it became darker and the commotion behind us quietened.

"How did they find us?" I whispered to Lucas as he caught his breath.

"I don't know but it doesn't matter now, we have got to get out of here."

"How far are we from home?" Isabelle asked.

"We can't go home, don't you get it." I whispered harshly. "They'll just follow us."

"Guys come on!" Jamie whispered from a little further ahead. "They'll be in here any second."

Lucas straightened up and we started sprinting again. We stumbled and tripped in the dark, crashing over roots and kidding on stone. I had hold of Isabelle's hand tightly, I wasn't about to loose track of her.

Abigail L. Marsh

After what seemed like hours we stopped. I couldn't breathe, Isabelle couldn't breathe and I had a horrifying feeling Jamie and Lucas had disappeared. It was dark still, and I'd been following the sound of their breaths, but now as our gasps for air calmed down, I couldn't hear them anymore and I wondered if I had been blindly following my own breathing.

"Jamie?" I hardly dared a whisper. No response.

"Where are they?" Isabelle murmured.

"Lucas, where are you?" I tried again; still nothing. Panic rose in my chest.

"They are around, don't worry." I said as much to reassure my self as anything. Iz's hand tighten around mine, but they weren't around, I couldn't see or hear them anywhere. We walked further and further until we came to the edge of the woods. The moon was out and spread some very much appreciated light on our situation. I had hoped the boys would be waiting for us, but Jamie and Lucas were gone. We fought through a hedge and popped out in a field with a light dusting of snow. I had forgotten it was early March and I hadn't realised how cold it was. Glad I had had the sense to put a jumper on I tightened the cords against the wind and clapped my hands together.

"Tilly, what are we going to do?" Isabelle asked a shudder in her voice. I looked around hopefully, desperate for any form of help.

Abigail L. Marsh

"You did survival training last... Remember what we need to do in the cold." I said, knowing full well my input was feeble.

"Build a *fire*." She snapped angrily. "But we can't do that can we?"

"No." I said matter of factly. Sucking in a breath of air through closed teeth to make a noise to fill the eerie silence, I pondered the next move.

"What's the next thing we do in survival?" I asked stamping my feet in an attempt to get some heat back into my toes.

"Arrgg, I don't know Tilly! Why didn't we just go with the police? After all we got kidnapped, they're not angry with us are they?" She said. I glanced over at her... I couldn't leave Cain, could I?.

"Ohhh that's right, you can't leave you're beloved Cain, can you?" She quipped reading my mind.

"Shut up Isabelle." I snapped.

"Look around you... He left you! He's gone!" She shouted stepping up to me and gesturing around the empty field.

"Yeah well... Yeah, WELL..." I couldn't think of anything to say. "He'll come back! I know he will." I retorted, turning away from her. The realism of his sudden abandonment hurt and she knew it.

She scoffed at me.

"Fine, if that's what you want, just GO! Run back home to little Johnny and Patty and see if I give a shit!" I all but screamed. Seeing a flash of red I gave her an almighty shove, she toppled backward into the muddy snow stunned.

"They didn't want me anyway." I grumbled, walking away from her.

Chapter Twenty-Two: If Not One Way, Then Another

The sun was now coming up and bathing the field in a warm glow, I marched towards a gate at the opposite side, praying some speedy movement would warm up my frozen toes. I got about halfway across the field before I heard a scream that shattered the early morning air. Spinning around to see what animal of the night had frightened Isabelle, I froze.

"Oh, Shit!" I said cursing myself for leaving her side while he was still knocking around. Harley must have been following us and at that moment had Isabelle captured, restrained in a chokehold. Raising my gun slightly I marched back over to them furiously.

"What the *hell* are you doing? Didn't I warn you!" I shouted as I approached them. It was clear he wanted me to be the one in his arms so I kept a wary distance, flashing my gun at him.

"Let her go." I said.

"I'd rather not." He smirked at me.

"Harley give me a break, there's police everywhere and I'm tired of your games. Just get out of here, it's you that will lose everything." I said with teeth chattering, as I gestured with the barrel of the gun for him to let her go.

He reached into the waistband of his trousers and pulled out the glock I didn't know he had.

"Harley, please." My voice cracked slightly.

"No, it's you that'll lose everything, no more baby sister." He almost laughed.

"Come on it's me you want, just let her go. Just me and you." I stammered my voice wavering as it did, giving away the fear I was so badly trying to hide. I could feel my hands shaking and had to grip my gun harder so Harley wouldn't notice.

"Tilly stop." Isabelle choked. I didn't look at her, I knew if I did my bravery charade would collapse just as fast as the Berlin Wall.

Harley quite clearly liked this idea. He thought about it for a moment "Put your gun down." He snarled. I glanced down at the weapon in my hand and shrugged tossing it to the floor. What was the point? I was already as good as dead. Harley roughly shoved the terrified Isabelle back onto the ground.

"Run." I said to her as she lay there helplessly staring at me.

"No! That's not fair!" She shrieked.

Harley laughed.

"Life's not fair."

The gun was now pointing at me, bang in line with my chest.

Abigail L. Marsh

"Tilly!" Isabelle screamed scrambling to her feet. "Stop please, STOP!" But I was calm. I was the calmest I had been all day. As I breathed deeply I looked straight down the barrel of the gun. Harley lined it up correctly, faffing around.

"Come on then, do it! We've both been waiting for this, pull the damn trigger." I spat verbalising what we were both thinking. Finally, he stopped moving and smiled a cold, nasty grin. I closed my eyes, this was it, my pathetic excuse for a life would be over.

BANG.

The shot screamed in my ears. Isabelle's screams rang in my ears, and then there was a soft thud. I felt nothing. So cold and so terrified I didn't dare to open my eyes.

"Tilly." Isabelle shouted, I felt her body collide with mine and as I stumbled backward my eyes flashed open.

Harley was on the ground, blood seeping out of the side of his chest and trickling down to the white snow underneath him, turning it into a pink-ish paste.

He was gone.

Isabelle held me in a vice-like grip, I had to pry her hands off me so I could move. What had hit Harley? I swooped down and grabbed my gun, saving it from further frostbite and nervously surveyed the field.

Abigail L. Marsh

I couldn't see anyone. There was no-one visible, but then as I traced back along the hedge line, I saw him… or them. Just adjacent from the gate, about a hundred metres down was the fluorescent colours of a policeman's jacket filtering through the hedge and in front of him was a gunman dressed in black.

"SHIT!" I exclaimed.

Isabelle stared at me, confused.

"Put your weapon down and your hands behind your head." A voice shouted. I scanned back to the gate, several policemen were jogging through it.

I didn't know what to do. Was it all over? I frowned, it was a bit of an anti-climax, standing in a big snowy field at ten to eight on a Tuesday morning.

Dropping the gun as a car approached the scene hope warmed my fingers as I realised it was a huge black Range Rover, just like Cain's, speeding up the lane. It came noisily through the metal gate and skidded in the snow to a halt. I prayed with all the fibres in my being that it might be Cain. Really I was just grasping at straws, it couldn't be him, he'd left me. As I surrendered, putting my arms in the air, I felt all power draining out of me. Had he been caught? What would happen to me now?

Abigail L. Marsh

Isabelle and I started moving across the field are hands behind our heads; I couldn't tell if she was relieved or scared. The policeman finally reached me, he grabbed me roughly and frog-marched me over to the Range Rover, hands digging into my wrists where I was pressed up against the freezing bonnet. Isabelle joined me moments later. Our hands were painfully cuffed behind us.

"Do you think they know who we are?" She asked me feebly.

I shrugged not offering her any hope. As I lay on the ice-cold car watching my breath curl up away from me, stones sinking in my stomach I heard the sound of screeching tyres approach.

"This is him, I told you he would come." I smiled. Doors slammed and I waited, any second now Cain would be here to save me.

"Emma Anderson and Charlie Jackson, MI5." I heard a woman's voice say. I frowned.

"MI5?" Isabelle whispered, trying to peer over he shoulder.

The voice made it's way over to us wearing black-heeled boots and a brown leather jacket. The woman crouched down next to the front wheel of the car and looked dead into my eyes.

"Hey sweetie, you're Tilly Carmichael aren't you?" She asked.

My breath hitched.

"There's no need to be afraid, you're safe now, I'm Detective Emma Anderson, and this is Detective Charlie Jackson, we are going to take you

Abigail L. Marsh

and you sister Autumn home now." She said pointing to the tanned skinned detective wearing a bulletproof vest behind me.

"Hey, can we get these cuffs off them?" Charlie barked at the police officers in fluorescent jackets and they hurried over to us.

I stood up rubbing my wrists. I wasn't at all sure about this whole 'going with the cop's' situation.

Isabelle's hand slipped into mine as she was released from her handcuffs and she squeezed it tightly.

"You are safe now, we won't let anyone hurt you anymore." Emma said. "Let's get you home."

I glanced back at Isabelle, she didn't have a clue what to do so I took charge and as much as I'd like to say I used some sort of karate kid moves and escaped, that's just not how my story goes… I surrendered, nodded and followed. There was nothing else to do standing in a field full of police officers. Without Cain, there was no point in fighting them.

"We've been looking for you two for a long time." Charlie said as we walked out of the field towards black unmarked police car with flashing lights flickering through the front grates. Bullshit. Isabelle was the one they'd been looking for maybe, but I was the forgotten girl and I had liked it.

Abigail L. Marsh

"Where have you been hiding out?" He asked. I didn't satisfy him with a reply.

The car journey was long and awkward. Emma kept reassuring us as we drove towards London that we were safe now, she repeated over and over again that they would catch the people who kidnapped us, and that was doing a pretty good job of making me feel even more sick to my stomach.

Chapter Twenty-Three: MI5 Headquarters

We arrived at a big black-gated building crawling with policemen, security personnel and dogs wearing little bulletproof vests. This was the place of Cain's nightmares and I was about to float right in.

"Where is Max?" I asked as we waited in a queue behind three police cars.

"Who's Max?" Emma asked, turning to look at me.

"My dog and Tommy too." I said.

"Are they at the house in Cromer?" Emma asked. She didn't look at me, but I knew she was probably feeling quite smug.

"Yeah." I replied hopelessly.

"Mason our animal handler will collect them, he'll bring them back her and check them over, then see what we can do." Emma said as we edged closer to the gate.

"What can you do?" I asked nervously, I didn't want them to be put down.

"Well, we can release them to a family or friend." She said. I grimaced. What family? What friends?

"Or we can see if they can be adopted." She added as there was a sharp rap on my blacked-out window. I turned around shocked. The lens of a huge square camera was pressed right up against the glass.

"Arrhh." I cried, falling away from it.

"Arg!" Charlie barked. He peeped his horn. A burly looking security man stepped down from his platform and created a barrier between the car and the cameras. Charlie manoeuvred our vehicle over the concrete block acting as the central reservation and the barrier came up, letting us into the private car parking beyond. He parked us up as near to the building as he could, but before he let us out he ripped his coat off. With Emma following suit he threw his jacket over me as he opened my door. I blindly climbed out of the car feeling his arms grab me and lead me away from the people shouting my name.

Tilly Carmichael.

Abigail L. Marsh

Finally we were inside. The hot air of the heater blew gently on my back as we went through the automatic doors and Charlie pulled the coat off my head. I had to blink a little to readjust my eyes from being under the heavy black jacket.

"What was all that about?" I demanded, my mind in a spin.

Charlie looked at Emma uneasily.

"Well you were on the news a lot, everybody's been looking for you for a long time." Emma said.

Yeah, okay. Spin me another.

"Oh right." I said vaguely, refraining from telling them what I really thought.

"Everybody wants to know where you've been and what happened, that's all." Charlie said. I nodded. Isabelle looked half scared, half relieved as I reached out to her.

"Come on, it'll be all right now, I bet your parents will be here real soon." I said, thinking her scared face needed some good news. She smiled and took my hand, squeezing it as I pulled her into a hug. Emma gave Charlie a sideways glance that piqued my interest, what was she hiding?

Abigail L. Marsh

"Right girls." Emma said brightly as I pulled away from Isabelle. "Let's get you something to drink, and are you hungry?" She asked. I was a little taken aback by her sudden change of demeanour.

"Uhh." I said, struggling for an answer. "Yeah, okay."

Isabelle agreed readily, it had been a while since we had last eaten something substantial.

"Okay, well let's get you settled and then we can talk." She said starting off down the corridor away from us.

"Talk?" I asked, shocked. Emma stopped and turned back to me.

"Yes." She said, confused. "We need to talk to both of you."

"Right okay… Yeah sorry, I thought you said…" And then my mind went blank of all words. "Had a bit of a mind blank." I said, awkwardly trying to cover up. Of course they wanted to talk, but what was I going to spin them? More to the point were Isabelle and I even on the same page? Emma smiled slightly before pressing on, Charlie bringing up the rear as we followed. I didn't dare look at Isabelle not with his eyes boring into the backs of our heads. We trooped down the corridors, people staring at us as if we had been brought back from the dead.

We obviously didn't look like we had been rescued from a life of being kidnapped. For a start I was wearing designer sunglasses. Emma pushed open a double door at the end of a long corridor revealing a canteen filled with people, the FBI or MI5 I presumed. Now, considering I had

Abigail L. Marsh

killed people before... So- a murderer.I went in with as much confidence as I could muster and nailed it. No one really looked our way, but I felt like if they did, they wouldn't know how terrified I was. I was an experienced emotion masker.

Emma got us both a ham sandwich and crisps with a promise of a full, hot meal later on. They wouldn't let us sit in the canteen for some reason and insisted we followed them to a better room, where we could eat privately whilst they sorted a few things out. I agreed if only for the sacred time alone Isabelle and I would get to discuss what we were going to say.

We had to get in a lift to reach the second floor and turn right down a long corridor with floor to roof window at the end. We stopped four doors shy of the window and went into an odd little room
The room had panelled windows all along the outside wall and I wondered if they looked like mirrors from the other side. My query was answered as Emma pushed the door open and led us in. They were just normal windows.

Inside was exactly like those rooms I'd seen on criminal minds, where they kept the kids. At one end there was a play area for the younger children who needed to be doing something, full of toys and a table

Abigail L. Marsh

scattered with pens and paper, all very brightly coloured. On the other side, there was a battered sofa in and a flatscreen television that looked as if it had about four channels. I didn't really care where we were, I just needed to speak to Isabelle without unwanted attention.

"Great, thanks." I said, turning to Emma. "Where are you going?" I asked squeezing my packet of crisps in a rhythmic pattern, seeing if I could play the 'We will rock you' song.

"We just need to run you through the system. We'll be fifteen minutes tops. Will you two be okay in here for a little bit?"

I nodded stiffly; I knew exactly what they were going to do, listen to us. They wanted information and they knew we weren't going to give up freely.

"Sophie's just across the corridor on reception. If you need anything she can put a call through to us and we'll come running." Charlie said smiling.

"Okay, thanks." I said. They left us, closing the door behind them. Isabelle flicked around and looked at me, but I shook my head subtly.

"I'm going to put the TV on." I said loudly. I set my sandwiches down on the table with the pens and paper on it then did a quick 180 checking out the room. In the far corner by the TV attached to the wall was a camera pointing right at me. I tried to ignore it as I went over to the TV and switched it on. I turned it up to a reasonably loud setting and then went back over to Isabelle. Looking at that side of the room there was another camera opposite the one by the TV, only definable by its red button that flashed every couple of seconds.

"Sit here and we'll eat." I said, pulling out a chair and angling it so she would have her back to the camera above the TV. She sat down, her facial expression suggesting she didn't really know what I was doing. When we were seated so that neither of the cameras could see what we were saying, I picked up a pen.

"What are you doing?" She whispered.

They're watching us stop talking.

I wrote on a piece of pink paper with a black felt tip pen. Isabelle's eyes widened, but before she got the chance to look around the room and blow our cover, I wrote another note.

Don't look, just trust me, we have to figure out our story okay?

She just nodded.

We need to look like we are doing something, so pick up a pen and draw something.

I wrote. Quickly she opened her crisps, grabbed a pen and began drawing lines. I joined in and after a few moments I whispered to her.

"Don't look at me, just keep doing what you are doing." I whispered keeping my head behind Isabelle's so the camera opposite me wouldn't see my lips moving.

"What's the story, something that won't get him into trouble, I don't care about the rest, just him." I whispered.

"Tilly he kidnapped us, surely it doesn't matter what we say, he's going away for a long time?" She whispered. I began drawing over the words I had written. We weren't on the same page which meant I had to waste valuable minutes explaining to her, trying to win her round. I looked at her desperately and when I realised I wasn't getting through, I proceeded to ask her.

"Isabelle please, for me. Lie and say nothing about training, nothing about the jobs, just that some other person kidnapped us, we don't know who and don't mention his name. Talk them around in circles, you're good at that." I pleaded. "Please."

"What are you crazy?" She hissed a little too loud, we immediately realised this and went back to colouring furiously.

"No, I won't." She whispered a moment later, head bowed looking at her drawing of a blue bear.

"Isabelle… Autumn, please." I begged her hoping that referring to her a real name may break through the wall she had risen up. Her angry eyes locked with mine and I understood there was only so much I could ask her to do, there was a line and I was on the brink of it.

"Alright." I sighed quietly, sitting back in the chair. I finished my drawing of a Monkey, then took my sandwich over to the sofa and sat down in front of the TV. The programme playing was the Antique Road Show

Abigail L. Marsh

and the remote was out of my reach. I had no effort to reach for it, so I sat in a slump and ate my ham sandwich bitterly until Emma and Charlie knocked on the door and came in, fifteen minutes later. Isabelle was still sat at the drawing table, the atmosphere in the room was silent and tense. I knew they could sense it.

"Everything okay?" Emma asked.

I looked over at them.

"Yeah, I'll go first." I said.

"Right okay! Well Isabelle sweetie, we will be just down the corridor." Emma said, going over to the table. She looked down at our messy scribbles and drawings but made no comment, I decided to rip them up as soon as I got back.

"We won't be too long hopefully, are you okay here?" She asked. Iz nodded.

She smiled at me then led me out of the room, Charlie closing the door behind us.

Chapter Twenty-Four: My Life

"Just in here." Emma said, pressing down on a door handle and pushing the door grey prison-like door inwards. I went in and was confronted by an interrogation room, three grey walls and a very large mirror. I started to think that maybe they already knew I had murdered people and they were here to make me confess so they could throw me in jail with Cain and the rest of The Pack… if they ever caught up with them.

There was no way out now though, I'd walked right into this one. Charlie was behind me and Emma was closing the door. I scanned the room, the mirror on the far wall I decided for sure, *definitely* doubled as a window and one real window above the table looked too small to climb out of anyway. I was trapped.

"Go on, sit down and we'll talk." Charlie said giving me a gentle nudge towards the table and chairs in the centre of the room. I bit my lip and pulled the chair closest to the door out so I couldn't be cornered in by the wall. Charlie sat down opposite me, groaning heavily as he rubbed his thighs.

"Have you got the recorder Charlie?" Emma spoke sharply as if telling him off for his unprofessional outburst. Charlie looked all around as if he had brought it into the room and managed to lose it between the door and his seat.

"I'll be right back." Emma said, leaving the room and tossing a glance full of annoyance at her colleague.

"So what's the deal?" I asked now I had Charlie on his own.

"What do you mean?" Charlie asked clasping his hands together.

"Well you want me to talk and I know how this works… So you're going to make it worth my while right?" I asked. He sighed, eyes rolling slightly as he realised my ploy.

"What is it you want?" He asked.

"My dog. I want my dog to live with me. If you can say you'll do that, then I'll talk to you about my life." I said phrasing the sentence into the perfect word trap.

Charlie rubbed his hands across his forehead, his eyes looked tired, I wondered if he'd been working nights that week as he'd gotten closer to finding us.

"We're often willing to help someone out if they are willing to help us piece together details of a major crime ring."

I'd tripped him up on my words and I knew it. Now to seal the deal.

"So if I tell you what you want to know about my life for the past ten years or so, you'll let me have Max back?"

"I don't see why not." Charlie said, "But…"

Emma re-entered the room, dumped the recording device that looked like a seventies radio onto the table and sat down in her chair, face flushed red.

Abigail L. Marsh

"I'm sorry for the delay." She said, not giving us any inclination as to what had happened. Then she smiled at me sweetly. "I'm going to record this for evidential purposes, there is nothing for you to worry about."

Yeah, the evidence against me.

"I want a lawyer." I said flatly. They both looked at me a little confused. "I'm not answering anything until I have a lawyer, I'm entitled to one, and I want one." I said.

Emma looked at Charlie, and a smile passed her lips.

"You are right, you are entitled to a lawyer, but this isn't an interrogation. You're the victim Tilly, that's not under question."

I could feel the sweat forming on my brow; they wouldn't be all smiles if I told them I had killed people.

"Tilly would it help if I told you we can't arrest you for anything you've done under the duress of the people who kidnapped you. Anything that you have done in the past ten years will not affect you now, you're essentially untouchable. We simply want to know what happened to you." Charlie said. I made eye contact with him, holding his comforting gaze.

"Nothing? I can't go to jail?" I asked, my tone more relaxed than I felt.

"Nothing, no jail I promise." He replied. Ha! That was sweet. He promised, but I didn't believe in promises. The room went quiet, and as I sat there with no real way to get out of the situation. Then the realisa-

Abigail L. Marsh

tion hit me as I thought back over the past decade. It was something Cain had told me when I was young. He'd said that 'when you're facing a brick wall, sometimes you have to be brave enough to trust someone to help you over it, no matter how hard it is, so that you can move forward.' Turning this over in my head I nodded at the pair, put a small ounce of trust in Charlie and Emma and tried to explain the last ten years of my life as best I could.

"I guess I'll start from the beginning, from when they took me into care."

Emma nodded.

"It just before Christmas 2004 when a social worker came and took Autumn and I away- What an amazing present huh? Our Dad had been abusing us, well me. They uh… They took us out of the house we'd been living in with Callie my older sister and our Dad. We went to a care home in Brooklyn, New York. I don't know why they took us so far or away from Callie." I began. I had started right at the beginning when things really started to go wrong.

"We lived there for a month or two just Autumn and I, we weren't allowed to see our Dad, and they said that Callie had been moved to a home in Indiana I think, so she was too far away to see."

"Did they say why you got split up?" Emma asked.

I shrugged, I couldn't remember and I didn't think that mattered now anyway.

Abigail L. Marsh

242

"Just after Christmas a family came in, well a couple actually, looking for a little girl to foster. They took a liking to Autumn, I tried to keep her away from them each time they came to see her. She didn't know what they wanted and didn't mind playing with them hour after hour. One day I came back from morning lessons, and she was all packed up and ready to go." I said, biting the inside of my cheeks, this was a hard story to tell.

"Pat and John?" Emma asked. I nodded.

"I had ten minutes to say goodbye to her. They promised to take good care of her and bring her to see me regularly, they even said I could go and stay with them sometimes."

"And did you?" Emma smiled as if the story I was telling was going to take an unexpected happy turn.

"No." I said bitterly. "I didn't see her again until I was sixteen."

"They shouldn't have said that to you if they weren't prepared to follow through." Charlie said. "I understand why you are angry."

"Oh I wouldn't worry, this story is full of lies, broken promises and crappy *crappy* people." I replied the taste of lemon lingering in my mouth. "For weeks, I pestered the care home manager and my social worker, but they got mad, they said that Autumn had a better life now, to leave it be. After being shut off so many times my heart was exhausted, so I shut her out. I shut it all out and forced myself to get on with life, there was no choice anymore." I said, my voice fading out. Emma

Abigail L. Marsh

and Charlie watched me as I fought to control my emotions, this wasn't a time in my life that was easy to talk about. I stayed quiet for a few moments before a thought occurred to me- the faster I told this story the quicker it would be over and I could shove it back in the box and nail it shut forever.

"It was the 9th of February 2005." I began with such oomph in my voice it not only made Emma jump but me as well. "I was kidnapped in the middle of the night. I don't remember anything after tea that evening, which was clumpy pasta and tomato sauce." I said pulling a face, recalling the vile food I was made to eat there. "When I woke up I wasn't in my bed anymore, I was lying on a sofa in a long room with lots of little windows, wrapped in my blanket from the care home. I was all by myself."

"You were on a plane?" Emma asked.

"Yes, but it wasn't like an airline plane, it was a private jet and at first I thought it was just a dream, my head was a little fuzzy so I tried to go back to sleep." I said.

"Why was your head fuzzy?" Emma asked.

"They gave me sleeping gas." I said.

"They told you that?" Emma asked, sounding shocked. "Did..."

"Yeah they told me, so anyway." I said cutting her off. "I couldn't get back to sleep. Later a man opened a door and came in, I didn't recognise him. I sat up and asked him who he was and where I was." I said.

"And what did he say?" Charlie asked when I paused to breathe.

Emma rested her hand on his arm, he was rushing me and she knew it.

"Not a lot, he said that uhh." I struggled to remember his exact words. "Something like…" I sighed heavily pretending the misty haze in my mind was thicker than it was.

"It's okay." Charlie smiled. "This happened a long time ago."

I nodded and decided to carry on, the less I said about Cain the better.

"I don't remember much, I wasn't really with it and after that, I don't remember waking up again until later when it was bright and I was in a bed."

"He gassed you again?" Emma asked. I shrugged.

"Maybe, or I just fell asleep, either way, I woke up and there was a huge dog next to me. Scared me stupid. I laid in the bed deadly still until someone came in like two hours later." I said, laughing at my childish fears.

"What's funny?" Emma asked she looked horrified.

"Oh, nothing.I was so silly, that dog had a puppy who became my best friend." I said smiling at the memory of Max when he was first learning to walk, he used to think he was top-heavy and his back legs would lift as if someone was pulling his tail up, until he would topple over on his nose.

"Okay, so who came in do you know their name?"

I remembered.

It was Melanie; she had brought me some toast and water. She'd shoed the dog whose name was Primrose out of the room and sat down on the edge of the bed. I had been so scared that I hadn't said anything to her for a long time until I finally got the courage to ask her where I was.

"You're in Cromer, in England." She'd said.

"I had been all alone in the care home in New York and back then to me, it didn't really matter where I was and looking around I had my own room and that girl that came in, looked after me." I said glancing back up at Emma and Charlie.

"What was her name?" Charlie pressed. I couldn't tell him, why would I do that to Mel? She'd been there at every scratch, every wound, every bad day, we were girls together, the only other one there.

So I ignored his question and proceeded with my story

"She looked after me until training started, then I was by myself again." I said a sense of dread filling my voice. I was about to describe training to them and that was almost worse than talking about Autumn. The inevitable question was asked.

"What's training?"

Abigail L. Marsh

I looked away from them, staring blankly at the wall trying to come up with some sort of explanation.

"I can't describe it." I finally said.

"What do you mean?" Charlie asked. I didn't look at him; the chipped paint on the wall had suddenly become far more interesting than my life story.

"Tilly, do you want a break?" Emma asked calmly.

"A break for what? It's not going to be any more describable in half an hour than it is now. I can't describe it." I said bluntly as I forced my eyes back to her. "It just… Hurt."

Emma looked at Charlie and I could see them having a silent conversation between themselves.

"Okay Tilly, we'll leave that for now. What else can you tell us?" Charlie said.

"Like what?"

"Well, did training end? What did you do afterward? When did Autumn come?" Charlie asked.

I nodded.

"Yeah training ended, and I had honed my skills, I could run faster, swim deeper and fight harder than ever before. I was like a miniature killing machine, you didn't want to be around me unless you could do what I could do *and* you were bigger than me." I smiled, remembering the fight I had picked with a kid I'd bumped into on the beach one day, when I was out with Kurt.

"What?" Emma asked.

"I accidentally went a little crazy on a boy when I was nine. He took my bucket and spade so I chased him down the beach with my dog who was only a clumsy one year old, tripping over his own feet. The boy was fast but not fast enough and I pounced on top of him and performed some of my karate moves on his face, let's just say that the guy that trained me wasn't happy, he had to chase me down the beach and rip me away from the kid; he had a black eye, a bloody nose and a bust-up lip. I was proud of myself, but when I got back to the house wriggling in Kurt's arms, I was in so much trouble for stirring attention." I said before gasping and covering my mouth with my hands. I'd dropped a name and it hadn't gone unnoticed.

"Why won't you tell us their names, Tilly? What they did to you is wrong. They kidnapped you." Emma said, sounding a little exasperated. I was furious with myself for doing something so stupid. I bit my tongue refusing to say another word, while kicking myself hard under the table.

"Tilly, did they threaten you so you wouldn't speak?" Emma asked. Charlie, who hadn't said a word, was staring at me with a hard glare. I reverted my eyes to him and gave him the same stare back.

"Stockholm syndrome." He finally said.

Abigail L. Marsh

"That's right and I don't care. I'm not giving you any names. I thought I made it clear when we made our little deal, I'll tell you anything you want to know about *my* life, not anyone else's." I said smirking, my whole attitude had switched. Clearly I couldn't hold my tongue while I was blabbing my life story so I would only answer them with short sentences from now.

"What little deal?" Emma asked, obviously annoyed that Charlie had done something he shouldn't. I looked at him.

"Should I tell her, or will you?" I smiled sarcastically.

"I told Tilly if she answered our questions we'd get her dog back for her..."

"And..." I prompted.

Charlie's face fell sheepishly.

"And that the dog could live with her."

Emma looked from me to Charlie, if I'd had a camera I would have taken a photo of her bulging eyes and taught jaw.

"We can't do that." She said shrilly. "The dogs need to be fully checked for drugs and anything else they have been exposed to. Then they must be deemed safe to be allowed out in public." She spoke, talking to me as if she was a robot.

I frowned.

"My dog is perfectly fine." I snapped. "This wasn't the deal...So we're done." I said, scraping the chair back and standing up.

"We're not done with you." Emma said.

"Well if you aren't going to help me and you aren't going to arrest me... Which you assured me you can't do... Then I can legally walk out of here. I'm not seven anymore no-one can stop me doing anything." I said triumphantly, before turning and walking towards the door.

There was a hushed discussion going on behind me and just as I pressed down on the handle, Emma piped up.

"Alright Tilly, we'll make you a deal." She said. I opened the door.

"I already made a deal." I said

"Yes, and it shouldn't have happened like that, but this deal I promise I'll keep." She said desperately. I stopped, there was that word again. Promise.

"Promise this promise that!" I snapped, turning around. "Promises mean nothing to me." I glared at Emma.

"Just hear me out?" She said. "I'll make it worth your while." She said. I let the door close but held my ground next to it so that she knew one slip up and I was gone.

"You give us a few names of the people who you've been around for the past decade, three at least, to give us a lead and I will personally make sure your dogs are fast-tracked through the process. Whilst they are de-

Abigail L. Marsh

tained you can see them any time you want and if they are deemed safe, then you can have them back. How does that sound?" She said hopefully.

I could tell her Chris, Rick, and Harley right now with absolutely no hesitation and my dogs safe return would be guaranteed, so I agreed. Relief flooded Emma's face as I went back over to the table and pulled my chair back in.

"You better stay good on this promise… Harley Rodriguez, Chris Hardy, and Rick Fox." I said sighing and worrying I'd set them on Cain's path for my own gain.

"Thank you, you've been very helpful. Let's take a break, we'll speak to Isabelle now and then maybe you can answer a few more questions a little later on?" Emma asked glancing at the mirror behind her, confirming what I had initially thought. I flashed it a smile. A thought occurred to me as I stared myself in the mirror.

"Emma, what's actually going on tonight, where are we staying?" I asked.

"Well you need to get checked over at the hospital, and you two will stay there tonight. Don't worry, they'll be an officer outside your door all night, no one will get in." Charlie reassured me. Like I cared about that.

"Checked over? Like a psych check?" I asked a little horrified.

"Amongst other things, but you aren't going to be sectioned." Emma added, a smile creeping onto her face as she read my expression.

Chapter Twenty-Five: I'm Out

Back in the 'playroom,' I glared at Isabelle as she as called for her 'talk.' When she was gone, I picked up my sandwich box and crisp packet and shoved them in the bin by the side of the television before going over to the table and looking at the drawings. Isabelle had been drawing while I'd been gone. There was a cartoon drawing of a wolf and a Monkey; the Monkey was in the wolves jaws. I knew what it meant, and as much as it pained me, she was right.

Quickly I gathered the papers up and spent the next five minutes, ripping them into tiny shreds so no one would ever know what they were. Satisfied, I sat back down on the sofa and flicked through the channels. Half an hour went by I was getting severely bored watching This Mornings repeat show. I stood and paced the room fretfully, what was I doing here?

No-one was coming for me. Isabelle would go back to Pat and John and I was confident that Roberts relapse had sent Callie back into care, so my future was looking pretty bleak. As I paced, my eyes fell on a window that hadn't caught my attention yet. Peering out of the glass in the door, checking t see there was no nosey bugger about in the corridor, I took a look out of the window.

We were on the second floor and the room looked onto an empty parking lot, it would be pretty simple for me to shimmy across the ledge, use the brick walls natural grooves to get to the window ledge below and jump to the ground. Where to next I didn't know, but hey at least I wouldn't be stuck there waiting for my impending doom.

I gripped the handle on the window and gave it a tug, nothing happened. I tugged again harder, still nothing and then I realised there was a key sat in the corner of the window frame, a bit of a stupid place to keep a key for a room they put flighty kids in. Grabbing it, I stuck it into the keyhole, wiggling and twisting until it made a satisfying click. When I tugged the handle again, it sprung open and the window glided up nearly taking my nose off.

I stuck my head out and breathed in the fresh air before assessing the situation. It was too high up to jump, I'd risk a sprained or even broken ankle and then I'd be up the proverbial creek without a paddle. Looking right, there was a drainpipe between me and the window in the next room. Perfect, the little rungs sticking off its would make it easy to slide

Abigail L. Marsh

all the way to the ground and then a flat parking lot that I could sprint across, over the fence on the other side and disappear into the busy streets of London.

Back in the room I checked around for anything I would need, my Ray-Bans were sat on the table. I wanted those!

I had learned that in situations like this it was always best to shut the window you were leaving from, people coming in won't assume you have made your exit that way and will search the building for you, before thinking you've leaped out the window. So I slid the window closed and pulled my sunglasses over my eyes as I shuffled precariously along the window ledge. I made a quick grab for the drainpipe and swung my body onto it, only just managing to hook my feet onto one of the rungs before my arms gave way with my weight. I stopped, breathing heavily for a moment; this was harder than it looked.

Once I had caught my breath and my nerve, I slid my foot down the pipe searching tentatively for another rung. It was a very nerve-wracking process, but a few minutes later my foot hit solid ground and I took off flying across the parking lot, dodging a few cars that were parked up in there before using a pile of rubbish by the fence to run up and vault it — horrible idea. I hadn't planned for what was on the other side...

Nothing, there was nothing on the other side and I fell through the air

Abigail L. Marsh

until I hit water. Icy cold water that knocked the air out of my lungs on impact.

The world went black for a minute and when I finally decided which way was up, I came out of the water gasping for air. My arms flailed above my head as my body was forced backward by the strong current, searching for anything to grab. Eventually I caught hold of a floating log and pulled myself together. Rubbing the water out of my eyes so I could see I looked around grimly. I was in a river, either side of me were the backs of houses and steep sloping muddy grass verge that fell away into the river. My sunglasses had gone, lost in the murky depths and I wasn't going back under for them. My first thought was that I had fallen into the Thames but it couldn't of been; the River Thames was much, much bigger.

Great!

I tipped my body forward and started swimming with the current, there was no way I was going to climb up a grass verge and clear the tall fences at the top, nor was I about to explain to a family why I was dripping water through their house as I tried to make it to the street the other side. I swam downstream a little bit going under a few concrete bridges before I started to go numb to the bones and just as I was about

Abigail L. Marsh

to give up and try to scramble up the banks and knock on some old woman's back door, the houses ended and the banks levelled out a little. At the top of the much lower bank stood a bunch of evergreens which I could hear people laughing and playing games beyond. I struggled against the current over to the banks with my now blue hands and hauled myself out of the water. I had to lie on the grass for a moment; thanking my lucky stars it was a sunny warm day, well for March.

Once I had retrieved my breath I pushed myself off the cold ground, forcing myself forward. I definitely looked like someone had kidnapped me now as I stumbled up the bank and appeared in the tree line on the edge of a park. I peeked out from my position hidden behind the great oak tree trunks across the field, where several of people were playing football. An ice-cream kiosk which had been shut up for the winter stood forgotten behind the game, but the sign that hung above it read: *Victoria Park Ice Cream Kiosk.*

Now I had my bearings- Victoria Park was on the upper East side of London, in the borough of Tower Hamlets. I routed around in my pockets hoping that I had brought my debit card with me. To my utter relief, I felt the hard plastic in the depths of my jacket. I pulled it out and looked at it, my heart sinking. It wasn't the right one. I had two bank accounts in case we ever got caught, Cain made sure one of them

Abigail L. Marsh

was hidden and protected, that had over £400,000 in it and this one had a little over £50, but for now it would have to do. I could get a taxi or a train to Cromer, go home and get my things. My card with the real money on it must also have been back at the house in my little chest hidden at the back of my wardrobe. Cain had saved it for me for if things went up in flames. I think this situation covered that. Then I'd go and hide somewhere until all this had blown over.

It seemed like a good plan at the time, but I was freezing and my hands were turning blue, March wasn't the best time to go for a dip in the river... The thought of being back at home was giving me the positivity I needed so spurred on, I made my way across the park trying not to draw attention to myself and when I hit the road at the far side, I took off in a sprint, trying to get warm. I found the signs for Homerton tube station and deciding the best way to do this was to go back into central London, to Kings Cross and find the trains for Norfolk. I hopped on the tube and kept a low profile as we hurtled towards the capital.

If you have ever been on the London underground, you will know that you could have three heads and a crocodile purse and no one would look twice. So, me being a little cold and wet wasn't a problem, no one batted an eyelid until had to change tubes at Camden town station. As I got onto the black line which would take me to St Pancreas, my arm was grabbed with a steely grip. I jumped out of my skin, thinking I had been caught, but when I turned around accepting my fate, I realised it was a bony, wrinkled hand and a warm smiling face that greeted me.

"Hello Deary, are you all right?" She croaked at me.

"Oh yes I'm fine, just got splash by a car." I lied, cheeks heating as my heart fluttered in awkwardness.

"Come and sit here." She said, patting the seat next to her. I groaned inwardly; this wasn't the time! Didn't she know I was a runaway? Of course not. Sighing mentally I sat down next to her and hid my grimace. She smelled severely of prunes; I hated prunes.

Well she got talking about this and about that until I wanted to box my ears off and when I stood up to get off at Kings cross, she stopped me.

"Here you go Deary, you look like you need this." she said, reaching into her bag that looked as if it was from the British Heart Foundation and pulled out a woollen cardigan. As I looked at it my *cold criminal* heart melted a little bit.

"Thank you." I said, taking it from her as the doors started to beep.

"Thank you so much." I repeated before spinning round and stepping out of doors.

The platform was crawling with people as I dragged the cardigan over my now drying arms. The first person collided with as I turned towards

Abigail L. Marsh

the exit was Detective Charlie. I gasped as he grabbed my forearms and stared at me, he was strong and there was no way he was letting go.

"Tilly, what are you doing?" He asked.

"Leaving." I snapped, my heart shooting into my throat.

"Where are you going? You're safe now." He clearly hadn't caught on. I shrugged.

"Does it matter?" I asked.

He looked confused.

"Get off me." I snapped, trying to pull away.

"Tilly. You are safe, calm down." Charlie continued, his grip held fast.

"I was safe before." I said. He stayed silent. "I'm bulletproof. I have nothing left to lose Charlie. I'm as safe as it gets." I said

"What about your sister?"

"How did you find me?" I asked changing the subject; I didn't want to talk about her. He laughed, his grasp on me loosening marginally as his attention wavered.

"I am a senior member of MI5." He laughed, "I can find anyone, any-where, anytime."

"Ohhh, I see... Well..." I said, before yanking hard, twisting and rip-ping my arms away from him. I had caught him off guard and his grip broke. I barged through the crowds charging away from him as fast as I could. I jumped the barrier that lead out into the train station filled with shops, which in return made a ridiculous squealing noise alerting the whole train station to where I was. I dived into Marks and Spencer's and crouched down behind a shelf of Percy Pigs, peering around the edge. I looked out of the open doors and saw Charlie jump the barriers after me and stand amongst the crowds scanning the mobs of people for me. Men wearing fluorescent jackets approached him, and he flashed his card at them. I sniggered. *He thinks he's such a big man.*

Backing away from the shelf I turned, looking desperately around for a fire exit. Someone came through a door leading out to a hallway over by the tills, just before it shut I saw a green exit sign hanging on the wall above an opened door. Relief flooded me. I made a move and shot across the shop floor, slamming my hands into the grey bar and disappearing out into the loading bay. There were a few lorries parked there, their back doors open and realising this was my only feasible escape, I jumped into one and crouched down at the back amongst the boxes.

Chapter Twenty-Six Making A Run For It

A few moments later, a man wearing filthy overalls and scoffing a Greggs sausage roll came out of a set of double doors at the back of the train station. He slammed the lorries doors shut and then we were mov-

Abigail L. Marsh

ing. I took my trusty Nokia that had survived everything out of my pocket and shone the dimly lit screen around. To my great pleasure, there were boxes in there from a load of charity shops. Not wasting any time I ripped one open and inside found all sorts of weird ornaments. "No, no, come on!" I hissed. I found another box and peeled back the completely overused gaffer tape. Sighing in relief as I'd found a box full of clothes I pulled out a jumper that was a lot nicer feeling than the granny cardigan I was wearing and a pair of black jeans that may or may not have been clean.

"Beggars can't be choosers Tilly." I sighed slipping my soggy jeans off and putting my newfound ones on, not forgetting to take my card out and being momentarily proud of that fact. I was just zipping up my blue jumper when the lorry stopped. Quickly I scrambled for my phone, closed the boxes and switched off the Nokia, crouching back down out of sight.

I heard the scraping of metal and the doors opened, letting in the blinding daylight.

"All right Jimmy, I'm coming, keep your hair on." My make-shift taxi driver said, stepping onto his lorry, grabbing a box and giving me a lovely flash of his builders bum. I watched him climb off huffing and puffing and disappear out of view, then seizing my chance snuck down the side of all the boxes and hopped down into Harrington street gardens, wearing a whole new outfit. Scanning the area I thanked my lucky stars there was not one mode of transport out on my predicament but three. A bus, the weird bank card bikes you find dotted all over London and, Mornington Crescent Tube station a hundred metres up the road. Sirens wailed all around me so I bolted into the tube station and disappeared underground. I paid for my tickets like a model citizen, or more to the point so I didn't alert anyone to my whereabouts with the bloody barriers, that loved to shriek at you the moment you stepped out of line.

I grumbled as I got to the platforms levels realising that I didn't have the money or the energy to go back to Cromer. I couldn't risk going back to Kings Cross; it would be crawling with police. I needed help, and I didn't admit that very often. The only person I could even vaguely put a name to a face was Carnaby, Cains suit man and all-round dodgy businessman who had been helping him fight the elusive Mr. Giannaville. So that was that I got on another tube and headed for Soho.

The tube to Tottenham Court was packed with people and when I looked at the digital clock on the train I realised I was in trouble with time. I'd be lucky if Carnaby was still hanging around work.

It was getting colder as the workday drew to a close. Soho was busy with people hurrying home from work and I didn't stick out like a sore thumb like I thought I might as I wound my way through the streets,

Abigail L. Marsh

trying with all the brainpower left in my body to remember which goddamn road Carnaby's shop was on. I couldn't for the life of me even remember what the shop was called. I was almost about to give up and go
into a little a place that looked like it served the best hot chocolates in
town, when I saw 'Threads' reflected in the cafe's window. That was the
one. Before crossing the street, I glanced cautiously around. Nothing
seemed amiss, nobody jumping out of sight so I crossed the road and
faced off the building. It was reasonably smart, although a lick of red
paint around the edge wouldn't have gone amiss. I climbed the stone
steps up to the door and was gutted to see the closed sign hanging in the
window.

"For God's sake." I groaned covering the glass with my hand and peering through. It was dark in there no doubt about it, but I figured taking a
look round the back wouldn't harm anyone. As I descended the steps,
there was a scraping sound above my head, I turned to see a thin lady in
her mid-thirty hanging out of the window in a black dress.
"What you want?" She asked with a very obvious fake cockney accent.
"Uhh." I stumbled.
"Well come on, I haven't got all day." She leered out of the window, fag
in hand.

Abigail L. Marsh

"I'm just looking for someone." I said, smiling edgily. The woman looked back into the room behind her and spoke in a language I didn't understand, her cockney accent seeming to vanish completely.

"Carnaby?" I added. The woman finally turned back around and spoke to me.

"You won't find him here at this time. Who are you?"

I swallowed, trying to come up with a name fast. Then to my utter shock and disgust the woman was pulled away from the window and Ricks' head popped out, chest bare and eyes popping.

"What the?" I demanded. "Rick?"

"What the hell are you doing here?" He asked, sounding not in the least bit amused that I should turn up out of the blue.

"You know her?" I heard the woman ask, her accent was flitting between some sort of Soviet slang and cockney.

"I could ask you the same thing." I retorted. "What the heck happened this morning?"

Rick looked up and down the street before angrily hitting the window-pane with his palm and sighing in anguish.

"Get your arse around the back, there's a key under the mat. Wait for me at the bottom of the stairs." He slammed the window shut, and as I walked round to the back, I wondered why someone who was invested in a crime ring would keep a key under a mat.

Abigail L. Marsh

Rick was fully clothed and not looking too pleased about it as he climbed down the stairs in the dingy light. He pushed me into what seemed like an office and closed the door.

"How did you get here?" He asked, scrabbling around in the desk and pulling out a cigar.

"Tube… Where's Cain?"

Rick gave me an evil smile.

"Did Daddy leave you?" He asked. I was exhausted and that little dig usually wouldn't have hurt me, but it did this time.

I nodded at him and left it at that. Rick looked slightly taken aback.

"I don't know where Cain went, he's probably hiding out somewhere like everyone else. He'll come and find you when it's over." He said, sounding surprisingly reassuring. I nodded again.

"I was at the MI5 base a few hours ago." I said.

"You escaped?" Rick asked, surprised.

I nodded.

"Fell into a river."

Rick laughed.

"Anyway, I'm screwed. I can't go back to the house to get…." Then I thought better of telling him my plans.

"To get what?"

"Max." I said expertly covering up my tracks, I didn't need him racing me for the money. Rick laughed, flicking his lighter which produced a small flame.

"You and that bloody dog." Then he looked around the room a little confused. "Where's your sister?"

I shrugged.

"I left her at MI5." I said. "This life, it was never for her."

Rick nodded before taking a huge drag on his cigar.

"Well…" He said. "I can't help you." As he exhaled the plume of smoke swirled up toward the ceiling and fanned out.

"Go figures." I said, rubbing my forehead.

"But, go down to The Three Fox Tails in Clapham. Carnaby should be there and if you tell him what's happened, he'll help you out."

"Doesn't he already know?" I asked. Ricks eyebrows furrowed. "I mean you're in his shop doing I don't know what with his wife." I risked a smirk.

"Natalia is not his wife! Now get out, I don't want to see you around here again you'll blow everything." He said, his face tinged with anger.

"Alright boss." I said nodding slightly. "And if you see Cain, point him in my direction."

"I will." Rick said. As I turned and started walking across the wooden floor, I realised something.

Abigail L. Marsh

"Why are you being so nice?" I asked, turning back to face the man.

"I'm not." Rick grumbled. There was a brief pause.

"Harley's dead." I said.

Rick looked up at me, shock and sadness riddled all over his face.

"Shot." I said. "By the police."

Rick nodded.

"They're looking for you Rick, you and Chris, they have your names and I don't know who else's. So don't stay put." I said. "Goodbye." I gave him a little wave and with that, I closed the door and left him. I knew I'd never see him again and I wasn't all that sad about it either.

It was starting to get dark and trickle with rain as I walked down the tiny backstreet to The Three Fox Tails. It was the only building on the street with it's lights on as ducked under the wilting flower basket hanging by the door and pushed it open. The room was full of men, some turned and looked me up and down, judging stares on their faces, others were too focused on their card games to even notice me. Smoke hung like a haze in the air, firelight danced in a fireplace at the far end of long wooden table and someone was lazily plucking a guitar string in the corner of the room. I scanned the faces as I wandered in, there were some I knew from pictures, some I could put a name too and others I didn't know at all. I was amazed by how well dressed everybody was.

Abigail L. Marsh

Suited and booted, they reminded me of Cain, a dark shadow cast over my face. *Cain.*

"What are you doing in here little lady?" A Russian voice shouted across the bar. A few other men grunted in agreement.

"I'm looking for Carnaby Hanson, I'm a friend of Cain Black."

The Russian nodded at me.

"Hey, Carny!" He shouted, looking to his right. I glanced over at a group of men surrounding a table. The cigar smoke was particularly heavy in that area, but as the group parted Carnaby's face came into view. He had a hand of cards in his left and a poker board in front of him. He looked surprised to see me, but the look on his face told me he a least recognised me.

"Someone here to see you." The Russian said. The whole pub had gone quiet and I felt a little edgy as I made my way through the uncharted sea of men. I had almost reached Carnaby's table when a particularly vulgar-looking man grabbed my bum. Without hesitation grabbed his hand and gave it a vicious twist in the wrong direction. He, who hadn't been expecting such a skilled move from the likes of me cracked under the pain, keeled over and shouted out. I held my ground, not letting go and brought my knee up fast, smashing him in the nose. Blood trickled onto the floor as I dropped his beefy fist. I paused for a moment, looking

Abigail L. Marsh

around at the crowds of men, thinking maybe that wasn't the best idea I had ever had. There faces dark and murderous, all snarling at me.

"Anyone else wants a feel?" I demanded.

"I don't want any trouble." The barman said firmly. I gave the men one last defying look and turned to Carnaby.

"Tilly Black." He said. I heard a few men gasp and put their beers down. I glanced around, eyebrows were raised. So some of them knew who I was. "Quite a first impression you've made." He said looking at the man behind me.

"Come on Carnaby, that was no first impression, you've known about me a long time." I said as smugly as I dared.

He frowned at me in contempt.

"We need to talk." I said. He looked up at the two men stood next to him, before looking back at me and nodding.

"Get a drink, I'll be over once the game is done."

I cleared my throat.

"I think you might want to hear this now." I said as he looked at the board in front of him.

"Hey Lenny, get Miss Black a drink." He said, not looking up. I glanced over at the lanky bartender now polishing glasses behind the bar. He winked at me. Ugh, men.

Abigail L. Marsh

"Raise." Carnaby said as I went over to the bar. The man whose nose I had broken had a bloody napkin pressed to his face and was giving me a decidedly menacing look.

"Don't mind him." Lenny said in a squeaky voice, as I pulled up a bar stool. The Russian was gone. "What can I get you?"

I turned my attention to Lenny. He was a spotty teenager, completely skin and bone who possessed no air of decorum in the slightest. I wondered if he got the shit ripped out of him at the pub.

"We got, vodka, whiskey, rum…" I looked at the many hundreds of spirits stacked up behind him.

"Um, just a vodka tonic please." I asked airily, unsure what the right thing to drink in that situation was.

He nodded and began throwing bottles in the air. I wasn't paying him any attention as I watched the men around the pub. They all seemed very surly, dressed up smartly, clearly they all had a ton of money, and I was pretty sure I knew how they had made it. Huge rings on their fingers, chains hung heavily around their necks and practically all of them were smoking cigars. I couldn't hear their conversations, the private ones were hushed and the others just became one solid hum that cancelled out any other noise.

My drink suddenly crashed into my arm. I looked at Lenny.

"How much?" I asked, picking it up and taking a gulp.

"On the house." He smiled.

Abigail L. Marsh

"You know I'm not quite eighteen." I said, taking another sip and placing it down on the sticky bar top.

Lenny smiled at me wryly.

"Does it look like we care?" He asked. I shrugged.

"Guess not."

My eyes were drawn to a screen hanging on the wall. No-one was paying it any attention, I couldn't even hear it, but what I saw made my heart leap out of my chest. It was Isabelle, and next to her, Detective Charlie Jackson.

"Who's that?" Lenny asked interrupting my thoughts.

"Uhh." I said, turning to him. "How should I know? Just put the game on, will you?" I asked.

"Sure." He shrugged and picked up the remote. It was Arsenal vs. Chelsea. "What's your team?" Lenny asked.

"Arsenal." I mumbled. "Hey Lenny, how long you worked here?" I asked.

"Let's see." he said, screwing up his face, he started counting on his fingers. "About five years, why?"

"How long has Al Pacino over there been coming here?" I asked, looking over at Carnaby who,with a dark face, looked very much like he was losing badly.

"Oh, Mr. Hanson?" I nodded. "Long time. He's here like clockwork, weird really, you'd think a man like him would be somewhere better

Abigail L. Marsh

than this crummy place- you'd think they all would." He said before going off on some waffling tangent about the Vietnamese gun trade.

"A man like what Lenny?" I interrupted. He looked at me.

"Well look at him, he looks like a proper gangster and they are supposed to have a load of money and be respectable, aren't they?"

I turned to him frowning, this kid knew nothing.

"Lenny, how often do you work here?" I asked as a cheer went up at Carnaby's table.

"Oh I'm only part-time, my uncle Bugs used to the place."

"Uncle Bugs?" I asked downing the rest of my drink.

"Yeah but that's just his nickname, his real name's Henry Bugsy Giannaville."

"Hold on." I said, stopping him chattering away. Lenny looked at me, excitement crossing his face.

"Yeah?" He squeaked.

"Giannaville used to own this place? Henry Giannaville?

Lenny nodded.

"But I thought they were rivals? Why would Carnaby be drinking in this pub if they're starting a war?"

"Bugsy went underground years and years ago, sold the pub, sold everything. Mr. Hanson has come here ever since."

"To taunt him? Is that a good idea?" I asked, thinking it most definitely was not. Lenny shrugged.

"I have no idea. I get ten quid an hour, that's not enough money to give a shit." Lenny said.

"Fair enough." I said holding my hands up.

My mind drifted as Lenny carried on his spiel about far less important matters. Why was Carnaby sitting in a pub that his biggest rival pre-owned? Was Lenny only still there to keep an eye on things? It didn't make any sense.

Carnaby was coming towards me as Lenny rabbited on about his nick-name 'The Len-mister'. I couldn't think of a more ridiculous name but there was no need to pass comment, I reckoned he got a fair amount of stick around there already. Carnaby's beefy hands clapped down on the bar top next to me as the man leaned heavily against it.

"What can I get you, Mr. Hanson?" Lenny asked jittering.

"Malt." Carnaby said in a low voice. As Lenny got to work, Carnaby looked over his shoulder at me.

"Why are you here, Tilly? What does Cain want?" He asked.

"Cains in jail." I said, looking him in the eye.

Carnaby turned fully to me, shock etched all over his face.

"Well, at least I think he is." I sighed. Carnaby grabbed my arm and pulled me off my seat. He led me through to the back and shut the door on Lenny who was following us with Carnaby's drink.

Abigail L. Marsh

"What's going on?" He asked, letting go of me his voice calm. I was tense, I had never been alone with this guy but I hadn't come all this way not to say what I needed too.

"You knew about New York?" I asked. Carnaby nodded quickly. "It was corrupt, we got attacked when we got back to England." I said. "They were waiting for us, everyone ran... Even Cain." I said.

Worry passed through Carnaby's eyes.

"Are they following you now?" He asked flicking a glance at the window. I shook my head, but it didn't settle him. He dragged the brown curtains across the window and pulled me away from them.

"I lost them this morning." I assured him.

"Who got out?" He asked.

"I don't know." I said. "Harley's dead, Jamie and Lucas, I saw them last in the woods outside Great Yarmouth in the early hours of this morning, and Rick... I saw him too." I said, thinking better of what I was going to say about his whereabouts. "But I don't know about anyone else."

"And Cain?"

"He left." I said matter of factly. "And I don't think he's coming back." A touch of acid in my voice.

Carnaby ran a nervous hand through his slicked-back hair caked in gel. He paced the small room for a moment, then there was a knock on the door. We both turned and stared at it. Carnaby pulled out his gun.

Abigail L. Marsh

I cleared my throat.

"Who is it?" I asked. There was a momentarily pause where I thought my heart was going to burst out of my chest.

"It's Lenny, I have your drink Mr. Hanson." Came the squeaky voice of the kid.

Growling in frustration I opened the door and snatched the drink from him, but before I could slam the door shut a muscly arm shot past me and grabbed Lenny by his collar. The poor boy went rigid, fear sparking up in his eyes as he realised his mistake. Carnaby yanked him forward, holding him millimetres away from his face.

"Did you hear anything?" He growled. I sighed and sipped the whiskey.

"N, No, Mr. Hanson."

"Good." Carnaby snarled, "Cos if you did, I'd have to kill you."

Lenny nodded. Carnaby let go of his shirt and using a thick hand peppered with golden rings smoothed out the creases.

"Glad we're on the same page, now beat it." He said. Lenny scarpered. Carnaby closed the door and turned back to me.

"Give me that." He said, snatching the half-drunk malt away from me. Misery crept up my chest and sat heavily in my heart.

"Look Carnaby, I need to lay low for a while, with half of London on my arse I'm not going to make it out. Will you help me?" I asked. Carnaby leaned against the radiator and appeared to be thinking.

"If I sort you out with something you have to do something for me." He said eventually. I nodded

"Sure, what?"

"I've got a little red-head, Cyrus. Best cat burglar I've got going at the moment, but she needs someone for a job coming up in a months or so." He said sipping his drink. "I've seen your work, help her and I'll put you up for as long as you need."

I thought about this, but I didn't need long. Without Carnaby, at that moment in time I was as good as caught. I nodded.

"Deal." I said, reaching out and shaking his hand. Carnaby held my hand for a little too long and I glanced up at him.

"Cain's not going to come banging down my door, telling me I kidnapped his kid, is he?"

Oh god, I wished he would.

 I shook my head.

"He's not coming back." I said, forcing emotion away from me. Carnaby let go of me and placed his heavy hand on my shoulder. Glancing into his suddenly soft eyes, I actually thought that he looked like he had some sort of feeling.

"He wouldn't have left you if he'd had the choice kid." He said. There was a knock on the door.

Abigail L. Marsh

"Boss?" A man said lowly.

"What?" Carnaby growled going over to the door and wrenching it open.

"Its time to leave, cops are on the beat." A rough-looking guy with a scar running down his forearm said. Carnaby turned to me.

"Let's go." He said.

I followed him back through to the bar, but instead of going through the main lounge we took a left and went down a narrow hallway and through a fire door. It spat us out at the back of the pub in the car park. I walked in-between Carnaby's two thugs over to a black Merc and got in the backseat.

We sped away into the night. The drive took us about fifteen miles out of London to a village outside south Croydon. It was warm in the back of the car, and the malt and vodka were starting to get to me as we pulled up to a mechanical gate.

I was surprised at how like our settlement in Cromer Carnaby's place looked.

"You can stay in the conversion." Carnaby said as we rolled into the courtyard. I nodded.

"Thank you." I said. The door next to me was opened and I got out into the nigh air. It was getting pretty cold as I followed the men away from the main house, across the courtyard and over to a cottage.

Carnaby pressed the handle down and let me in.

"Up the stairs, first room on the right." He said. "Come over to the house in the morning, someone will be there to talk to you."

"Thanks." I replied stepping into the warm kitchen.

Carnaby closed the door on me as a sinking feeling grew in the bottom of my stomach. *What was I getting myself into?*

"Pull yourself together, Tilly." I said harshly to myself.

The kitchen was dimly lit by a light on in the hallway beyond. I was too tired to look around that night and seeing the staircase at the back of the kitchen I went over to it and climbed. By the time I'd reach the top my eyes were closing, I hadn't slept properly in over twenty-four hours, I'd been almost murdered, captured by and then escaped the police and then managed to find myself in a group of what can only be described as more bloody criminals, all in one single day.

I stumbled into the first door on the right, pushing it open with my body weight and wandering into the room. It was warm in there and the last thing I remember seeing before my head hit the pillow, still fully clothed was a bay window. I had always wanted a bay window.

Chapter Twenty-Seven: Strange New Beginnings

I woke up the next day very late. Still sprawled out on my snowdrift of a bed and still fully clothed. I glanced around the room, seeing it for the first time in daylight. It looked new, as if no-one had touched it since it was built. Everything was made of pine wood. I was laying on the double bed in the centre of the room, A chest of drawers was next to me and a very tall, creepy looking wardrobe that reminded me of the terrifying scene in The Conjuring, stood opposite me the foot of the bed. I sat up groggily and rubbed my heavy night's sleep away from my eyes. The little clock on the nightstand said it was half eleven. Movement outside my door had me on my feet, my door was open a crack, and I cursed myself for not closing it properly. Anyone could have walked in! Creeping over to it I braced myself before grabbing the handle and wrenching it open.

A girl with fiery hair behind it jumped in fright and backed up, crashing into the wall behind her with a bump. I stared at her, thinking she must be the tiny little red-head Carnaby needed me to help. Before I had a chance to say something to her she bolted, running back down the corridor, around the corner and slamming a door shut in another part of the house. I wanted to follow but tripped on a stack of clothes I hadn't seen

Abigail L. Marsh

sitting in front of the door. I looked down at them feeling very bewildered by the whole ordeal.

Back in my room, I dumped the clothes on my bed. There were a few pairs of jeans, a jumper, a couple of tops and a dress that I would not be wearing in March. I lifted my arms and caught a whiff of myself. "You need a shower." I mumbled to myself. So taking a pair of black jeans and a t-shirt and left my room in search of the nearest bathroom. Two doors down, I found it and spent the next hour in the shower behind a door that thankfully had a lock on it.

By the time I was out, dressed and had blowdried my hair, I was starving. I left my room as quietly as possible and found my way along the thickly carpeted hallway back to the top of the stairs.

"Cyrus sit down and finish your lunch." A woman who was clearly at the end of her tether was saying. I crept down a few steps, quietly listening.
"Cyrus, I won't tell you again." The woman snapped. I heard a chair scrape and somebody huff in great disapproval.
"When is that girl coming down?" A girls voice asked.
"When she's ready, now if I have to tell you again Carnaby will be informed."

Abigail L. Marsh

There was silence after that. I stayed silent on the stairs for a moment before my stomach grumbled and I decided to descend the rest.

The kitchen came into view and so did the commotion I had been listening to. There was the little girl that I had seen outside my room sat at the table with her back to me with, a rather strict looking chubby lady wearing an apron watching her, her hands on her hips. They both looked around at me as I came down the last few steps.

"Ahh, nice of you to join us." The boss lady said. I smiled awkwardly. "Hi."

"Hello, you must be starving. Now sit down and I'll make you something to eat, what do you fancy?" She asked. I was looking at Cyrus, who was staring back at me wide eyed. The girl from earlier *was* Cyrus. She was a tiny but I suppose I couldn't really be that shocked, I had been a pretty good burglar at her age.

"Oh umm." I said, tearing my eyes away from her. "Anything, I'm starving." I said.

"Full English it is." The lady said, "I'm Faith by the way."

"Thanks." I said, "I'm uhh Tilly." I said going over to the table and sliding a chair across the stone floor.

"Are you sure about that?" Faith asked as she began getting pots and pans out onto the side. I glanced up at her, confused. "You just don't sound that sure."

I smiled at her.

"Well, that's my name."

"It's a very pretty name." Faith said. I twigged onto her immediately.
She was poking around for information.

"Thank you." I said, "My dog gave it to me."

Cyrus laughed into her glass of water and I had to bite my tongue as
Faith glared round at me.

"You don't have to be so rude." She said.

"Sorry." I replied quickly and looking over at Cyrus winked.

Cyrus finished her lunch long before I had finished mine, but she waited for me and then Faith kicked us outside into the fresh morning air.

"Take Tilly to see Carnaby." She said closing the door behind us.

"Who does she think she is?" Cyrus moaned. "My chuffing mother?"

I laughed.

"What are we supposed to do around here?" I asked, pulling the zip up
on my jumper two ward off the chill.

"Whatever you like really, no-one cares." She shrugged.

"What do you do?"

"Well when I'm not training or revising layouts I sometimes play tricks
on the boys." She said with a glint in her eyes.

I smiled, raising an eyebrow at her. She was the spitting image of me
when I'd been her age.

Abigail L. Marsh

"How long have you been here?" I asked as we wandered across the courtyard towards the house.

She shrugged.

"Long as I can remember, Shaun picked me up when I was about five, my Mum was a druggy, she was no good to me, sold me for money." She said as if it didn't bother her a bit. "He brought me to Carnaby. He didn't like me at first, got really mad that I'd turned up out of nowhere." She added pulling her top down at the back to reveal a scar running down the back of her neck.

"He did that?" I asked, feeling a small sense of dread fire up in my chest.

"A long time ago, he likes me now, thinks I could be the best criminal he's ever seen." She laughed, reaching out for the handle on the green door we'd come to.

I smiled weakly.

"Get in there and when you're done, come round the barn. I wanna show you something." She said, pushing the door open and turning away. I watched her skip across the courtyard and down some steps out of sight.

"Close the damn door!" A man voice snapped. "You're going to let all of March in here."

I turned and stepped inside, closing the door on the cold.

"You must be Tilly Black." The voice said. The man it belonged to sat at a round table on the far side of what appeared to be the kitchen. He had

Abigail L. Marsh

a newspaper in his hand covering his face and a gun lying on the table next to him. Cigar smoke rose it's way up to the ceiling above his head.

"Yes." I said. "Carnaby said that…" I was interrupted.

"How's Mr. Black doing these days?" He asked. I had to swallow my words and bite my tongue hard. That wasn't a subject I wanted to talk about.

"I wouldn't know." I said tightly. The man put his newspaper down and I got my first look at his ugly mug. He looked older than I had expected. Wrinkles covered his time-worn face and his grey eyes the only features that stood out. A pale scar ran down the side of his rugged cheekbone on the right side of his face and there was an aura about him that had me making a mental note to watch my back when I was around him.

He stared at me from across the room laughing a horribly croaky laugh and sat up dropping the newspaper to the table, his white shirt and slacks coming into view.

"You are Tilly Black, though, are you not?" He asked,

"No." I said in a funny tone that even I couldn't grasp. He looked over at me, slightly confused.

"My names just Tilly."

"Well, just Tilly I have something to talk to you about." Carnaby said, coming into the kitchen and making me jump. I glared at the old man at the table. How dare he make me feel belittled!

Abigail L. Marsh

"You're too sensitive." Carnaby said grabbing my arm. I let him lead me out of the room still seething.

We walked down a daylight lit corridor and through a tall oak door sitting at the bottom of a particularly wide staircase. The room was tall and wisps of smoke hung in the beams of light coming through a gap in the curtains high up. There were numerous of paintings hanging on the walls of men on horses, the carpet thick, a swirly green pattern running through it. I was pushed into a chair opposite a large wooden desk piled high with papers. Although I didn't like being thrown around, I held my tongue- now wasn't the time to be antsy.

Carnaby went round to a chair at the other side of the desk and began rifling through some papers. I waited, watching him carefully.
"You are all over the news!" He said suddenly. I swallowed hard as he grabbed a remote off his desk and pointed it at an ancient-looking box, which was smothered in dust. The first thing that came on was channel one, snooker. Quickly it switched over and sure enough on channels two, three, four and five there was some report going on about me across all of them. I could see Carnaby was mad but I'd told him what was going one, nonetheless his jaw was clenched hard, shoulder tense. "And who's this guy?" He asked furiously, chucking a piece of paper at me. It flew off his desk and landed upside down on the thick carpet. I

Abigail L. Marsh

reach down to pick it up. Flipping that piece of paper over was the first thing I did wrong that morning and staring at it a little too long was the second.

"Well, who is it?" He demanded.

I tore myself away from the man in the photo, whose eyes bore a hole into my head and met another pair.

"No-one." I lied.

"Don't lie to me Miss Black." Carnaby said, lighting a thick brown cigar. I sighed, nervously scratching my head.

"He really is no-body." I said.

"One of Cains friends?" Carnaby asked.

"I don't know him!" I retorted. Carnaby glanced up at me. My knuckles turned white as curled against the carvings on the chair.

"What did he do to you?" He asked, twisting in his chair to look at me properly. I reverted my gaze back to the floor.

"Nothing, I don't know him, and he definitely does not know me!" I said forcefully. Carnaby sighed.

"What is your problem? It seems the men involved with you, always get screwed one way or another..."

"Do they?" I asked nonchalantly.

"Yes, they do. There's this guy. God knows what's happened to him." He said, snatching the photo from me and holding it up to see. My insides were screaming as I stared back at my father's printed face. "Half the guys you worked with are in jail, Cains on the run… Harley's dead. You are a bad omen, Miss Black."

"My name is *Tilly*." I choked angrily, standing abruptly. "All these men have screwed me over! All of them! Why should you or anyone else give a damn about them? Let them rot."

Carnaby sat back in his chair, his eyebrows raised.

"It's the line of business you're in." He said matter of factly. "Choose your friends more wisely Tilly, and never fall in love."

"I don't have friends."

He raised his eyebrows.

"That's a very clever move." He said. "Sooner or later people like them, people like me will use all of that against you."

"It's a good job I don't love anyone then, isn't it?" I said. "I don't need anyone."

"So why did you come looking for me?"

I looked up at him.

"I don't want to be this 'princess' anymore. People think they can just discard me and get away with it. I want people to be afraid of me, afraid to hurt me." I continued to stare him down with my fiery eyes. "I want to make the people who hurt me suffer. I want all of them to regret ever

Abigail L. Marsh

meeting me."

"And why do I fit into this plan?"

I shrugged.

"You're the only person I know left."

He nodded.

"Prove it to me."

I knew he was talking about the heist. I nodded.

There was a brief moment's silence before the subject was changed drastically.

"Alright." He said, reaching for his ashtray and knocking the ash from his burning smoke. "That's not what I wanted to talk to you about… I liberated something of yours in the early hours of this morning and I wondered if you wanted him back?"

"Him?" I asked, looking up.

"It's not Cain if that's what you were thinking." Carnaby said. "Bring him in Louis." He shouted. I turned back to the door as it opened. I could hear exciting whining and clattering as a blur of fur ran towards me.

"Max!" I cried excitedly, dropping onto the floor to greet him. He threw himself into my arms and I was engulfed in fluff and a wet nose.

"I thought they'd got you." I spoke into his fur. He gave me a woof in response. When all the excitement was over, I turned to the boss man.

Abigail L. Marsh

"How did you get him?" I asked

"I went back to London last night, grabbed him out of his cage in the back of a police truck." He said. I stared at him wide-eyed.

"Why? Why risk it?"

"Take him back to the cottage, Faith will feed him." He didn't answer my question. I waited for a moment. "Cyrus needs you to revise the notes, so get going."

I stood up taking Max by the collar.

"Oh, and Tilly." Carnaby said. I turned back to him. "Don't... Wander."

"Okay." I said and led Max back through the house. The man from the kitchen was still sitting there reading his newspaper, but I ignored him.

Cyrus was waiting by the steps across the courtyard when I came out. She looked sad, but her face lifted as she saw Max trotting along next to me. He sat down at my feet when I reached her.

"He's a very good dog." Cyrus said, reaching out to stroke Max. He grumbled lowly and she stopped.

"It's alright, Max, she's a *friend*." I said, using the term only for Max. The grumbling stopped immediately and his tails waved backward and forwards.

Cyrus looked up at me, her eyes searching mine for permission.

"He's fine now." I said, crouching down and stroking his head. She patted him gently as the cottage door opened and Faith stepped out.

"Max." She shouted. Max turned and looked at her but didn't move.

"Send him in Tilly." She called. "I'll feed him."

"Go on, Max." I said, giving him a little nudge. He bounded off towards her.

"Come on." Cyrus said, grabbing my hand and pulling me to my feet.

"Where are we going?" I asked as she tugged me down the steps and across a dirt track.

"The barn, where'd you think?" She laughed. She was quite light on her feet, I really should have expected it, but I managed to overtake her as we skidded round a corner and approached a vast red, wooden building.

"That's a big barn." I said as Cyrus hauled the doors open.

"Go in." She said. I obliged and went into the warm dust-filled room. Cyrus followed and closed the doors behind her with a dull bang.

"You work here?" I asked unzipping my coat. It may only have been March, but that barn was warm.

"Yeah... Well, I'm not supposed to. I have a room in the house with all my techy stuff, but I'd rather be in here."

I stared at the young girl thinking she was crazy, but as Carnaby's words echoed around my head I followed her over to some hay bales knowing this was my only chance. A bunch of papers lay messily across the bales, boxes and bags full to bursting sat scattered all over the place. "It's organised chaos." Cyrus laughed at my raised eyebrows. "This is it here." She said pointing to the paper's on a neatly packed bale by the edge of the barn.

"What is all that?" I asked, sitting down on the hay opposite Cyrus. She gave me one of the pieces of paper strewn across it. It was an address and underneath was a screen-grab from google maps.

"The plan." She said.

Chapter Twenty-Eight: Plan in action

It was odd. I'd only been at Carnaby's for a little over six weeks, but it felt like an age had passed. Cain was no longer on the cards. I didn't have the slightest inkling of where he was. There was nothing on the news of his capture so I figured he must be somewhere about, but I was sure by now that he wasn't coming back for me. Carnaby had in a sense taken me under his wing, but I was not treated as Cain had treated me. I wasn't precious to Carnaby, I was replaceable, and that made me want to work for his gratitude. I didn't know how long it was going to last, but I was heading fast for the heist and I didn't have much time at all to be thinking of anything else, not if I was going to prove myself to Carn-

aby and get what I wanted. Cyrus and I trained hard together day and

night, we needed to see how each other worked otherwise we'd never

get in and out alive.

We were in the barn two days before the heist when I realised I didn't

fully understand why we were doing what we were doing. Cyrus was

sprawled out on some hay bails revising the layout of the house, so I

went over and asked her.

"Carnaby's had a long-running issue with Mr. Sykes. He owes a lot of

money to Carnaby, and he won't pay it back."

"Owes money for what?" I asked. I was sure Carnaby wouldn't be send-

ing us in to rob him blind if it wasn't something huge.

"Suits I guess...." Cyrus shrugged. "No-one tells me anything. I go in, I

pick the stuff up and get out. The rest is dealt with."

"Oh." I nodded.

"Now look at this layout, the backdoor around the side of the house is

bound to be guarded by their dogs so when you get there with the audio

dialler, be quiet and shimmy up the drainpipe next door. I'll be on the landing of the second floor with the safe."

I nodded.

"Remind me again why I have to come?" I asked.

Cyrus sighed.

"I can't walk in there with an audio dialler. Mr. Sykes will let me in to have a sleepover with Minx, but he's super tight on security, he checks everyone and everything that comes into his house. I can get in there cos I'm a kid... You know like you did." She said, talking to me as if I was five.

"Yes I'm well aware, but..."

"Tilly, please stop asking questions, you have to bring the audio dialler and bring the loot back here. I have to act like the little girl I am on a sleepover and go back to bed."

I rolled my eyes.

"Okay fine, I was just confirming."

"Okay well we're all set now.. I'm going to go and check we have what we need, go and walk Max or something."

"Go and walk...?" I frowned as I watched Cyrus walk away. "She is far too big for her boots."

Cyrus disappeared the morning of the heist. Mr. Sykes sent a car to pick her up outside the main gates and after that, it was all down to me to get the audio dialler to her. I sat around all day twiddling my fingers, praying to god all would go well and I wouldn't be shot at or arrested. Carnaby called me into his office just before I was leaving. I was dressed from head to toe in black with a small black rucksack, a flashlight and an audio dialler strapped to my belt.

"Don't I need like some sort of weapon?" I asked the boss man who was sat in his chair by the fireplace, smoking a thick cigar and sending plumes of smoke up into the haze filled ceiling.

"You can knock someone out with that torch." He said, cracking his knuckles and sitting forward in his chair. "You ready kid?" He asked.

"Yep, all set, see you back here in a few hours." I said brightly. I felt like the work experience kid going out on her first real job.

"One word of advice Tilly." I looked down into his eyes, listening intently.

"Trust gets you killed."

I frowned at his crypticness.

"Who said that?"

Carnaby looked at his watch.

"Get going."

I turned from Carnaby thinking about his comment and walked back towards the door.

"Good luck." His voice came.

Abigail L. Marsh

I spun back to him, but he had picked up the TV remote and was watching the screen intently.

I closed the office door and left the darkening hallway for the car parked across the courtyard. Sheets of icy rain pelted me as soon as I opened the front door, what a night for it! Pulling my jacket over my head I stepped out. Unfortunately for me, the jacket over my eyes prevented me from seeing pretty much anything and I collided with someone who shoved me hard back into the house. I wrestled with the coat as the door clicked shut tearing it off my head ready to shout at whoever had got in my way, but as my eyes met his I couldn't even whisper.

"Hi Tilly." Cain said. I stared at him, my stomach turning knots. *What the hell?*

"Uhh...Um" I stammered trying to coherently string a sentence together in my head. My eyes wandered his suited body, not a scratch was on him. His hair looked in immaculate order, not even his flick was astray and his shoes shined like the first time he'd bought them.
"Tilly, what are you doing here?"
My head whipped up sharply and looked at him.
"Where the HELL have you been?" I growled at him. Eyebrows raised, he looked taken aback by my anger. The clocked chimed behind me, I

Abigail L. Marsh

was already running late and I didn't have time to slip any further. My life was depending on this. I barged past him, shoving him roughly out of my way, but as had happened before his secure grip was around me and I was yanked back.

"Where are you going?" Cain asked an air to his voice that made me want to smack him down to the ground.

"GET off me!" I snapped. "I have a job, and I'm late!" I said, trying in vain to shake my arm free. He scoffed at me.

"Job? What kind of job? What are you talking about?"

"That's classified information." I snarled and before he had a chance to respond, I stomped hard on his polished shoes leaving a muddy mark and pain behind as I darted out of the house. I splashed across the courtyard and jumped into the back of the four-door black saloon car waiting for me on the drive.

"Where the hell have you been?" Louis shouted over the noise of the pelting rain and car engine.

"I was dealing with something." I snapped slamming the door hard. We set off not a second later, but only got a few feet before I was thrown forward. I looked up sharply to see Cain in the headlight of the car, gun pointing at Louis's head. He was shouting something maniacally.

"Just drive." I said. Louis revved the car to scare Cain. Bad mistake.

Abigail L. Marsh

The force of the bullet shattered the windscreen and punctured Louis's head, spewing blood across me and the leather interiors. I sat stunned for a moment as Louis slumped over the steering wheel and the horn letting out a continuous wail.

"CAIN!" I yelled in angry frustration, slamming my hands on the back of the seat in front. My door was wrenched open and Cains' hand shot in. Through my frantic efforts to boot him away he managed to get a hand on my forearm and yank me back into the rain.

"What the hell are you doing?" I growled colliding with him, the rain was starting to trickle down my back and I was horribly late. Cyrus was relying on me to be there and I wasn't going to be if I couldn't shake Cain.

"We're leaving!" Cain shouted. My brain was struggling to fathom what he was saying as I stared at him.

"No! No you don't get to do that. You don't get to leave me alone for all this time and then walk back in." I yelled. "I'm not going with you."

"What is going on?" I heard a voice shout behind me. I turned to see Carnaby and his men running over to us. "What have you done?" He shouted, grabbing Cain round his throat. I watched in vein at the men tousled with each other, but being on home turf gave Carnaby the upper hand when Ross and the other men joined the fight. Cain by himself was no match. I looked down at my blood-spattered hands as Carnaby knocked Cain to the ground, he turned to me clenching and unclenching

Abigail L. Marsh

his fist.

"Get in the car, go." He said, pushing me back into a second vehicle parked on the the drive. I stared at Cain laying in a puddle of blood as Jake climbed into the diver seat and slammed on the accelerator.

We were in London thirty minutes later.

"Here, get rid of the blood." I heard Jake say as he passed me back a piece of cloth. "But for God's sake do it on the way." My mind had been thrown and I struggled to focus as I climbed out of the car and looked up at the tall house. Thankfully there was no moon standing guard over London that night and as Jake drove away, the rain from Croydon subsided and all that suggested that it had ever been there all at all, was the glisten of water on the pavement. I stood and listened to the silence. It was the kind of night I yearned for, in the stillness I felt like the only person in the world. Shaking Cain from my mind, I quickly hoisted myself over the stone pillar and dropped down quietly on the other side of the metal gates.

The courtyard was empty, but I stuck to the shadows making my way around to the gutter on the far side of the house. It was the easiest one to climb up. Unfortunately the torch had twisted itself around and was now tucked painfully in it's holster digging into my waist. The house was big but I knew the layout by heart, the gutter was by the back door and I made it there without fault. I glanced up at the window I would be entering in by, Cyrus would have left it open for me while she went for the safe hidden behind a painting in the hallway beyond. Checking my watch confirmed I was15 minutes late- Cyrus would be bugging out by now, without the audio dialler she'd just be standing there like a lemon.

Putting one hand in front to the other, I shifted up the guttering feeling the familiar burst of adrenaline that came with the job. Maybe that's why I kept doing it, I much preferred the feeling of excitement and fear that came with the rush, rather than feeling nothing at all. The window ledge came into view and I became aware that something was wrong, the window was wide open but I could see yellow light spewing out into the darkness.

"What the hell is she doing?" I whispered, reaching up and getting a hand firmly on the stone window ledge. Using it I levered myself across, still holding onto the metal guttering and took a quick peek into the room. I couldn't make out much, the light was shining from the hallway beyond. I wasn't sure what to do. Who had turned it on? I waited for a good minute and a half, just watching and waiting, nothing happened. Hoping nothing was awry I used the guttering and kicked off

Abigail L. Marsh

it, scrambling onto the window ledge and crawling unnoticed into the bedroom inside.

The rain had cooled the sudden spring warmth down in the outside world, but inside the house it was warm. Making sure there was no-one in the bed I padded over to the door and cautiously poked my head out. I was wrong, Cyrus wasn't standing there like a lemon. She wasn't there at all. I stepped back into the room and cursed my luck. Assuming she had gone back to bed after I didn't arrive I had to make a decision, do I risk getting caught and find her, or do I risk it all and go home empty-handed. Decisions, decisions, neither of them easy.

Of course, being who I was, I decided to go into the house and find Cyrus, I knew where she would be from the plans and I wasn't going to get chucked out of the team for not delivering.

Taking my torch out of my belt and holding the thin end tightly in my hand, I crept along the hallway feeling very vulnerable.

Minx's room was down the hallway I was in, then I had to hang a right and it was at the far end of that corridor. Creeping along in the dark by myself I felt a horrifying urge to leg it, but I managed to dodge any squeaky floorboards and make it to the door with the words 'Minx' Written on it in purple wooden blocks.

Abigail L. Marsh

Holding my breath, I pushed open the door and went in. Minx had a weird glowing moon next to her bed that shed pink light across the room, so my eyes found Cyrus curled up in her bed on the floor easily. Minx was completely out, so I didn't worry about her as I clasped my hand over Cyrus's mouth. Her eyes flashed open.

"Shh." I said, pressing my finger to my lips. I slowly let go and she sat up glancing around the room.

"Where were you?" she hissed. "I waited for ages…"

"I got held up, now hurry up." I said standing up and offering her my hand, she took it a frown on her face.

We made it back to the safe unscathed and I lifted the photo off the wall, passing Cyrus the little black machine that would help her unlock it. It was a painstaking 3 minutes and 40 seconds until there was a satisfying click and the safe opened. Cyrus grabbed the handle and held it open while I shined my torch in.

"Whoah." Cyrus said, reaching in and taking out a diamond necklace.

"Right just be careful." I said. "There could be sensors or something…"

Before I could finish my sentence the hallway was filled with a loud screeching bell and the light inside the safe turned red. Cyrus spun around and looked down the corridor as a bedroom door was opened. Thinking fast, I shoved my hand in the safe and grabbed a handful of stuff, tossing it into my backpack and zipping it up tightly. I slammed the door of the safe shut and watched Cyrus freeze.

"Move." I hissed, grabbing her shoulders and shoving her into the bedroom I had come in through.

"Who's there?" I heard a man shout. "I have a gun."

"Get out." I snapped hoisting Cyrus up to the window.

"I'm supposed to be in bed." She panicked.

"Not now you're not, climb." I instructed. With little other option, she began sliding down the guttering, one foot after the other. I heard the sirens in the distance as I reached the ground.

"The alarm goes to the police station." Cyrus recalled as I turned to face her.

"Just run." I said. We took off, sprinting towards the back fence. I clasped my hands together and launched Cyrus over before hauling my self over. We landed on a deserted back street, the only thing there a cat with yellow eyes watching us. We bolted down the street, took a right and appeared onto the main road.

"Bayswater road." Cyrus said.

"Hyde Park?" I asked.

She nodded.

Watching for traffic, we raced across the road and vaulted the black metal spikes of the fence, disappearing into the trees.

Abigail L. Marsh

"Do you think Sykes will split on us?" I asked

"No, we know that. Once he finds out who it is he'll dismiss it all."
Cyrus said. "He knows what will happen if he doesn't." I grimaced, I
had a pretty good idea as well. We half walked, half jogged across the
park, crossed over a bridge and eventually stopped just behind the trees
closest to Park lane on the other side of the park.

"Now where?" I asked. Cyrus looked around looking lost, "Come on,
you know London." I persisted.

"We can't go home." Cyrus said "The Police will pursue us tonight,
that's what Carnaby always says. If things go wrong, never go home,
lay low."

"Great." I tutted. "Well if they really are following us we can't stay
here, this will be the first place they look."

I noticed Cyrus was shivering and softened my tone.

"I don't know anyone in London Cyrus. Is there anywhere, or anyone
that could help us tonight?" I asked.

Cyrus was staring out into the lights of park street seemingly mes-
merised by them.

"Whitechapel." She said suddenly. She turned to me. "There's a place, a
B&B that Carnaby uses sometimes. They'll take in anyone who needs
help... If you know what I mean"

I nodded.

Abigail L. Marsh

"They take in criminal reprobates."

Cyrus raised an eyebrows in confusion.

"They look after criminals and don't tell the police. " I said dumbing it down for her. She nodded enthusiastically.

"Yeah, Mrs. Bassey is an old convict, and Cameron's..." Cyrus stopped short.

"Cameron's what?" I pressed.

"He's, well he's nice." She said, sounding unsure. A second later a police siren had us running for Marble Arch Station.

Chapter Twenty-Nine: The Grange

When we arrived on Fieldgate street almost an hour later and I realised what Cyrus had been talking about. We rang the doorbell and took a few paces back. It was a cute little place on the outside, a mix of two ter-raced houses, a rusty old sign hanging from the wall with 'The Grange' painted on it, in years old chipped paint. More to the point it was one in a million guest houses in London and we would be safe there for the night.

Cyrus, who was now wearing my jacket shivering away next to me smiled, when a doddery old lady opened the door.

Abigail L. Marsh

"Mrs.Bassey." She said in a sweet, butter wouldn't melt kind of voice that made me sick.

"Rachel?" The doddery old lady said peering over the rim of her glasses.

"Yes Mrs. Bassey, this is my friend Rose. We've found ourselves in a spot of bother, could we come inside?" Cyrus continued.

"Of course you can, can't have two girls like you running around London on a night like tonight, sirens everywhere, you'd think there was a mass murderer on the loose."

I looked at Cyrus slightly un-nerved as we were led through to a reception desk. My nose shrivelled as I took in the scent of wet dog and prunes… More prunes.

"We need a bed for the night, Mrs. Bassey." Cyrus said. "Is there a room free?"

We were led up some rather rickety wooden stairs that opened out onto a long dark corridor.

"It's late my lovelies, get some rest and come down for your breakfast in the morning." The old crone said, letting us into a small room. At least it had a double bed. I was exhausted, and my adrenaline was starting to fade. Cyrus shut the door and locked it tight before putting a chair in front of it for extra measures. I closed the curtains on the bright lights of the city and collapsed on the bed.

Abigail L. Marsh

It was a long night, Cyrus tossed and turned and I kept hearing sirens in my head, which accompanied the sounds of the springs in the bed whenever either one of us moved. By morning my head was heavy and my eyes bleary. Cyrus was awake at seven; bright-eyed and bushy-tailed.

"Don't even start." I said as she opened her mouth to say something. I took a long shower in the grimy en-suite and then threw my clothes on from the night before.

Cyrus was looking at the breakfast menu when I came back through feeling a little more human.

"Come on, it's almost eight, they'll stop serving and I'm starving."

"I don't know if you've noticed." I said, "But we haven't got any money, so unless you're planning on stealing the lot then…"

"Cameron will give it to us for free." She said, sliding my black jacket over her dark onesie. I looked her up and down. Thank god the girl had the presence of mind when on a job, to wear something at least half sensible and some sturdy slippers, in case it all went tits up. It had done for the night, but I knew deep down we'd have to find her something else to get home in.

"You keep talking about this Cameron, who is he?"

Abigail L. Marsh

"One of Carnaby's pals, he lives here, kind of like an agent that lives in the field, but Mrs. Bassey lets him help out in the kitchen when money is short."

I nodded disinterestedly. Now I thought about it, I was hungry as well.

"We need to find you some clothes, we'll get spotted a mile away with wondering around in a onesie and slippers."

"I'll ask Mrs. Bassey…" She began.

"No, just." I said rattily. "Just leave it to me."

Cyrus's eyes widened, and she held her hands up.

I sighed and rubbed my head. I needed an aspirin.

"I'm sorry." Cyrus said, the soft tone of her voice had me looking up. She was upset. I remembered quickly that she was just a kid and all this drama was probably scaring her.

"Come on, let's go and get some breakfast." I said in a kinder tone. I took her hand and pulled her out of the room. It was still dark and dingy in the hotel due to the lack of windows, but we trooped on down the stairs and opened the doors to the breakfast room.

I stopped dead as I scanned the few guests in there. Jamie and Lucas were sat there bold as brass, Jamie had a bowl of Shreddies and Lucas was reading the Daily Telegraph.

"Go and sit down." I said to Cyrus.

Abigail L. Marsh

"Why?" She said.

"Just find us a seat." I said, pushing her in the opposite direction.

Jamie looked up from his shreddies as I walked towards them. I didn't know whether to laugh or cry. He tapped the newspaper in Lucas's hand with his fork, and Lucas popped out from behind it.

"Tilly." He said, smiling when he saw me. "You're a sight for sore eyes."

"Am I?" I asked tightly.

"I told you she'd be pissed off." Jamie said, I looked at him in confusion. "We saw you come in late last night; we assumed you'd be down for breakfast." He explained.

"Where the hell did you go? I almost got shot by that imbecile Harley."

"Yeah, but you didn't." Lucas said, still smiling. "Who knew you'd be able to make it out from under Cains watchful eye."

I squinted at him.

"Where've you been?" Jamie asked.

"Here and there, you spoke to Cain since?" I asked.

Jamie nodded.

"Spoke to him a few days back, nothings very safe at the moment, so it was only brief."

"What did he say?"

"He said he was looking for you." Lucas said.

Abigail L. Marsh

"Yeah, I figured when he turned up last night and now I've got the whole of London police force on my arse."

"You saw Cain?" Lucas asked, shocked.

"Yeah, why? Haven't you?"

"No-ones seen him, he's been AWOL since that night."

I shrugged.

"He showed up yesterday."

"Well you must be pretty special to that guy kid." Jamie smiled. "For him to risk coming back to London for you."

"Yeah well I don't need him. He screwed me over big time on a job last night."

"Oh, that was you?" Jamie asked slurping a mouthful of milk off his spoon.

"What was me?"

"All over the news you were last night." Jamie said.

"My face?" I gasped.

"No no, just the job but it was dropped, some geezer, Sykes, dropped it all."

"I told you he would." A voice came from behind me. I jumped and spun around. It was just Cyrus.

"Jeez! I told you to go and get a table."

"Who are these guys?" She asked, leaning on me like a four-year-old.

"No-one." I said.

"But they look like some…"

"Cyrus!" I snapped. She jumped and looked up at me, her eyes wide. "Go and order some breakfast you've been whining about it all morning."

Her face fell, and she ran away. Rolling my eyes I felt a twinge of guilt.

"Who's that?" Lucas laughed.

"Just a kid I work with, she's great under pressure, but she's a kid and you know…"

"Kids have that awful habit of being kids." Jamie smirked winking at Lucas.

"I was not that annoying."

"Wanna bet?" Lucas laughed. "Cain! Lucas hit me, waa, waaa."

"I was eight and you broke my arm." I said acidly.

Whilst Lucas finished his laughing fit, Jamie looked at me seriously.

"What's your plan?" He asked

"I'm going back to base with Cyrus." I said.

"Wheres base?"

"Croydon." I said not wanting to give too much away in case Carnaby found out I'd been blabbing about him.

"You went to Carnaby?" Jamie said, slightly taken aback. I winced.

"Yeah, Rick told me to…"

"You saw Rick?"

"Yes, why?"

"He's dead." Lucas said matter of factly.

"What?" I gasped.

"Knife to the throat, the day after we got back."

"But…I saw him that afternoon. He was with a Russian girl at the suit shop."

Lucas shrugged.

"Must have been one of his miss's… Carnaby's, not Ricks." He clarified.

"Jesus." I sighed.

"Listen." Jamie said. "If you're with Carnaby, be careful. He's not all he seems and if it fits with him, he'll stab you in the back. Things can never go back to the way they were before. Cain is your best bet out of here, he cares about you. Find him and get yourselves as far away from London as you can. You guys can settle down somewhere and live off the money we've made." He said.

"Well, what about you? What are you doing?"

Jamie shrugged.

"Who knows where the wind will take us, but the important thing is you find Cain and get yourselves out while the going's good. Do you understand?"

Lucas agreed.

"Will I see you guys again?" I asked, feeling a touch nostalgic.

"Who knows, we have to bounce anyway, been here a few days. We're heading up north and getting out of the country." Lucas said. Then he looked at Jamie, who nodded.

"We could take you with us if you want?" Lucas said.

I admit the thought was tempting. I was angry and tired, and they could have solved most of my issues, but something was holding me back. I glanced over at Cyrus sitting at a table across the room, head in her hand and plate of bacon and eggs in front of her.

"I can't abandon her." I said. "But good luck, really and I'll…"I stopped short, doubting I would see them again.

The boys nodded understanding.

"Any chance you could lend us twenty quid?" I smirked, knowing full well it would never be repaid. Jamie gave me a wry smiled and after opening his wallet handed over some notes.

"Thanks." I smiled pocketing them.

"Well good luck." I said and with that they stood up. Lucas folded his newspaper under his arm and they walked away, looking like two ordinary people going out to do something totally ordinary. I watched them leave through the doors at the far side of the room, then feeling somewhat saddened by their exit returned my attention to Cyrus and sat down opposite her.

"Hey." I said. She looked up at me with teary eyes.

'I'm sorry if I'm being a bit crabby." I begun.

"I don't want to get caught." She sobbed into her eggs. I sighed. "They'll be angry I didn't…"

"I won't let that happen, okay?" I said softly. Cyrus stopped talking as I dragged my chair around to the side of the table closest to her and pulled her into a hug.

"We're going to eat this, find you some clothes then go home, okay?"

"Okay." She said, sniffing loudly in my ear.

"All right, just breathe, we're going to get out of this."

Chapter Thirty: Left for Dead

The journey back to Croydon was sickening. The tubes were all delayed, grumpy tourists jammed up the busses, and nosey commuters kept wondering why we were dressed so appallingly as we fought to make it home. I didn't dare call Carnaby for fear of making him even madder than he was already going to be.

I stumbled up the steps of the house late that evening, with Cyrus nervously loitering behind me. I couldn't believe we'd made it back. I rapped on the door hard and waited, nothing happened. I banged again. "Maybe they're all out?" Cyrus said in a decidedly unhopeful tone. I glanced down at her, she was wearing a knitted jumper with a cat on it that Mrs.Bassey had said was specially made for her. I had laughed to the point of crying when she put it on, but now the joke was old and I was starting to understand what Jamie had meant. Were we falling head-first into a trap?

"Yeah, probably." I said as brightly as I could. Pulling Cyrus down the steps we walked around to the back of the house, through a gated arch-way and to the back door. I knocked on that. No- one came.

The cottage was the same; the garages were empty of cars, they'd all left.

"Cowards." I muttered looking through the window at the empty house. "They must have moved somewhere else after the police started poking around, everything's gone. For god's sake, why did we mess up so bad-ly!" I said, turning and storming back across to the cottage. I picked up

Abigail L. Marsh

a brick and lobbed it through the window. Cyrus grabbed my arm in horror,

"What are you doing?" She exclaimed

"Getting my stuff." I said, picking up a stick and sliding it around the window form, knocking out all the shards of glass, before climbing through.

Cyrus followed me somewhat cautiously, and we went up to our rooms. Most of my stuff was there. Shoving a few clothes into the bottom of my backpack, I grabbed a few rounds of ammunition and gun from the drawers and a took my passport and bank card from their home in the floorboards, before looking at Max's old collar on the floor. I picked it up and studied it, his name in shiny golden letters against the navy blue leather before shoving it in my bag. I hoped to God he was safe with them wherever they were. I went over to the window and looked out at the garden, wondering how long they had been gone, an hour? A day? My eyes were drawn to the smoke smouldering from the bins that sat a little way down the garden. Poking out of the closest one was a bright pink top I had seen Cyrus wear. *Poor kid, they'd left her.* I turned to see her standing in the doorway, looking tired and miserable.

"They've taken it all." She suddenly sobbed. I slung my backpack over my shoulder and went over to her.

"They're probably waiting for you somewhere then." I lied. "Come on let's get out of here." I said gently turning her around and pushing her out of my room. We went down to the kitchen and she dried her eyes with the back of her sleeve whilst I opened the well stocked fridge and grabbed some snacks.

"Cyrus, where does Faith keep her money?" I asked, closing the fridge.

"In the jar behind the fireplace." She said without a doubt.

"You're a good spy." I grinned going over to the fireplace and crouching down. She gave me a teary smile as I pulled the back off the hearth and stuck my hand into the black hole. Sure enough, there was a jar in there. I pulled it out, hoping against all hope there was some cash in there. There was! Four £50 notes and five £20 notes.

"Awesome!" I said, shoving the cash into my bag and zipping it up.

"Right!" I said brightly turning around and smiling my best encouraging smile. Cyrus was eating from a packet of biscuits she'd found.

"Hey! Save some for me." I said, groaning as I got to my feet. I dropped back to the floor almost immediately cracking my knee painful as I did. Across the courtyard a man dressed in black was wondering about holding a gun up as if he had the skills to use it.

"Get down!" I said, grabbing Cyrus's arm and yanking her to the floor. Her eyes widened in fear.

"What?"

I crawled over to the window and poked my head up praying it wasn't about to get blow off. The man standing by the side gate was joined by another. I didn't recognise either of them, but they didn't look like peo-

Abigail L. Marsh

ple you wanted to trifle with, massive muscles and suited down to the pristine cufflinks on their shirt sleeves. You didn't mess with suited men unless you knew, without a doubt you could win. Very quietly, I un-zipped my bag and pulled my gun out. I singled for Cyrus to come over.

"They don't look like cops." I whispered.

"No... The war?" Cyrus said. I nodded. If we were right and the war had started, the deserted house had nothing to do with us messing up. "Haha! Carnaby's running scared! Get Mr. Giannaville on the phone." I heard one of the men say confirming our thoughts. Cyrus sat back on her heels, jaw clenched.

"Reckon he's gone to Rapsgate?" The other man asked.

"Yeah, most likely... Get the boss for god sake!"

I peeked over the rim of the window and watched the men disappear round the back of the house.

"Right let's go." I whispered. Silently we climbed back out of the win-dow.

"Where are we going?" Cyrus whispered as was jogged quietly towards the open gates. I looked up the street and almost laughed at their stupid-ity. The goons had left their car parked just outside on the main road and as we got to it, I was ecstatic to realise they'd left if with the keys in.

"Your chariot ma'am." I said, opening the passenger seat door.

Cyrus climbed in and we were flooring it down the road before they'd had a chance to stop us.

"Where are we going?" Cyrus asked as I turned sharply onto the main road at the end of the street.

"What's Rapsgate?" I asked, looking over at her. She reached out and fiddled with the dials on the car.

"Hey, dude, what's Rapsgate?" I asked again, she didn't answer and began pressing buttons.

"HEY, Cyrus! Stop, we don't know what this car has in it! You could eject yourself out, or blow us up." I said grabbing her hands and shoving her back against the seat, she glowered at me before turning abruptly away and pulling my dirty jacket over her face. I sighed in frustration, whoever said 'never work with children or animals' was a goddamn genius. There was a satnav built into the car, and I typed in Rapsgate.

"Two hours and twenty-eight minutes to your destination." The satnav said. "Turn left in 500 yards."

We took a left and drove along for a few hundred yards before I heard Cyrus crying softly. I looked over at her curled up against the door and my hard expression softened.

Abigail L. Marsh

"Cy, come on, it's fine." I said. She didn't respond. "Cy, why are you crying?" I asked, she'd never once cried before, not properly. The jacket fell away from her face and she looked around at me.

"There's a reason they left without us." She said shakily.

"They left because I messed up, I was late and the heist fell apart." I said adamantly. "And this stupid war. Giannaville chased them away." She shook her head.

"Tilly that's not why! They've been planning this for a long time, that heist went wrong for a reason, you were late because Carnaby wanted you to be late."

"And why's that?" I asked, completely bewildered.

She sighed.

"They've been trying to get rid of me for a while now, they…"

"Cyrus.."

"No, listen. They needed a way to get rid of me, I…The police are getting close to.…"

"Why?" I asked as the satnav told me to take the next right, I obediently took it. Cyrus looked over at me glisten of fear shimmering in her eyes.

"What have you done Cyrus?" I asked in a low warning tone.

"Tilly… My names not Cyrus."

I didn't know what Cyrus was about to tell me, but I could tell from her deadpan expression that is was not going to be good.

Abigail L. Marsh

"Well, what is it?" I asked as if it was the most important question I could ask at that moment.

"Ella."

"Why does everyone call you Cyrus?" I asked as we swerved around a particularly tight corner.

"Because that's my undercover name."

"Undercover..." Once I'd realised what she'd said my brain stopped. I slammed on the breaks jerking us onto the grass verge roughly.

"What are you talking about?" I said sharply.

"I'm not Carnaby's secret weapon. I'm the governments."

I stared at her, wide-eyed.

"So all this?" I said gesturing to the past two months of my life. "It's all an act...Do you know who I am? You know I'm a runaway? You know..." She had been nodding through my questions.

"But then, does..."

"Charlie knows exactly where you are. He has done since the first day I had lunch with you."

I shook my head incredulously.

"But, you're a kid!"

"I'm twelve!" She retorted. "You were way younger than me."

"No." I said. "There is absolutely no way you could pull this off, just no."

Abigail L. Marsh

"I'll prove it." she said.

"With what?" I asked, looking around the car for something that would corroborate her story.

The pained expression on her face proved she had no means of identification. I shook my head.

"See this is it." I said. "If you were working for the police, why would you want to prove it, why would you want to infiltrate a London crime ring and then just sit there? Why would you be telling me all this?" I asked.

"For the same reason, you did." Cyrus spoke softly.

"What are you talking about?"

"I have no family. I was tossed from one foster home to another, no -one wanted me. I spent my life shoplifting, vandalising, robbing houses, people. I got picked up when I was younger, it was young offenders or some special police programme for me. It was a dog eat dog world. You did what you had too. A police officer took a liking to me, told me about a job, going undercover, doing a job no adult could do, so I jumped on it. They delivered me to the gates and left there, to show Carnaby what I could do. He hated me at first, but no-one was coming for me, why would they? That was three years ago. The detective… Got bored and I was left hanging, but I couldn't just leave, that would blow everything out of the water, and I wouldn't be safe anywhere, and neither would you. An MI5 agent picked it up last year."

Abigail L. Marsh

"What do you mean, I would be safe? What has any of this got to do with me?" I asked.

"Well..." She began, looking sheepish.

"Wait, wait, wait." I interrupted. "What have you been doing since the detective left you? I mean for a start they don't do that, but we'll just airbrush over that for now because you're just joking, right?. None of this makes any sense."

Cyrus shrugged.

"I'm not lying... I became one of them." She said. "A criminal. I fitted into the lifestyle, I did what you did, I built myself a family from the ground up."

"And when the agent picked you up?" I said allowing myself to enter-tain the story.

"My com started beeping one day, I thought I'd gotten rid of it, but it was in the crawl space hidden behind my bed, I picked it up... It was a janitor in the basement of MI5. He'd found the detectives old com. I told him what had been going on, we'd talk for hours. I never knew his name, I think he just wanted to hear the stories and I didn't have any-thing better to do so I told him everything. Next thing I know there's an MI5 agent on the line wanting to know what the hell I was still doing here. So I told him my ride never arrived." She smiled. "He didn't find it so funny. Anyway, the case was re-opened, nothing happened for a while, they just wanted to be updated, they're building a case against

Abigail L. Marsh

Carnaby and Henry. Nothing exciting happened until you turned up and now my coms always beeping, a lot more people are involved."

"Who is Henry Giannaville." I asked.

"He runs the rival gang in Manchester, in this particular strand. Word is he's going to make a move on our lot, and when he does the police are going to arrest them all."

"And then what happens?" I asked.

"We get over to Rapsgate's, demand they take us back in, watch what happens and when something does we lead MI5 there." she said.

I frowned.

"You wanna blow your family out of the water- so to speak?"

This was clearly quite a difficult question for such a young girl, but when her eyes met mine, they had the answer.

"I don't have a *real* family. I'll get placed on another mission, like this one and I'll begin again." She said.

"And me?"

"You go home." She said.

"Home?" I laughed. "What's that?"

"With Robert and your sisters, in America." Cyrus said very matter of factly. I almost choked on the air I was breathing.

"How do you know that?"

Cyrus smiled.

"I have my ways." She said, smiling.

"What do you mean, home with Robert and my *sisters*?" I asked, suddenly on guard.

Cyrus looked at me uneasily.

"I didn't want to tell you." She spoke softly.

"Tell me what?"

"I didn't because I was so afraid I couldn't trust you not to leave." She stopped, but I didn't speak. I waited for her to continue.

"Autumn's gone back to live with your Dad and your other sister."

I sat back in my seat, slightly dumbfounded.

"Cyrus, Ella, whatever you're name is, My Dad he's an…" I faltered, not sure how to explain it to a child.

"An alcoholic?" Cyrus said.

"Yes." I said, relieved she already knew. "We're not allowed to live with him; we don't even know where he is." I said.

"I do." Cyrus said. "He was waiting for you the day you ran from Charlie. He was waiting for you just downstairs, he was right there."

"What?" I breathed barely able to hear my own thoughts as they fought over each other to be heard. I glanced in my rearview mirror and saw two men dressed in black running towards the car, guns poised. I pushed Cyrus's head down and rammed the car into first gear. The wheels spun agonisingly in the mud, spraying it across the road and waisting precious seconds that I thought might have us killed, before

Abigail L. Marsh

shooting off down the road as if a rocket had been shoved up our rears. There was a loud ping as a bullet hit the boot of the car, but I pressed the accelerator to the floor and we were out of range a second later.

We drove in complete silence, only the satnav breaking the quiet with her occasional directions. My mind was all jumbled up. I had no idea Robert was back and had been waiting for me. That Isabelle was now living with him and Callie in America. How had I not seen that Cyrus wasn't who she said she was? How on earth was I going to break it to her that I'd have to put a stop to her plans, her life mission, because I couldn't watch Cain go to jail, not even if he could do it to me.

It got dark in no time at all. I grabbed a coat from the back seat, draping it over a sleeping Cyrus. Rapsgate wasn't somewhere I wanted to go. Whatever was waiting for us was daunting, but we didn't have any-where else. I had to find out where they had taken Cain and Max and why he had left me. I had to find out what was going on between the rival gangs. Maybe I could put an end to this, perhaps it would carry on and I'd get swept up into another life of crime, either way, as night closed in Rapsgate was my new destination and I was hurtling towards it as fast as I possibly could.

Chapter Thirty-One Rapsgate

Rapsgate turned out to be a tiny hamlet in the middle of the Cotswolds. Regrettably, I had to wake Cyrus up when we got there because there was just nowhere I could see Carnaby hiding out. We took a narrow winding road away from the hamlet and a few minutes later pulled up outside the gates of a long driveway.

"Okay, ditch the car, and we'll walk up." Cyrus said.

"Absolutely not. This is the nicest most expensive car I've ever driven." I said. "Just wait here."

I got out and ran over to the gate. It had a keypad on it with a button to call the house. I pressed it.

"Hello?" Came a slightly nervous voice.

"Well, well well." I said. "Look who's been promoted. It's Tilly and Cyrus, let us in Michael." I said.

"Tilly? Bloody hell kid, you scared us. What are you doing here?"

"Open the bloody gates Mike, and I'll tell you." I said.

"Right, okay."

There was a mechanical scraping noise and the gates moved. I climbed back in the car and looked at Cyrus.

"The story?" I asked.

"We made it back, no-one was there so we presumed they'd all gone to Rapsgate to avoid any connection to the house." Cyrus said. "We hijacked a car that was parked at the front of the house, we don't know where it came from and we drove over hoping they would be here." She said. "And that's it, we don't know anything about anything else, okay? If they think those men working for Giannaville know we're here, they will do a runner."

I nodded at the twelve-year-old.

 I edged the car up the driveway and parked it in front of a big wooden door. An overhead light came on as Cyrus unbuckled her seatbelt. It wasn't much warmer this side of the country and I was thankful when the door opened and Mike let us into the house.

"What is this place?" I asked, looking at the stone walls with huge tapestries hanging off them.

"Carnaby's holiday home, he's a stickler for an old house and some clay pigeon shooting in the summer." Mike said.

"I would never have known." I said as Cyrus slipped her hand into mine. Knowing what I did, it felt odd that she would act so childishly, but I realised she was playing the part again.

"Where the hell did you guys go?" I asked suddenly to Mike.

"Sorry Tilly, we had to get out." He said apologetically. "When the heist went wrong it was a case of every man for himself."

"The police came knocking?" I asked.

Abigail L. Marsh

Mike nodded.

"But not just them, Henry's lot were on the prowl, we'll be lucky to get the house in Croydon back, it's a complete wreck."

"We know." I said. "We came looking for you."

Mike acted surprised he led us through to the kitchen.

"You went back to Croydon?" He asked. "Did you see anyone?" He asked.

"No." I lied, following Cyrus's story. "Where is everyone?" I asked realising the big kitchen was empty, the only movement came from a flickering fire and the arms of a ticking clock.

"Bed mainly, there are only a few people here and there's no chance we are leaving the house until everything calms down." Mike said, opening the fridge. "Want some food?"

I had always liked Mike, he didn't deserve to be stuck in their lifestyle. I watched him as I ate my ham sandwich, wondering what had gone so wrong for him.

A door banged somewhere beyond the kitchen and I turned around to see who it was as the door was opened. Carnaby strode in and got the shock of his life when he saw us.

"Alright, Carnaby." Mike said. "Look who's showed up."

Carnaby's face had gone all twisted and white.

Abigail L. Marsh

"What are you doing here?" He asked quickly.

"Well we managed to get away from London after a day, but you'd gone, the whole place was all shut up" I said.

"Giannaville came around, took us by surprise we didn't have a choice." Carnaby said.

"Well, Cyrus said you may be here… Thought it was worth a try." I shrugged, then reached for my bag and routed around in it. I pulled out a long diamond necklace, a ring with a sparkly blue sapphire in it and wad of cash, purposefully avoiding Cyrus's angry eyes I stood up and went over to him.

"There you are boss." I said, dropping the stuff in his open hands. "Told you I wouldn't let you down, now is Cain here? I have a bone to pick with him."

Carnaby looked from the loot in his hands to me, to Cyrus and Mike then back to the loot.

"He's in a room upstairs, the second one on the left." He said bewildered. I nodded and set off.

"But Tilly." He said suddenly, his tone making me turn. "He took heavy fire when Giannaville descended, he's not doing so well, don't expect much from him." He said. My heart dropped, what?

"And your dog..."

"What?" I said, turning back to him.

"We tried to patch him up on the way over here, but there was nothing we could do."

"He's dead?" I asked tears clouding my vision.

Carnaby nodded.

"He's out in the shed, we were going to... bury him in the morning." He said. I didn't believe for a second that he was going to do that, but at least they had brought him here. Cyrus ran over and threw her arms around me.

"What happened to him?" I choked.

"He took a bullet for your pal upstairs." Mike said.

I'd forgotten about Cain and pulling away from Cyrus I practically flew up the stairs, taking three or four at a time and bursting through his bedroom door.

At the back of the room pressed up against a wall, there was a double bed. A small bedside lamp illuminated a ghostly pale figure propped up by pillows, his eyes closed.

"Cain?" I whispered, wiping tears from my cheeks as I stumbled over to the bed. When he didn't move, I said it louder. "Cain wake up."

I climbed onto the bed and knelt as close to him as I could get. His skin was tinged with grey, the bottom half of his torso wrapped in a bloody bandage, beads of sweat rolled down his forehead, but he was so still I feared the worst.

Abigail L. Marsh

"Cain!" I said a hitch in my voice, "Please wake up." I sobbed, reaching out and touching his bare chest.

"What?" He grumbled. My heart rate spiked as I sat forward on my knee's. His eyes flickered open and a small smile appeared on his face. "Princess."

"What, what happened?" I stuttered through uneven breaths.

"Took a bullet or two." He croaked. "Don't worry I'll be right as rain in a few days."

"No, no, you need a hospital, Cain." I begged. "Please, you're gonna die otherwise."

He wavered in and out of consciousness for a moment, his head lolling to the right.

"Cain." I said with a firmer tone. "You need a hospital." I pulled his head back around gently and with trembling fingers forced his eyes open. It took a moment to get him back.

"No, Tilly, we can't risk it, just get me some water." He said. I shook my head.

"No! This time it's my choice and I'm calling an ambulance." I said, taking my backpack off and turning to go and find help .

"Tilly wait...Look." I watched as Cain reached for his filthy jacket laying on the bed next to him. I pulled it over.

"What are you looking for?" I asked as he strained, face contorting in pain whilst he struggled to locate whatever it was he was searching for.

"In the inside pocket." He finally sighed, giving up and dropping the jacket next to me.

Taking it from him, I reached into the inside pocket where sat a piece of plastic safely tucked away. Bringing it into the light I realised that it was my real bank card.

"Just in case." Cain wheezed.

"You're not going to die." I said shoving it into my bag. "I promise. I'll be back." Tucking the bag under the bed I headed for the door.

"Tilly." His croaky voice came from across the room as I reached it. I looked back at the greying man propped up in the four-poster bed.

"I shouldn't have left you. I'm sorry."

I nodded not knowing what else to do. Then without wasting anymore valuable seconds I scrambled out of the room and disappeared into the corridor to find a phone, Cains calls not deterring me. I finally found one on a dresser at the top of the stairs. I grabbed it and punched in 999.

"Tilly, what are you doing?" Cyrus asked coming out of nowhere and snatching the phone out of my hands.

"Cyrus he's gonna die." I growled trying to snatch it back, but she dodged expertly and stepped away.

"Tilly think about the bigger picture." She whispered harshly. "There is nothing they can do at this moment, if you call it in now, we'll lose everything."

I shook my head grimacing.

Abigail L. Marsh

"Cain has been there for me, for as long as I can remember. You think you know me because you've kept tabs on me? Because you think you saved me? You don't know anything about any of this. You *can't* save me because *you* are *just* a kid Cyrus."

Cyrus swallowed this attack like a saint, only her eyes giving away the sudden pain I had inflicted with my sharp tongue.

"I'm sorry Cyrus. There's no winning here. Why don't you just get out while you can?"

She shook her head.

"I can't let you do this Tilly." Her voice came back stronger and more fierce than I thought it would, I had to change tactics.

"What are you going to do to stop me?" I asked. "Look at you."

She may have known her stuff, but so did I and she was much much smaller than me. I made a lunge and knocked her off balance, but she was quick to regain it.

"Tilly stop." She snapped.

"I don't want to hurt you. Just leave." I snapped back, but she was stubborn. Just like me.

Using my height as an advantage, I loomed above her, grabbing her shoulders and spinning her around, I managed to get an arm around her neck, securing the win.

"Give me it Cyrus." I said using my free hand to finally wrestle the phone from her. She tried her hardest to squirm out of my grasp, but I

Abigail L. Marsh

wasn't giving up. I didn't want to hurt her, I really didn't but Cain was my priority. I managed to grab the phone and using the arm I had around her, I flung her away from me. As her grip on the telephone released she collided with a door frame, knocking her head and falling to the floor. I stared at her for a moment, she was just laying there, motionless, her eyes closed.

My hands shook as I turned away from her.

"Hello?" A tiny voice was speaking from the other end of the phone. I realised quickly that during the fight, one of us must have pressed the connection button.

"Hello, hello?" I said.

"Are you alright?" A worried voice said at the end of the phone. "What was that noise?"

"Is this 999? I need an ambulance, someones been shot." I said.

"Alright honey, what's your name, have you got an address?" A woman asked.

"Somewhere in Rapsgate, but I don't know where…" I stuttered

"Okay, hold on." She said. "I'm going to pinpoint your exact location."

"Okay." I said, staring over the banister at the floor below, praying no-one was listening.

Abigail L. Marsh

"Okay honey I've got you. What's your name, who's been…" The line suddenly went dead.

"Hello?" I said. "Hello?" Yanking the phone away from my ear I stared at it in horror, the screen was blank.

"No." I snapped shaking the device hard, as if somehow violence would bring it back to life.

"Tilly just wait a little longer." I heard a voice say behind me. I spun around to see Cyrus standing up, one hand on her head where she had hit it and next to her on the floor lay the disconnected phone socket.

"Cyrus!" I cried angrily.

"What's going on?" I heard Carnaby's voice shout from the floor below, I stopped yelling at Cyrus and went down the stairs, Carnaby was stood at the foot of them with a face like thunder.

"Cains sick and no-ones doing anything about it?" I demanded.

"There is nothing we can do." He said.

"There's plenty we can do, why don't we call somebody?" I suggested arms falling in fury.

His eyes widened.

"Absolutely not, get back up to the room and stay there."

"You can't just leave him, he'll die."

"That's not my problem." Carnaby shouted his face quivering with anger.

"Clearly!" I shouted back. "But it is mine."

"Oh yeah?" Carnaby said a sickening smile appearing on his face, throwing me off guard slightly. He moved towards me at frightening speed and grabbed my arm.

"Get the hell off me!" I screamed angrily as he yanked me painfully down a long corridor. We clattered down some stone steps and went along another short corridor, all the time fighting with all my strength to free myself.

"Cyrus!" I shouted. "Cyrus!"

Carnaby laughed.

"Calling for an eight-year-old, come on Tilly, that's not like you."

I gave him a swift but hard kick in the shins which he apparently didn't feel.

"She's twelve!" I shouted as he threw me back into a dark room. The door was slammed shut.

"Sweet dreams." Carnaby said before a bolt was slid across and I was left alone in the black, the only light the moon shimmering through a window high up in the wall. I looked around assessing the situation for any evidence that I could escape. It was useless, the door was the only way in or out. The room was a tiny square, only a desk and chair on the thinly carpeted floor, it wasn't a concrete cell like I'd been expecting, the walls were wooden panels and the ceiling corniced. After a few vain attempts on the door, I sat with my back to it cursing my ever awful luck.

"Well, now what?" I asked myself, tapping my foot rhythmically against the floor. Nothing came to me and quite suddenly I felt the mists of sleep clouding my vision. I wasn't surprised to be honest, I hadn't slept properly in a very long time. Against my better judgment, I crawled over to the dark side of the room, below the window and closed my eyes, the floor was uncomfortable but my body didn't care, I was asleep before it had a chance to.

Chapter Thirty-Two: Escape

A loud crash above my head woke me with a start. I sat up flustered, not recognising where I was in the slightest as I glanced around the odd room. It came back to me when I looked up at the window where dim daylight now filtered through it. Was it morning already? There were another few bangs and then the unmistakable sound of a gunshot. I was on my feet in an instant, dragging the table over to the window wall and climbing on it. It was still only very early morning and the light was not very useful, but looking out across the gravelled front driveway now level with my eye line, I could see half a dozen cars strewn across it, and behind the cars were men, all dressed in suits, all holding guns.

Abigail L. Marsh

I banged hard on the window.

"Help! I'm trapped down here!" I screamed as loud as I could. I watched in utter frustration as the men behind the cars advanced towards the house. I didn't know what defences Carnaby had, but as the first man closest to the house hit the floor, a glazed look in his eyes I realised we were probably in for a big fight and I was trapped underground without a hope in hells chance of getting out.

Gunshots came thick and fast. Tiny projectiles cutting through the air without a single care to their purpose. Each one ripping into something, something inanimate or something real it didn't matter. Everyone was out for blood. As I watched a bullet ricocheted off a drain pipe not far from my room and hit the gravel less than a metre in front of my eyes. I ducked down and turned to the door, I wasn't sticking around in this room awaiting a fate I wasn't clear on. I ran at the door and gave it an almighty kick, kicking it over and over until the locked on the other side bent. The door opened ajar but got caught on the remaining metal. It was all I could do to stick my fingers out and wave pitifully at the hall-way beyond.

"HELLO!" I screamed. "CAN ANYONE HEAR ME! I'M TRAPPED DOWN HERE."

No-one came, either they couldn't hear me or they were leaving me in there for a reason. I pulled my fingers back through and stepped back.

Abigail L. Marsh

"Okay Tilly you've seen this done a hundred times." I said, turning slightly and holding my shoulder up. I ran at the door and crashed into it. The pain reverberating through my arm seemed to spread across my whole body, but I carried on there was no other choice. It took four runs and two more colossal kicks, but the lock finally gave way, and I fell out into the corridor. Now for a gun. I knew someone was bound to have one hidden away in their rooms and thanks to Cyrus and Cain, I knew exactly where those hiding places were likely to be.

I snuck back through the house as fast and as quietly as I could. The entrance hall was full of Carnaby's men, so I swerved to the right into the sitting room and using the rear door that led into the kitchen I found myself running up the backstairs and onto the landing of the second floor. I could hear the shouts and gunshots echoing around the house, but they were in the distance now. Going into Cains room, he wasn't in a good way, his body shook with pain as I rested a hand on his shoulder. "Cain?" I whispered.

His eyes flashed open.

"Tilly? What's going on?"

"It's okay, I just need a gun. Have you got one? Mines almost out of bullets" I asked. "With this many people it's not going to be enough." He shook his head.

"Carnaby has one in his… Pocket, Tilly in his red… Red jacket pocket." He said as his eyes rolled back.

"No, no stay with me." I said tapping his cheek. "Don't leave me." I cried, desperately. To my great relief, his eyes rolled forward again. "Find his red jacket, the key. A big gun in the wall with lots of bullets." That was all I got from him before he was unconscious again.

I breathed in deeply and held my breath for a second before exhaling slowly. I was shaking like a leaf.

"Okay" I breathed wringing my hands. "Find the key, get the gun and… And kill some bad guys." I said out loud sounding foolish even to myself, but I could do that. Right?

Unfortunately, I didn't have a perfect idea of the layout of the house, so I spent valuable moments searching desperately Carnaby's room. It took me ages and all the time I could hear the fight going on as I fumbled with doorknobs and burst into bathrooms and cupboard alike. The house was full of rooms I didn't want to be in. Eventually, on the second to last door on the second floors third corridor, I found it. I could tell because his red jacket was lying on his bed, I practically flew over to it. Thankfully the coat was not in the least like the house and only had three pockets in it, the key hidden in the zipped up pocket on the inside. With my heart racing and people getting injured every second, I ran around the room pressing on every wall until the panel above Carnaby's

Abigail L. Marsh

bed head popped open. Inside was a big metal safe with a keyhole. I shoved the key in and twisted. The vault made a satisfying click and I pulled it open.

"No way." I breathed staring at the black handheld machine gun sitting in there on stilts in all its glory just waiting to spew bullets and tear through lives. There was another colossal bang from downstairs that had me reaching in and pulling out the handheld gun. It was almost the size of my whole torso. In the back of the safe were long strips of ammunition and a bulletproof vest. I'd never used a machine gun before, and I had to fight with it to get the bullets rigged up.

"Okay." I breathed, reaching as far back into the safe as could and grabbing the vest. It was way too big for me, even after pulling the straps it was slipping to the right. It sounds silly, but I felt like a proper little assassin as I crept out of Carnaby's room and snuck back to the landing above the fight.

The battle had calmed down considerably as I knelt behind the banister and poked the end of the gun through the railings. I looked over the bloody scene. A few of the men had been hurt really badly, there were splurges of blood smeared across the wooden floor. Jason lay in the middle of the room motionless, except for the blood dripping out of his stomach and winding its way across the ground creating a pattern, not unlike the ones stitched into the tapestries hanging on the walls

The double windows either side of the oak door were smashed to smithereens, providing me with a distorted glance at the outside world. A few men were scattered on the floor their black suits making them look like lumpy rocks in the ever-growing light.

"All right men." I heard Carnaby say from somewhere underneath the landing I was on.

"Five down, seven to go, Roger you go around the back with Harry and Jake. Rod, Si, Mark and I will cover the house from here and the living room, and Mike you take Cyrus and shoot from the second-floor windows."

"Harry's bleeding bad sir." Jake said. There was a moment of silence in which I presume Carnaby checked it out for himself.

"Tie a bandage around it and suck it up." He said. "We've almost beaten them we can't give in now."

I held my breath as Cyrus and Mike came towards the stairs. I could see them now and if they came up any further, they would surely see me too.

"Mike!" Carnaby snapped. "Are you trying to get yourselves killed, go up the back stairs." They disappeared again.

It went silent for a few minutes. I laid patiently on the ground, knowing that I had to get rid of Giannaville's lot before I could take on Carna-

Abigail L. Marsh

by's. I waited, biding my time and hoping that if I left it long enough, Carnaby would wipe out Henry for me.

Nothing happened for a while. I could hear Carnaby talking in a low voice on the floor below. He was biding his time too, hoping Harry, Jake and Rodger would do his dirty work. Suddenly there was a huge bang, and a crack shot down the middle of the front door. I held my breath as two men appeared at the windows on either side of the doors. A bullet came whizzing across the room below me and skimmed the man's head, a moment later another hit him square in the chest, he fell backward. I watched in horror as another of Henry's men caught his body and used it as a shield, climbing through the window, brandishing a machine gun much like the one I had hold of.

Before I had a chance to decided what to do, he tapped the trigger. I closed my eyes as I listened to him murder Carnaby and his three allies. "For god's sake Tilly." I growled at myself. I opened my eyes to see the man looking around for someone to shoot as two more men began climbing through the windows. Taking a deep breath I aimed my gun and fired at the first man, before swinging it around and pointing it at the other two. Blood sprayed across the floor and up the walls dramatically, causing my stomach to convulse in sickening terror.

Abigail L. Marsh

An eerie quietness settled over me as I watched the boys fall in slow motion, thumping against the floor like hollow trees. I swallowed hard as another man climbed through. He saw too late what I had done and fell back through the window with the force of my bullets.

"Tilly!" I heard a voice shout from down the corridor. I yanked my gun from between the railings and pointed it down the dark hallway.

"It's Cyrus! It's me." The voice squealed desperately.

"Come out where I can see you." I snapped. The young girl ran out into the light hands held above her head as I stared at her intently. She was smothered in blood, it dribbled down her arms and stained her clothes red as she clenched a handgun in her visibly shaking hands.

"Mikes dead." She said.

"Hey I think they're all dead, we can get in!" I heard a man shout from downstairs. Spinning my gun around and tapping the trigger, I shot the man in the window. He looked up at me as the bullet penetrated his stomach.

"They're upstairs." He choked. I hit him with another round. Scrambling to my feet I peered over the banister at the gory bloodbath.

"One, two, three... Four, five and he makes six." I said, counting on my fingers all the men I knew to be dead.

"There's one more." I said, looking up at Cyrus. Her eyes were wild with fear.

Abigail L. Marsh

"Okay just go back through…"

My blood ran cold as I heard a tickling of metal skim across the wooden floor and hit the bottom of the staircase. I looked over the banister to see a small dull green pineapple spinning around ten feet below me. Grabbing my gun, I shoved Cyrus as violently as I could and dived after her landing on the floor as the world around me shook.

The bang was astounding and it rang in my ears as I fought to keep my consciousness. Squinting up I saw Cyrus screaming, hands covering her ears and dust raining down around us. I don't know what happened or how I did it, but I forced myself off the ground, picked up my gun, grabbed Cyrus and bundled us all down a few doors and into Cains room. Slamming the door we raced to the other side of the bed.

"Okay, you've shot a gun before?" I said as she popped her ears by widely opening and closing her mouth, she nodded.

"I want you to stand here, point the gun at the door and if someone other than me comes in, shoot them." I said putting the machine gun, still glue to its stilts on a strategically positioned table. "Do you under-stand me?" I said.

"Yes but, where are you going?" Her voice wavered in panic.

"I have to end this. Please, please stay here, don't come out until I tell you to. Protect him. He, he's all I have."

Abigail L. Marsh

Although Cyrus perhaps thought she knew better, she didn't say; instead, she nodded and gripped the trigger. I looked over at Cain, paling by the second. His wandering eyes found my face and he opened his mouth. I stepped around the bed, putting my ear close to him.

"Remember, you're a wolf and you are *not afraid*." He said. A tear fell from my eye, landing on him and trickled across his cheek.

"I'm not afraid." I said. He smiled. Sliding my backpack out from under the bed I took the faithful handgun out, checked on the six bullets I had left and headed out of the door.

The house was deadly silent, shards of glass spewed across the floor, ripped paintings hanging lopsided on walls, the people in them looking a little worse for wear. The bodies on the floor downstairs oddly reassured me, there were seven, I reckoned there couldn't be many more out of sight. Holding my gun tightly, ready to shoot at anything that moved, I made my way down the thickly carpeted staircase to the ground floor. My footsteps echoed as they splashed gently int the pools of crimson liquid covering the tiles in the lobby. Through the splintered front door and smashed windows there was no movement, I wondered if my bullets had taken the lives of all the men that presented danger. A small cough behind me told me otherwise. I spun, almost skidding in the blood to where a pitiful sight met my eyes.

Slumped over in a doorway, with red saliva running down his chin and a nasty bullet wound to his stomach was the infamous Carnaby Hanson, not looking as great and glorious as he once had done to me. I crept towards him gun raised and aimed as he watched, helpless to do anything else, but his expression didn't translate to that of a helpless animal. With a horrible smile He chuckled at me, showing once pearly white teeth now stained the colour of fury.

"You're not going to shoot me, are you Miss Black?" He croaked. "You wouldn't do that, after all I did for you." He croaked.

"You tried to kill Cain. You wanted to be the last man standing, he is going to die and you did nothing." I spoke with venom.

Carnaby laughed as the cold, sadistic smile spread further across his face.

"And there it is, that mouse." He spoke the words as he spat a gob of bright red spit onto the floor. I lowered my gun slightly, confused by his words.

"You haven't got it in you Miss Black. You see a lion can raise a mouse, but when it comes down to the fight, that mouse is still a tiny, fearful mouse. I tried it with that red-headed kid, Cain tried it with you. No matter what, a lion cannot change what you are." This was a long spiel for someone who was knocking on death's door, and he hacked up a disgusting mix of mucus and blood that reminded me of the pile of guts I had once seen when Cain had made me watch Saving Private Ryan. It had scarred my ten year old self at the time, but I could see then why Cain had done what he did. Carnaby leaned back against the door, eyes closing.

"Good job I wasn't raised by lions then, isn't it?"

Carnaby's eyes opened again, a look of contempt crossing his face as if to say- 'can't you just let me die in peace?'

"I was raised by wolves." I spoke firmly.

"What's the difference?" He sneered. I raised my gun, his death now definite in my mind.

"The difference? I will never, ever perform in your goddamn circus." BANG.

Chapter Thirty Two: Short and Sweet

As the ringing in my head faded, I stepped back from the corpse slumped over on the ground.

"Cyrus." I yelled with all the voice I could muster.

"Well, well, well." A gravelly voice croaked from just behind my shoulder. I spun, but there was no time to aim my gun. A giant hand swiped it from me and sent it spinning across the bloodied hall. Taking several rapid steps back I crashed into a wall painfully.

"Oh, no, no. Don't you go running." The man said only a second away, using his thick hands covered in shiny golden rings and chains to trap me tight again the wall.

"What do you want?" I demand, holding my nerve as the man looked over me with beady eyes.

"So you're the girl everyone's been talking about?" The man breathed on me, his whiskery chin only centimetres from my face. "You're Cain Blacks kid."

"Who are you?" I growled.

"Ha! Didn't he ever tell you? I'm his old pal. My name's Henry Giannaville, not so pleased to meet you. You're the brat that murdered my men."

So *he* was Henry, this brute of a man covered in chavvy bling, with a suit on that looked like it had seen better days and definitely smelt like it had. This was the man everyone was so panicked about? My

Abigail L. Marsh

unmistakable unimpressed look angered the man, who then grabbed me by the throat hard, forcing me to cough. His meaty hands sliced through my oxygen supply as adrenaline shot through my veins, hands grasping his, trying fruitlessly to rip them away. My visions wavered for a second and I was horrified to think the last thing I was going to see on earth was this ugly man. With lungs screaming for air as if a million burning nails were being driven into them, my foot jerked forwards colliding had with his golden jewels. Henry flinched, readjusting his position and allowing me a single shallow breath before they were clamped back.

I gave up hope pretty quickly after that, until in my drifting mind I heard a dog bark. Confused at the sudden presence of an animal, my eyes opened. Another bark and another. Henry was looking around too. Then he let go completely and backed away. I fell to the floor, drained of energy as I grasped at life. A pattering of feet came into the hall, then a ferocious growl. Oxygen returning to my body I opened bleary eyes and watched in complete bewilderment as my dog- my apparently very much alive dog- Max flew across the door and hurled himself at Henry. It was almost comical as Henry screamed like a giant baby and if I hadn't been about to pass out, I would have laughed. Max made a loop of the room, sweeping past me and giving me a lick as Henry backed into an office and slammed the door.

"You're alive?" I said, wrapping my arms around his neck and using him to pull myself into a sitting position. Woof. He licked me again.

"I love you too." I laughed, breathing hard. My laughter quickly faded as the door to Henry's room flew open, gun exiting first as he aimed for Max.

"NO!" I yelled as two bullets flew across the room.

On impact, Max yelped, fell to the floor and then he was gone. The breath inside him, disappearing in a split second, forever. My eyes found Henry at a complete loss; the same cold, sadistic smile spreading across his face that Carnaby had given me as he raised his gun to me. I looked back at my dog, my always, the one constant thing in my life, hand bunched up in his fur I closed my eyes.

BBBBBBBBBRRRRRRRRRRTTTTTTTTT.

The rattling sound of a machine gun echoed around the room, but nothing touched me. Gasping I looked up as Henry's eyes bore into mine, a twisted expression etched across his paling face. He turned his head to where the shots had come from. I looked too. Laying on the floor at the top of the staircase, machine gun in hand was Cain. With one more

Abigail L. Marsh

round Henry's fell to the floor, blood mixing with the rest of the innards drying on the ground.

Blue lights reflected against the staircase as I struggled to my feet, lifting my enormously heavy dog with me, breathing hard.

"Cain!" I breathed taking two steps towards him.

"No Tilly, go!" He said, pointing to the corridor. He was in no fit state to go anywhere, I knew that and the likely hood was the game was up for him. As I turned to go he called after me. "I promise I will find you."

"Goodbye." I cried, choking back a sob as I staggered down the back corridor drying my eyes on Max's fur as I went.

"It's alright, Maxy." I whimpered. "We're going to get out of here."

We made it almost all of the way down the corridor to the back door and out to freedom before I heard a familiar voice call out for me.

"Tilly! Tilly is that you?"

The voice caught me so suddenly off guard that my body refused to go any further and stopped.

"Is that you?" The voice asked. Stumbling slightly I managed to stead-ied myself on the doorframe of the dining room. I looked back down the dimly lit hallway. A man stood outside the living room door, his hair a silver shining grey.

Abigail L. Marsh

"Tilly Carmichael?" I recognised the second voice as it shouted through the house for me, Charlie. I tensed up, this was the craziest decision I had had to make in all my life.

"Tilly it's alright, it's Robert, it's Dad." The silver haired man said. I gripped Max tightly. I knew exactly who it was. I couldn't bring myself to speak to him. Instead, I used the little strength I had regained and forced myself to cary on down the hall. Robert came after me, I could hear him as I burst into the kitchen and raced for the back door. To my complete horror, it was locked. I fumbled with the window next to it, fighting to see over Max's body as he weighed a hundred tonnes in my aching arms, but all the power had drained out of my body and adrenaline alone would not shift it.

I kicked the door hard.

"OPEN!" I yelled in rage as tears flowed openly down my cheeks now. All at once, I felt warms arms reach over my shoulders and hold me tightly.

"Tilly, it's alright. You're safe." Robert's voice whispered in my ear. I ripped away, stumbling on a chair leg as I fought to free myself from him.

"Tilly, why don't you put the dog down." Robert asked reaching out for me, pain and fear swimming in his eyes .

"No. Don't you touch him!" I growled ferociously as my arms burned with he thought of release. "Charlie! Charlie, I'm here." I screamed, my voice breaking as I backed up against the sink.

Charlie burst into the room moments later, door clattering back on the wall as he did.

"Charlie." I said, bypassing Robert as I ran over to him. "Please please wake him up."

Shocked I'd shoved a dog into his arms, Charlie looked down at Max who was clearly dead.

"Tilly, I don't…" He shook his head.

A shaky sigh fell from my lips as a wave of sickness passed though my stomach. That was a feeling I knew.

"Come on, let's get him in the back of the police car, we'll find a place for him okay?" He said, the tone in his voice making him sound like he was talking to a three-year-old, and not a grown teenager. I nodded, comforted by his suggestion. I walked purposefully in front of Charlie back to the massacre in the lobby not wanting to look at my father. We weaved around the dead bodies, and paramedics seeing to them and were just about to step out of the front door when I heard Cyrus call my name.

"Wait, Tilly, wait!"

Abigail L. Marsh

I stopped and turned around to see her being carried down the stairs by an armed guard. He brought her over to me and set her down on the floor on the only clean spot there was left.

"I thought he might have got you." Cyrus said, throwing her arms around me.

"Nah, not me." I said battling burning tears as her eyes fell on Max.

"Max?" She whispered. I decided to keep what Max had done for me between him and I. Cyrus thought he died a while ago and no-body needed to share in our precious last moments. "I'm really sorry about him." She said, But, we won!" She grinned, going from sad to happy in an instant as we walked out onto the sprawling driveway covered in police cars and people walking around in fluorescent coats looking like fireflies in the every growing morning light.

"Yeah. We did." I said, giving her the answer she wanted and drying my eyes, the kid's spirit-raising my own. "Are you coming with me?" I asked, then looked at Charlie who was laying my dog down on a tarp in the back of the police van we'd stopped next to.

"Yes, for now." He said. "Jump in."

Cyrus and I shared the back seat, as I leaned heavily back against the headrest keeping my backpack safely at my feet, I realised how exhausted I was. I let my eyes flutter shut and the last thing I remembered was Cyrus's warm body curling up next to me before I was out like a light.

Abigail L. Marsh

Chapter Thirty-Three Hospital

We were driven to a hospital in Oxford, which had a helipad on the rood and I found out later on that that's how Cain had arrived. Charlie woke me as we pulled up. We were parked outside the front doors, the bright lights burned my eyes like the lights of a thousand suns as I squinted hard. Cyrus was still asleep on me and it took me a second to realise where we were and what had happened. I glanced up at the detective.

"Now don't you get any ideas about running away, you're on lockdown." Charlie said. I nodded, in all honesty I was far too exhausted to even attempt an escape. I shook Cyrus off my tingling arm, she sprang awake before giving me an almighty karate chop to the leg and scrambling away from me, her eyes wide.

"Oh my god!" I groaned clutching my leg.

"I'm sorry." Cyrus cried falling back towards me and clasping her hands over mine. "I'm sorry." She repeated guiltily, I took a deep breath and through clenched my teeth replied.

"You've got power kid."

The armed guard chuckled opening the front passenger door and getting out.

"Funny?" I snapped at him.

Abigail L. Marsh

"Tilly I…" Cyrus began.

"Hey its fine, no sweat." I said, unplugging myself and allowing Charlie to give me a hand out of the car. Even he had a smirk on his face.

"You know I could give you one." I said. "And I guarantee it'd hurt about a hundred times more."

Charlie held his hands up and I sneered at him shaking my heading disgust.

"Ladies." The armed guard said, stepping through the automatic door and prompting us go through first.

"Thanks, James." Charlie replied following us through. "You sticking around?"

"Yeah I'll be with you guys until the evening, then I'll swap and Danny will be with you until MI5 get down here tomorrow."

"Brilliant." They took us through to A&E where apparently they were expecting us.

Cyrus and I were triaged straight away. The poor girl was covered in other peoples blood and was shoved into the shower, scrubbed clean and then forced into a hospital gown that drowned her. She had a size-able cut on the back of her leg which she'd confessed she'd not even noticed.

When the nurse came back with my results, I was snoozing on my bed in the cubicle. Charlie was positioned right next to me, he wasn't taking any chances this time and I could already see him eyeing up my bag. After explaining that I had almost been choked to death, I was rushed through a bunch of tests where I was prodded and poked until I wanted to scream. Both Cyrus and I were given a private room where Charlie and James, the armed guard they had brought in could keep an eye on us and told we'd be staying overnight.

I was almost happy with my results. It meant I could take a breath, I wasn't going to be dragged back to London and forced to make any decisions.

James, sat on a chair stationed in the hallway, opposite our open door, I think this was more so he could see us more than we were reassured by seeing him. Charlie stayed with us for a little bit, but he soon got bored and wandered in and out all day bringing coffees and magazines too and fro. The first chance I got I took my backpack down to the toilets and slid my card into the lining. Charlie could have my passport if he went looking in my bag and that would hopefully be enough to keep him at bay. Cyrus slept most of the day, she was exhausted and I didn't blame her, she was so young and had been through so much already, it was scary to see even for me.

Abigail L. Marsh

I was content with watching the TV on the wall opposite us. I flicked

through channels and half read a magazine Charlie bought back for me.

It was half-past three when I finished reading an article about a ghost

who apparently lived in a basement under a pub in Wiltshire. Closing

the paper I looked up at Charlie.

"Charlie?" I asked.

"Hmmm?" He said putting his phone down.

"If you knew where I was, why didn't you come and get me?" I asked.

Charles soft expression wavered. "Ella told you, didn't she?" He asked,

looking over at Cyrus a glint of frustration in his eyes.

"Don't look at her like that, she was frightened." I defended. "How

could you force a little girl like that to do what she's had to do?"

Charlie sighed.

"She didn't tell you it all did she?"

I frowned.

"She told me about having no family, about getting busted for trivial

stuff and ending up in a special police programme, about some corrupt

police officer dumping her and not coming back... everything?"

Charlie shook his head.

"I didn't ditched her, and I didn't know that you'd moved until a few

hours before you called. Ella got so deep into the crime ring world she

switched sides. It wasn't clear for a long time whether you were still in

Abigail L. Marsh

England or if you were in Outer Mongolia."

"Wait you were the police officer? She's twelve Charlie!" I said, shaking my head. "Kids don't pull that kind of shit off."

"Tilly think about it, the police force you know, have they ever for one second stopped looking for you, have they ever put a child in danger for the wrong reasons? Have they ever stopped fighting for what is right."

"Is there a right reason to put a child in danger? Because if there is, then there are definitely some corrupt police officers."

"But not me. I delivered Ella to that house for two reasons. One, she was our only chance, and two she wanted to go. She wanted to make something better of her life. She had a tracking device, she had an emergency phone that she could have used any time. She had a way out. She chose that life."

"But why didn't you go in after her? When you realised she was becoming corrupt?"

Charlie sighed.

"And blow the biggest operation we have ever had out of the water? We had to find you Tilly, we had to find Autumn. We were so close, and we'd been working on taking down that trio for years. Sometimes you have to let go of the little things to achieve the bigger picture."

"Little *things*?" I said appalled. "She's a person... Not a disposable cog in your machine."

Abigail L. Marsh

"I know you don't like it." Charlie said. I shook my head angrily and turned away from him, curling up and closing my eyes.

"Tilly look around you, she may have been corrupt for a little time but look what she's managed to do. She's the one who gave us the tip-off about the flight back from France, she's the reason you were found. She may have gone a little rogue, but she never forgot what she went in to do."

"Wait, what?" I asked springing back up.

"You may not like it now, but Ella saved yours and Autumns life."

"You mean all this, all of it, its all connected?" I asked, thinking it all through. All the time I'd been with Cain, knowing of Carnaby and Giannaville, the plane disaster, finding Cyrus. All that time, this little girl had been fighting to get me out of that. My brain collapsed in on itself as I looked sorrowfully at Cyrus.

"What's wrong?" Charlie asked.

"I thought you'd given up looking for me, I thought I'd be in that situation forever."

"So you made the best of it." Charlie said.

"I kinda liked it." I admitted. "Being capable, you know."

"You still are, nothings going to change that now." Charlie said softly. "No-one stopped looking for you, you were just hidden so well that only someone on the inside had any chance of finding you."

I smiled.

"Charlie, my Dads an alcoholic, I can't go back to him." I said, "Isabelle she has to come back, away from him."

"Your Dads doing really well, he's been sober for four years now. It was the alcohol that made him do those things Tilly."

"No, he hasn't."

Charlie looked at me, quizzically.

"What do you mean?"

I sighed and debated whether or not to tell him.

"Last..."

"Tilly." Charlie interrupted. "Your Dad has coped really really well with having Autumn and Callie back in his life. He has a relief worker who watches over him and the girls have an allocated social worker who is on call 24/7 if something goes wrong. Your Dad knows the stakes and he's making a genuine effort to give you the best new start possible." Charlie explained. "I know how scary it is to go back to something you think is unstable and dangerous."

"I'm so scared." I confessed. "You don't know what I do."

"I think I do..." He admitted hesitantly. I frowned at him. How could he possibly know?

"And trust me it's a far better thing for you to do to trust him, otherwise you throw it all away before you've given him a second chance."

Abigail L. Marsh

"You know?"I asked.

Charlie nodded.

"And I will call it in if that's what you want. I don't have to tell you that Callie and Autumn will be taken from him immediately and he will be reassessed in rehab and by the courts before he can even think about getting you back again. You won't see him beforehand, and that could take months, even years and not to mention the damage it could do to your sisters and your Dad's mental wellbeing."

I watched him talk, there was something else there, something almost selfish. I didn't understand why he wanted this so bad.

"And you?"

"I'd lose my job for withholding information and interfering with the wellbeing of minors."

There it was.

"But what if he does it again? I'm not going back to all that because you made a cock-up."

"He won't do anything Tilly, he's a changed man."

"That's a lot of faith you have in him." I said, not knowing if he even had the right to have so much trust in a person he didn't know.

"Your Dad and I go back, far back." Charlie said as if reading my mind. "I met with him a few months after you'd been officially stated as a missing person worldwide. He's been a good friend to me, he helped me through my divorce and I've helped him back on his feet. I intend to carry on helping. Nothing bad is going to happen Tilly."

I could see Charlie had slipped out of his professional demeanour and was now begging me, as a friend to give my father one last chance. The sincerity in his eyes had me second-guessing myself. I turned over and pulled the hospital blanket around me.

"I can see you need to think about it." Charlie said gently. He got up and I listened to him go over to the door. "I'm going to get a coffee, James will stay." And with that he was gone. I looked over at Cyrus, who was still fast asleep. I wanted so badly to disappear into the ground and never resurface. I glanced over my shoulder, yep, James was still there with his gun, held tightly. I closed my eyes on the world, not wanting to think anymore.

Two hours later, my eyes flashed open, images of my Dad and sister drifted away from me as I rubbed my eyes and sat up. Charlie was back in his chair, he had the remote and was watching the news quietly. I watched it for a little bit in silence and then watched as James and Danny switched over. James waved at me, and I nodded at him as he left.

"I'll do it." I said quietly.

Charlie's head flicked round to face me.

"You will?" He asked. I nodded.

Abigail L. Marsh

"But I need to see Isabelle first, can you do that?"

He returned my nod.

"Yes."

"Where are they?" I asked.

"You're Dad's been in England since Thursday." Charlie said.

"And Isabelle? I'm guessing she's in the US?"

Charlie shook his head, and my eyes lit up.

"Your Dad brought her over with him... Tilly she's not doing great, she's been so worried. Since going home she's changed her name back to Autumn. Robert says she won't eat or sleep. I've spoken to him today, he was going to put her back on a flight to LA, but she refused to get on it."

"So long story short?" I asked a little rattily, desperate to find out exactly where she was.

"She's in London." Charlie said, ignoring my backchat.

"Can you bring her here." I said suddenly feeling like I needed her with me there and then.

"I'll make a call." He said, standing up. Charlie left the room and came back fifteen minutes later.

"They're sending her over in a car, but it's going to be about two hours." He said. I nodded.

"Thank you, Charlie." I said in genuine appreciation. "Is my Dad here in the hospital?"

Abigail L. Marsh

"Yes."

I nodded again.

"Charlie?"

"Yeah?"

"How did you know about what happened? The shootout and stuff."

"You called, remember?"

"I called 999 yeah, but the line was cut off before I could say barely anything."

"It took us a while to figure it out." Charlie smiled. "But you said enough."

There was a brief pause, and I thought the conversation was over until Charlie asked another question.

"Tilly that bag you've kept an iron grip on, you know I'm going to have to take a look before you leave." He said. Although my mind was fretting, I smiled at him.

"I knew you were going to say that, here you can see." I said sitting up and taking it from underneath my pillow. Charlie looked surprised at how easy it had been as he came over to me. I laid it out on the bed and unzipped it.

"You're not going to be thrilled." I warned as he reached in and pulled out one of the only three thing in it he could reach. The first thing that came out was Max's dog collar. I looked away from it my heart aching.

Abigail L. Marsh

Charlie saw my expression and put it to one side. Next out came the roll of money I had pilfered from Faith. He made no comment and then last out came my passport.

"Nellie Watson?" He asked, surprised.

"Now you can see where I've been to and from my whole life, it's like your own personal tracker for my past excursions." I smiled.

Charlie tipped the bag upside down and shook it, but nothing else fell out. He routed around in it, but my card was safely hidden in the linings, exactly where I had left it.

"You can keep the bag and the collar, but you know I have to take the money and passport."

I nodded.

"Yeah, I know." I said, taking the collar back and shoving the whole lot back under my pillow. "Where is Max."

"We've taken him to the pet crematorium like we talked about. Would you like his ashes?" Charlie asked.

"Yeah, I want to take them to his favourite place." I said.

"Where's that?"

"The beach, Cromer beach."

"What are you talking about?" Cyrus said, suddenly sitting up. I looked over at the kid in the bed next to me.

"You're a big fat liar." I said grumbled. Her face fell and I realised I couldn't be angry at her. Life screws everyone over, I was no different to her, my cards were just as bad.

"But the best big fat liar I know." I said smiling. I climbed out of bed and sat on the edge of hers, pulling her into a hug.

"Thank you." I said.

"I thought you didn't want to be saved." She said looking from Charlie to me. I tipped my head from side to side, unsure of how to respond.

"You didn't know that and now I'm here I reckon things will work out." I smiled.

"It's always better to be with your family Tilly, no matter who they are." I looked down at the child in my arms, she was wise beyond her years and she didn't even know it.

Chapter Thirty-Four: Back in my arms

Cyrus and I convinced Charlie to buy us a film and we sat and watched Harry Potter for the next hour. Much to my frustration, the nurse forced me to put my oxygen mask on, and Cyrus laughed at how much I sounded like Darth Vader.

Abigail L. Marsh

I was just finishing an impression of him, making Cyrus laugh uncontrollably when there was a knock on the door. I turned and my stomach did a little flip, she was here. I ripping my oxygen mask off I smiled. "Isabelle!" I said. Autumn almost fell over herself as she scrambled across the room and flung herself into my arms. "Autumn even." I said correcting myself but she didn't even hear

"You're here." She sobbed into my shoulder as I wrapped my arms around her.

"I'm here." I said, holding her tightly. "I'm here." Her whole body shook as I looked up at Charlie, he smiled sadly.

"Autumn it's okay."

"Please don't leave me again." She sobbed.

"I won't, I promise, I promise." I said feeling a massive amount of emotion creep up in my chest and strangle me. Cyrus looked over from her bed, I could see the tears in her eyes. I hadn't realised how much damage I had caused by just leaving her the way I did.

"It's alright." I said, rubbing her back trying to soothe her. Although her fingernails stayed lodged in my arms Autumn started to calm down, eyes distracted by the screen across the room, as Charlie read a magazine quietly in the corner. After a while Autumn looked up at me with her big golden eyes.

Abigail L. Marsh

"I didn't tell." She whispered. "About Cain." She said even quieter.

Then she turned back to the TV, eyes closing. Charlie threw a glance

over at us, I gave him a confident smile, knowing then that I could beat

them.

When I looked down at her only half an hour after she'd come in she

was sound asleep. I studied her face, it was pale and thin almost as if

she were disappearing, she was hanging onto me so tightly even so deep

in sleep. I looked up at Charlie's melancholy face.

"What happened to her?" I asked.

"It's not what you think." Charlie said, assuming I was thinking Robert

was neglecting her. I wasn't.

"She was distraught when we came back to the room we'd left you in all

those months ago, you'd gone, and I had to go back and tell her I

couldn't find you. Robert had come. She'd been just as afraid and angry

as you, she remembers less obviously, but the pain, the memories

they're still there. Eventually a few weeks of being in England and in

the company of Robert and Callie we persuaded her to go and check out

Oceanside. She loved it, but not long after arriving, Robert said she

would wake up crying in the middle of the night, she was scared."

Charlie began the story.

"Of what?" I asked. "Of Cain?"

"No… Well yes and no. She was terrified that he'd caught up with you again."

"But she knows he would never hurt me."

"She was scared that if he had gotten to you, she would never see you again."

"But she'd survived without me for years before all this." I defended myself.

"She'd become so attached to you, so reliant on you being there that she struggled to do anything for herself anymore."

"What do you mean?"

"She wouldn't eat, she couldn't sleep, she didn't want to leave the house." Charlie gave me more examples than I needed and I stared down at the girl in my arms, feeling sick.

"It got better quickly though, she went to see a psychiatrist, and they helped her a lot, she snapped out of it. But since the news came of you being involved in another crime ring, or more the same one, just a different branch, she fell back into old habits." Charlie said. "She's a terrified little girl. I know you did what you did because you were scared too, and I don't blame you, but you can't do it again, for her sake and your own. I won't bail you out again Tilly. You run away this time, it'll be deemed as your own choice and they'll arrest you."

"I'm not running away again." I said, holding Autumn even tighter.

"I'm going to hold you to that."

I glanced over at Cyrus, who had drifted into a fitful sleep. She had tossed and turned for a while, but it seemed as if she might have settled down.

"What happens to her?" I asked.

"She'll be safe, don't worry about her, you need to focus on getting yourself back on your feet."

I nodded.

"I'll go down and talk to Robert." Charlie said.

"Okay… Tell him, tell him… I say hi." I said, feeling my cheeks flush.

"I will." Charlie smiled as he left.

The next few hours, I spent watching Autumn sleep, feeling her even breathe against my neck and having her close to me. I had missed her more than I'd realised. Her long chocolate hair lay in loose curls on my chest. I wrapped a strand around my fingers and twirled it gently. The second Harry Potter film of the say played in the background, but I paid it no attention. All I wanted was for Autumn to be happy and I had taken that away from her, now I was going to make it up. I would suck it up and go to Oceanside if that's what she needed to be happy and healthy. The rest I could deal with when it came. I had trained hard and beaten all the odds. I was a child abused by her doting father, kidnapped at the age of seven, grown up in a crime ring and cheated death multiple

Abigail L. Marsh

times. Despite the statistics I had come out on top, unscathed and now it was time to settle back down, to save someone else instead of saving myself.

I closed my eyes and turned slightly so I could get some sleep. It was late and I could feel the weight of tomorrow already on my mind.

"They're asleep." I heard someone say.
"I better take her to the hotel, we'll come back tomorrow." I heard my Dad say. As much as my mind wanted to stay with Autumn, I knew she needed to be with our Dad. He lifted her away from me, so I let my arms slip over her only opening my eyes fractionally, as I watched him carry her carefully out of the room. Then I was asleep.

I woke up the next morning early. Seven o'clock was far too early for my liking. I stumbled out of my bed and reached for the jug of water next to Charlie chair, which was peculiarly half empty. I poured myself a cup of water and downed it in one, wiping the dribble from my chin as I did. I ended up emptying the jug and decided to go and find the bathroom to fill it back up again. *How kind of me.* I turned around to find my jumper but realised it had been taken away. A new set of clothes had been left at the bottom of my bed.

Abigail L. Marsh

"Oh, a lovely lime green jumper." I groaned to myself. "And oh, what a surprise, a pair of purple jeans."

Despite the running theme of terribly coloured clothes, I was thankful I didn't have to wander around in a hospital gown where your arse hangs out.

I opened the door and was surprised to see the new armed guard fast asleep in his chair.

"Danny." I said, kicking his leg gently. He was on his feet in an instant.

"What!?" He stuttered. "I'm awake, I'm awake!"

"I'll take your word for it." I chuckled before turning and walking towards the bathroom.

"Where are you going?" He asked, suspiciously.

"Just to get some water from the bathroom, you can come with me if you like." I smirked.

"No, no that's alright, just come straight back." He said with a slightly irritated tone.

The bathroom was deserted. I went about filling my water jug up and then caught my reflection in the mirror. I looked different than I had done the last time I had seen myself. My muscles were more prominent, my jawline more visible (which for me is all I ever wanted out of life), and despite what I had been through, my eyes were sparkling. I smiled at myself for the first time in a long time, not because I had anything

necessarily to be smiling about, but because I deserved to see it.

When I got back to my room with my water I found Danny dozing in

his chair again. This time I left him and went back into my dark room,

muttering about him being a lazy git and that if he really wanted to be

fired, well I wasn't going to stand in his way.

It was still only early, so taking the bit of change I had laying on the

bedside cabinet next to my bed, I put on my socks and shoes that had

been cleaned and left on the floor and abandoned the room in search of

some much-needed greasy breakfast. I didn't know what time breakfast

was served or what time Charlie was coming back, maybe he didn't

even stay the night at all, but either way I was hungry and there wasn't

anything Danny was going to do about it.

I wandered through the ward, trying not to inhale the disinfectant smell

that always made me feel sick. There were two nurses on the reception

desk, but I didn't think that having an armed guard positioned outside

my room warranted me much trust. I veered away from them and found

the backstairs at the other end of the corridor. The stairwell was breezy,

so rubbing my hands together I descended it quickly, all the way down

the three floors to the bottom and out into a long deserted hallway. To

Abigail L. Marsh

my right was a long line of vending machines, but to my left, through the automatic sliding glass doors, and across a road was a glorious sight- McDonalds. Godsend.

Now in hindsight, it was not a good idea to leave the hospital, but I was starving and a girl's got to eat. So without much hesitation, I turned my back on the vending machines and went out into the cool morning air. McDonald's was practically deserted and with my £7.48 I bought a huge bacon and egg McMuffin and all extras you could ever want to go with it. It was like Christmas had come in May. It was already half gone by the time I had crossed the road and entered the sliding doors. I wandered slowly back up to my room cramming as much into my mouth before I bumped into Danny or Cyrus, they were bound to want some and I was in no mood for sharing.

I made it back up to the third floor and was just walking around the corner that led back to my room when I heard a whole load of commotion coming from inside. Someone was crying and another person was shouting. I ran down the hallway and rounded the doorframe. Charlie was blue in the face and yelling at Danny who looked horrified and Autumn was sat on my bed, my Dad holding her in his arms, she was distraught.

Abigail L. Marsh

Amongst all of this Cyrus was sat drinking a glass of water not looking the least bit amused at all the people crowded in her room.

"What the hell is going on?" I asked. They all stopped and turned to look at me, their faces a picture of anger and relief.

"Where have you been?" Charlie and Robert cried at once.

I held up my McDonalds bag.

"Maccies, I was hungry." I said. I glanced over at Cyrus, who had a smirk on her face.

"I told you she'd come back." She said. Charlie looked over at her and glared.

"We thought you'd run away." Robert cried coming over to me, then he pointed at my hysterical sister. "Look." He said.

"I'm sorry!" I snapped at the man I hadn't seen in months, it wasn't the way I had wanted to start our clean slate."I didn't think anyone would be here this early, I just went to get some food, okay? I'm not running away." I said going over to Autumn and pulling her into my arms. "I'm not going anywhere." I told her. Her hot tears soak through my jumper as I held her tightly and my heart sank. Charlie turned back to Danny.

"Get your things and go, I'll be speaking to your superior this morning." He said. I looked over at Danny a twinge of guilt in my stomach, the man had been up all night keeping an eye on us.

"Charlie go easy on him." I said as Danny left the room a grim look on his face.

Abigail L. Marsh

"You! Pack your stuff up. We're going back to London in twenty minutes." He snapped, pointing angrily at my bag. I sighed as he left the room with Robert. I tried to let go of Autumn so I could reach for my bag, but she held on tighter. I had to bite my tongue and count to five. None of this was her fault, but I desperately just wanted to get my shit and get out.

"I'm not going anywhere Autumn, okay? You can let go of me." I said. There was a brief moment when she didn't move but thankfully her arms loosened and I was released. I tried not to look at her as I flipped my pillow over and pulled out my backpack.

"Are you coming back with us?" I asked Cyrus. She shook her head.

"My ride is coming this afternoon, I'm going up north." She said. I looked at her quizzically.

"My superintendent rang early this morning. I'm talking a refresher programme then going back out in the field." She said.

"What? Why?" I asked horrified.

"It's what I want to do, it's what I'm good at." She replied.

"But...What about...?"

"Go to Oceanside Tilly." She smiled. "Don't worry about me, I'll be fine."

I was just about to open my mouth when Charlie came back into the room, throwing his hands up in the air.

"There it is." He growled, picking his phone up from his chair.

"Charlie I want to see Cain before I leave." I said

He stopped and gave me a stony glare, if looks could kill I would have absolutely been dead.

"No Tilly." Autumn said, pulling on my arm.

"It's my one condition. I won't go without saying goodbye."

"Fine." Charlie spat. "But you're in and out, then we're leaving. If there is any funny business, I will drag you out of there and personally…" He trailed off, but I got the gist.

"Tilly please?" Autumn begged, pulling on my arm again, I looked down at her little face full of worry.

"I have to Autumn. I have to close the book before I start again." I said, brushing her fringe out of her eyes. "I promise I won't do anything stupid, okay? Do you trust me?"

She stared into my eyes, all I could see was the panic behind them, but she nodded bravely. I let go of her and gave Cyrus a hug.

"Stay safe, stay in touch and I'll see you again, that's a promise." I said.

"You too." She agreed, squeezing me tightly.

"Tilly, get a move on." Charlie said from the door. Pulling away from Cyrus, I blew her a kiss, then took Autumn's hand and we left the room.

Robert was standing outside in the hallway, looking bedraggled and exhausted.

"I'm going to take her to see Mr. Black and then we'll meet you out in the car." Charlie said. Robert gave me a broken look as if I had stabbed him through the heart again. I swallowed and proceeded to try and explain.

"I'm coming back with you, but I have to say goodbye. Cain's been good to me for all these years, I know you disagree." I said. "But it's really important that I say goodbye. I hope you can understand and if you can't, I hope you can forgive me." I said.

"I've waited for you your whole life." Robert said. "I can wait ten more minutes."

I smiled at his acceptance as Charlie took hold of my arm and led me out of the ward.

Chapter Thirty-Five: Time to Say Goodbye

We were in the intensive care ward a few minutes later, and I was led to Cains room, which was guarded by two policemen. He looked like a very sick man as I went over to his bed. I had asked to be alone, and

Charlie told me he'd be right outside. Cain looked up at me as I sat gently on the edge of his bed, machines beeping all around him.

"Tilly." He began, his voice was hoarse with pain. "I'm sorry."

I tilted my head in dismay.

"I should never have taken you from…"

"Don't." I interrupted. "I don't have a lot of time."

"Tilly, you must hear this." His voice interjected. "I have caused you…"

His face creased. "So much pain."

"Stop!" I snapped getting off the bed. "Who knows what would have happened to me? Where I was headed. I sure don't, but it wasn't looking great, was it? What's done it done, we can't go back and we can't change what's happened, so why waste what little time we have left talking about it?"

Pain crossed his face in a furrow of eyebrows.

"Don't look at me like that." I said, sitting back down. He tried to reach out and take my hand, but the silver chains he was bound by prevented his efforts. He tugged on them hard.

"Tilly." He said, struggling against them. "We could get out of here, they're not watching." He said rattling the chains in anger and trying to force himself off the bed in delirium.

Abigail L. Marsh

"No, Cain… Hey, it's okay. It's alright, here lie down and I'll get you some water." I said, resting my hand against his chest. Sweat beaded on his forehead as I looked into his eyes. There was so much fear running wild in them, my heart sank. I didn't want to do this.

"Come on." I said with as much conviction as I could muster. "Lay down."

His body relaxed, and I was able to push him back against his pillows. I turned to a little jug of water on the desk next to him and biting my tongue hard to keep my own crippling feelings at bay. I poured him a glass of water.

"Here." I said, holding a bendy blue straw to his lips. He took a few gulps and much to my relief the atmosphere calmed down. He lay back on his pillows and stared up at me miserably.

"Where are they taking you?" He asked.

I shrugged nonchalantly staring at the creases in the his bed sheets.

"Tilly…" He pleaded with me. "I need to know." his voice penetrated a nerve I didn't know I had, sending horrible shivers throughout my body and my eyes full of hurt and anger looked up into his.

"I gotta go home." I said.

"They're sending you back?" He asked horror crossing his face.

"Yeah." I whispered, looking away. "Iz will be there." I added a smile appearing on my face, anything to lighten the mood.

Abigail L. Marsh

"But your Dad… I swear if he lays a finger on you I'll…"

"I know." I smiled. "Kill him?"

Cain squeezed my hand.

"No matter where I am, what they do to me, I won't let him hurt you."

"Cain?" I said.

"Yeah?"

"Thanks."

"For what?" He asked.

"You raised me, you saved my life."

He smiled up at me.

"I love you as if you were my own Tilly. I always have, never forget

that."

I opened my mouth to reply, but there was a loud knock on the door

which annoyed Cain.

"Piss off!" He shouted angrily.

"It's alright." I said, squeezing his hand. "My times almost up." I added

getting to my feet. The door opened, and Charlie's face appeared.

"I'm just saying goodbye." I said. He glanced at his watch.

"Two minutes, then we have to go." He said. I nodded as he closed the

door before turning back to Cain, He looked so sick with his pale,

sweaty skin and bruised body. I leaned down and wrapped him up in my

arms.

Abigail L. Marsh

"I'm scared Cain." I whispered into his ear.

"Fear is a choice Tilly. It does not control you." I heard him say before he went stiff in my arms. I pulled away in shock as his whole body shook. The machines he was wired up to went crazy, screeching, and flashing.

"Charlie!" I screamed, reaching out and trying to hold him still, but he slipped through my hands. The door flew open smashing into the wall, Charlie grabbed me and hauled me away as a blur of blue descended on Cain. Clutching my chest I watched wide-eyed from the corner of the room, Charlie's hands firmly attached to me.

A nurse turned and looked at us.

"We need you to leave the room immediately." She insisted and before I had a chance to say anything, I was pulled from the only person I wanted to be with and forced out of the building. I stumbled as we went out into the sunshine.

"Just keep walking." Charlie said as he supported me all the way to his car. He opened the door to Autumn, I could barely see her through my tears. She reached out to me but I shoved her away, turning into the window and pulling my hood over my head. I couldn't bring myself to talk to anyone, in my head it was all their fault

Abigail L. Marsh

Chapter Thirty-Six: Endings

We drove in silence back to London. I couldn't think of anything else except Cains body shaking uncontrollably and the machines screaming in my ears. Was he alive or was dead? It was killing me not knowing. We arrived back at MI5 headquarters just after ten o' clock. I sat subduedly in the car until Charlie had me out and was forcing me into the building. The first face I saw was Emma and it was plastered with a ridiculous smile.

"Tilly, lovely to see you! How have you been doing?"

I barely registered her as Charlie pushed me through to the family room and into a chair. I looked around and realised we'd somehow lost Autumn and Robert. Emma came in and sat down opposite me, placing a thick blue file on the table in front of her labelled with my name. With bleary eyes, I looked up at her.

"Is he dead?" I asked with a definite shake to my voice.

Emma opened my case file and picked up a pen.

"Tilly, I know how important he was to you." Emma said in a sickening tone.

"I'm sorry, did I stutter." I snapped rudely. "Is he dead?"

"Okay Tilly. I know you're upset."

I shook my head in utter frustration.

Abigail L. Marsh

"What the hell am I doing in here? Put me on a plane and let me go." I said standing up and storming over to the door, but before I had a chance to open it, Charlie came back in.

"Whoah!" He said. "Where are you going?"

"Let me take a wild guess." I quipped. "America."

I watched Charlie risk a glance at Emma.

"What? Has he decided he doesn't want a total raving lunatic after all?"

"No, no, not at all." Charlie said. "Here sit down, we just want to have a quick chat and then you're free to go if that's what you want." He added going over to my chair and pulling it back out. I shook my head.

"Charlie I don't want to talk, to you or anyone. You're pretending I have a choice, but you're lying to me. There isn't one."

"There is a choice, of course there is." Emma said.

"Will you tell me the truth about Cain if I sit down?"

Charlie nodded.

So I found myself sitting staring at the pair right where I had been two months previous.

"Your Dad is ready to take you home." Emma began.

"Is Cain alive?" I asked disregarding her comment entirely.

Emma looked at Charlie.

"Yes, he's alive and stable." He said honouring his promise.

"What's going to happen to him?"

"If he pulls through…" Charlie began.

"He will..." I was quick to interject.

"He will go to jail." Charlie nodded.

"For how long?"

"The rest of his life, the crimes he has committed will be investigated, but for yours and Autumns kidnapping alone, it will be a life sentence."

I sat back for a moment, I had to do something. He'd taken care of me, practically my whole life, I had to do something to repay him.

"Well, what did Autumn say?" I asked suddenly remembering what Autumn had said to me in the hospital and that I hadn't told them anything about Cain.

"We want your side of the story." Emma spoke firmly.

"What side? I don't know what you're talking about." I said, sitting back in the chair.

"You already gave a statement." Charlie said.

"But what does any of that have to do with Cain?" I asked, knowing for a fact I hadn't dropped his name into anything tinged with crime.

"Pardon?"

"Well, have you got any proof that he was connected in any way?" I asked, "Did Autumn actually tell you anything?"

"It's pretty obvious." Emma said, frustration entering her voice.

I laughed,

"She didn't, did she? And Cyrus, she has no real way of knowing."

"Tilly, we have significant intel that proves you've been living with him."

"Yes, I've been living with him, but quite freely. Do you have any actual proof, evidence, confirmation? You know that proves I was kidnapped by Cain Black?"

Emma leaned forward on the table.

"Are you saying he didn't kidnap you, only a few months ago you told us it was him."

"No, actually I didn't." I said shaking my head.

Emma raised her eyebrows.

"Look back through my reports, nothing I told you said anything about Cain, because it wasn't him." I lied.

Charlie and Emma passed confused and aggravated glances at each other.

"He didn't kidnap me." I shrugged.

"Well, who did then?" Emma asked gritting her teeth.

I shrugged again.

"Who knows, I was seven and I was drugged. It could have been anyone." I smiled folding my arms across my chest. I had them by the balls.

"Charlie, can I speak to you outside please." Emma said, standing up. They left the room, and I sat back in my chair, a smug smile on my face. They had lost, and they damn well knew it.

I was let go that afternoon where I went to a hotel with Autumn and Robert. I'd started to come around to going to California. Being there with Cain, the sun had shone, people laughed, and the sea was warmer! The hotel was middle ground. Autumn and I watched films, Robert and I talked with the police, detectives, or just him and I. Everything was truthful and honest. I was kept an eye on pretty much at all times, but what was there to run to now? Autumn needed me, and it was her turn now, it was her turn to be happy.

Two days later, Emma and her team had come to a decision, and I was called back.

Emma came into the little conference room where I was sitting, she was holding a small silver pot and had a resigned look on her face which told me she was defeated.

"Alright Tilly, we have both Carnaby Hanson and Henry Giannaville dead, Chris Hardy, Wesley Anderson and Cain Black in custody. You helped us to do that, so we're going to let you go."

"Very kind of you." I smiled.

Abigail L. Marsh

"You're going to go back to America with your father and your sisters. I don't want to see or hear of you ever again, do we have an understanding?"

"Yes." I sighed. "No offence but I don't exactly want to see you either... Are those Max's?" I asked. She nodded and slid the pot across the table. I took it carefully.

"You will be assigned a social worker when you get to California, each one of you has a different one, and you will attend singular counselling twice a week and family counselling once a week. If anything goes wrong, if you feel like Robert is drinking again, or you have any concerns whatsoever, call your social worker! They are there to sort it out for you. Do not run away or get into any more trouble. Do you hear me?"

"Yes, I hear you. I'll be a good little girl." I swore blind, grinning as I crossed my fingers under the table. For who could promise to be perfect? Definitely not me!

"Okay, your father is waiting outside. You're going to Norfolk?" She asked a little suspiciously.

"Only to spread Max's ashes, then we're going to go to Oceanside." I replied. Emma nodded then stood up, and I followed her lead.

Abigail L. Marsh

"Well, have a brilliant life." She smiled, reaching out to shake her hand.

"Yeah, you too Emma." I said, shaking her hand. Holding Max's ashes in one hand, I opened the door and walked back to the lobby. Cautiously optimistic about my new life. Robert and Autumn were waiting for me, I took my sister's hand as we left, smiling for the first time in a while.

Up on a windy sand dune, we all stood, the blue waves crashing onto the Norfolk coast below us.

"I miss you so much buddy. I love you." I whispered lifting the lid off the pot. As I launched the ashes into the sky I closed my eyes, holding on to our last few seconds tightly.

"Thanks!" Autumn cried, interrupting the moment. I turned to see what she was moaning about and realised both Robert and Autumn were now wearing Max.

"The wind is very precarious around here." Robert said trying to wipe his tongue with his sleeve.

Autumn smiled first, then Robert and then me, and then came the laughter. Real, happy, laughter.

Abigail L. Marsh

A final acknowledgement...

To Georgie, because even though life get's hard sometimes, you're always there. You're

my best friend and I love you.

Authors note: Please join Tilly as she takes the next step in this whirlwind of a life.

Part three and four coming soon.

Cover illustrated by Daniel L Martin

Abigail L. Marsh

Printed in Great Britain
by Amazon

34830481R00232